Finding Freddie Venus

Have Body, Will Guard Adventure Romance

by Neil S. Plakcy

Copyright 2013, 2020 Neil S. Plakcy. This book is a work of fiction. Names, characters, places, and incidents either are products of the author's imagination or are used fictitiously. Any resemblance to actual events or locales or persons, living or dead, is entirely coincidental.

All rights reserved, including the right of reproduction in whole or in part in any form. This book was originally published by Loose Id. Maryam Salim did an awesome job of editing this book, and the rest in the series.

Reviews for Neil Plakcy and the Have Body series:

"Never slows down" – Literary Nymphs Reviews on *Three Wrong Turns in the Desert*

"Plakcy's characters… charm" – Kirkus Reviews

"An engrossing writer" - Publisher's Weekly.

"Plakcy's Tunisia is the perfect exotic locale for your fantasy summer vacation, if you don't mind dodging an assassin or two along the way." – Dick Smart, reviewing for the Lambda Literary Review

For Marc, who showed me the highway of stars across the heavens. And for Brody and Griffin, who regularly remind me that it's time to have fun.

1 – New Client

Aidan Greene stood in the reception area of the Nice office of Agence de Securité, where he and his partner worked as close protection associates. Through the tall, thin window that looked into the conference room behind the receptionist's desk, he saw a muscular fortysomething man in jeans and a baggy white T-shirt. The stranger was turned in profile, and Aidan recognized his rounded chin, his sharp Roman nose. As the man moved in his chair, one shoulder of his loose T-shirt slipped down, revealing the edge of a distinctive tattoo that clinched his identity—a pair of angel wings stretched from one shoulder to the other.

Aidan turned to his partner, Liam McCullough, who stood beside him. "Do you know who that is?" he asked.

Victoire, the sweet middle-aged woman who managed the office of the Agence de Securité, taking calls and sending bodyguards out on assignments, looked up. In French, she began, "His name is—"

"Freddie Venus," Aidan interrupted. "I'd recognize him anywhere."

"Monsieur Venus," Victoire said, giving the name the French pronunciation. "*Il a appelé ce matin. Il croit qu'il est traqué.*"

Aidan associated the word "*traqué*" with hunting or tracking an animal, and it took him a moment to make the connection. "He called this morning because he's being stalked?"

Victoire understood English much better than she could speak it. "*Oui*," she said and nodded.

"And who is this Freddie Venus?" Liam asked.

"You don't know?"

"Aidan, if I knew, I wouldn't ask, would I?"

Liam was like that, Aidan thought. Always so logical. And it wasn't that much of a surprise that Liam didn't recognize the man. Liam had only come out of the closet and left the military toward the end of the Don't Ask, Don't Tell era, and Freddie had retired by then.

"He's a porn star," Aidan said. "Very sexy. Though it looks like he's put on some weight."

"And you know this gentleman how?" Liam asked, raising his eyebrows.

"Only as a fan." Aidan had spent many happy hours watching Freddie Venus perform, in the privacy of the bedroom he had shared with his ex-partner Blake back in Philadelphia. Blake had lost interest in sex several years before he lost interest in Aidan completely, and Freddie had filled that void.

Seeing Freddie there reminded Aidan of those days when he and Blake had been nothing more than roommates. Looking over at Liam, Aidan was glad that their relationship was still strong.

Aidan and Liam had met and fallen in love in Tunis, where Liam had settled after leaving the military. He had maintained his physique even though it had been years since he was an active duty Navy SEAL: his shoulders were broad, his biceps bulged, and his waist was as narrow as it had been when he was a teenager. At six-four, he was a couple of inches taller than Aidan.

Aidan had fled a bad breakup with Blake, landing in Tunis for a job teaching English as a second language. He had spotted Liam showering naked in a private courtyard and fell immediately in lust, which had deepened to love as he helped Liam with an assignment.

Since then, Aidan had put muscle on his skinny frame and learned how to shoot a gun and immobilize an opponent, and they had become a team, eventually relocating to the south of France a year before to join the Agence.

"Anything we need to know before we go in?" Aidan asked Victoire in French.

"He passed his credit check," she said. "That is the most important."

Liam was evaluating Freddie through the window, and Aidan took a moment to observe his partner. Liam was as handsome as when they met nearly six years before, though the years were taking their toll on both of them. Liam worked out nearly every day and maintained his awesome physique, but Aidan had noticed a few of his chest hairs going gray and the way his partner's joints sometimes creaked when he got up from playing on the floor with their little dog.

Aidan thought he'd maintained his body well too. He was never going to be as muscular as Liam, but he watched his diet and ran with Liam, and though he was starting to feel some aches and pains himself, he was still in good shape.

If he was honest, their sex life wasn't as exciting as it had once been. Though how could it be when they knew each other so well they could predict each other's movements, needs, and desires? When was the last time they'd had sex, anyway? Had it been a week, or more?

"He looks pretty agitated," Liam said, and Aidan snapped back to reality. "We'd better go in there."

They walked into the conference room and introduced themselves, and Aidan refrained from becoming a gushing fanboy, though he wondered briefly if sharing one of Freddie's videos with Liam might be the ticket to bringing excitement into their bedroom.

"You believe you're being stalked?" Liam asked after they'd sat down.

"I *am* being stalked," Freddie insisted.

Up close, Aidan thought that Freddie Venus still oozed sexuality, though it had been some time since he'd acted in a film. Aidan had assumed the man was dead—a casualty of AIDS or drug abuse—when he'd dropped out of sight.

"Can you tell us why you believe that?" Liam asked.

"I was walking on the Promenade des Anglais a few days ago, and I had the sense that someone was watching me. I shook it off." Freddie paused. "Back in the States, I was a performer, and people occasionally recognized me on the street. I assumed that's all it was."

He coughed, and Aidan turned to the pitcher of ice water Victoire had placed on the table by the door. He poured a cup for Freddie and handed it to him.

Freddie nodded in thanks and drank the water down in one gulp.

"I live in a quiet neighborhood off the Rue de Canta Galet," he said. Aidan knew that road, which snaked up into the hills, one switchback after another.

"Two days ago, when I was returning from the *hypermarché* on the Boulevard du Mercantour, I was sure that a white Fiat was following me, staying far enough back that it didn't appear so. But not many roads run through the hills, so I ignored it, especially when the car drove on after I turned into my driveway. But then yesterday…"

He paused to take a breath, and Aidan and Liam both leaned in to listen.

"I have about an acre of property, so you don't end up peering in my windows by accident. I do film editing, and I work in a studio with large windows that look out toward the ocean. It's a very calming view, and because of the steep hill, it's very private. I was in the middle of an edit yesterday afternoon when I looked up and saw a man outside the window staring at me."

"Could you describe him?" Aidan asked.

Freddie nodded. "A big man, tall and fat, with shaggy blond hair. From his plus-sized polo shirt and baggy jeans, I'd say he's American. He was circumcised."

"How could you tell?" Aidan asked. "If he was wearing jeans?"

"Because he had his pants open and his dick out, and he was jerking himself off in a patch of my lavender."

2 – At the Hypermarché

The hypermarché off the Boulevard du Mercantour was crowded on a Sunday afternoon, full of French families doing their weekly grocery shopping, and Newt Camilleri vowed to do his shopping on weekdays in the future. He pushed his cart behind an Arab woman in a head-to-toe burka, two squealing toddlers with her, and thought about including a woman like her in his next book.

What if that wasn't a woman under all that black after all, but a man? A man wearing nothing more than a jockstrap and work boots. The burka also concealed the bat-like wings that sprouted from his forearms and a long, forked tail, which snaked out of the crevice of his ass.

After years of writing Tolkien pastiches full of elves and hobbits, Newt had stumbled into writing gay erotic fantasy, imagining sexy couplings of angels, devils, and other fantastical creatures. His most popular character was a half man, half unicorn named Fledglis. Like a centaur, he had a man's head, arms, and torso over a horse's body, with a spiral horn sticking out of his forehead. He was pure white except for dark hooves and a mane with all the colors of the rainbow in it.

His mission was to skewer every antigay government official—literally. When he found a homophobic mayor, sheriff, governor, or legislator, he'd use his front hooves to knock the man down. He'd strip the man naked, then pinion him to a floor or wall, his legs open and his ass exposed. Then Fledglis would turn his horn into a giant penis and fuck the man into oblivion. By the time the jerk awoke from his sex-induced stupor, his attitude would have taken a 180-degree turn.

Newt loved to write those books, taking his revenge on everyone who had ever picked on him, teased him, or ignored him. And people loved to read them too—he sold a few hundred e-books in the Fledglis series each month and got fan mail from timid teenagers who found Fledglis an inspiration, and from straight women who were turned on by the raunchy male-on-male sex.

Newt was happy writing unicorn sex scenes because he could make up all the details, and no one would know how little sexual experience he had. In the past, when he'd tried to write realistically about sex, he'd been skewered by online reviewers because he often got the details wrong. He'd never been with an uncircumcised man, for example, and so had no knowledge of what happened to the hood during sex.

It was so much easier writing about unicorn sex. If there was a right and wrong way to describe it, at least no one had caught him yet.

Ahead of Newt, the burka woman's two kids were tugging at a pyramidal display of kitchen tools. Newt wanted to get as far from them as he could, but he was trapped in the aisle behind them. He watched in horrified fascination as the display toppled and rubber kitchen tools flew everywhere.

One of the large plastic forks caught on the neckline of a burly man a few feet ahead, dragging the fabric down and exposing the man's tattooed shoulder. Newt peered ahead at the tattoo, the tip of an angel's wing.

The man turned to remove the offending fork and tug his shirt back up, and when Newt recognized his profile, an electric shock ran from his brain direct to his groin. He recognized that tattoo and that face. It was Freddie Venus.

Freddie had been a star when Internet porn was exploding in the mid-1990s. He was in his twenties then, topping the cutest boys and bottoming for the hottest studs. His back was tattooed with the wings of an angel, but Freddie fucked like a devil. Newt had become addicted to his videos, but Freddie had long since dropped from sight.

And now here he was, buying milk, juice, vegetables, and toilet paper at a hypermarché only a few miles from where Newt was renting an apartment, across the street from the main train station in Nice.

Newt pushed his way around the burka woman and headed directly for the checkout. Nervously, he waited in line, keeping an eye out for Freddie. He paid for what he'd picked up and then loaded his bags into the tiny smart car he had bought. It was the very first new car he had ever owned, and even though it was difficult to squeeze his considerable bulk behind the wheel, he loved the new-car smell, and it was all he could afford.

Then he waited. Freddie Venus had to leave the store sometime, and Newt would follow him home and then… Well, he'd figure that out as he went. That's the way he wrote, after all. He was a pantser, figuring out his story by the seat of his pants, not a plotter.

He didn't have to wait long. Freddie walked out of the store, and Newt got a good look at him. The man had aged very well—strong jaw, prominent cheekbones, and a few lines that gave character to his face. It was hard to tell if he'd maintained his physique, because he wore a baggy, oversize T-shirt and nylon workout pants, but Newt was certain that no matter what else had happened, the man still had the dick of death.

Freddie pushed his cart through the lot, stopping at the trunk of a new-looking Mercedes sedan. He loaded the groceries, then got in the car and backed out.

Newt's pulse raced. He'd never followed someone covertly, but he'd watched enough TV shows to have a basic idea of what to do. The black Mercedes turned onto the Boulevard du Mercantour and headed south, toward the Mediterranean. Newt followed, careful to stay several cars back. This wasn't so hard, he thought.

Freddie, if that's who he was, drove the speed limit and signaled his turn onto the La Provençale highway early. Then things got difficult. The Mercedes took the first exit and began to wind through narrow, twisting roads. Newt had no idea where he was going or what would happen when he got there—which was exactly what he'd come to France for, wasn't it, to shake up his life?

A cascade of events had driven Newt from his comfortable town house in Lawrenceville, New Jersey, to the Côte d'Azur. For nearly twenty years, he'd been a minor cog in the grand state bureaucracy, a paper-pusher with a two-year college degree who rubber-stamped applications for government assistance because he had a soft heart for the disenfranchised and downtrodden.

To celebrate his fiftieth birthday, he had put the finishing touches on his newest novel, *Unicorn Triumphant*, the third in his series, and self-published it.

A week later, his boss was replaced by a woman who immediately began reorganizing the department. Newt was given more work and expected to stay late without overtime pay. His new boss constantly criticized his case decisions. He had no time to write and no enthusiasm for anything.

Then, after a positive review on an M/M romance website, *Unicorn Triumphant* took off. Fans downloaded the e-book by the thousands, gushing about it on bulletin boards, giving him hundreds of four- and five-star reviews online. The day the first big royalty deposit landed in his bank account, Newt quit his job and put his town house on the market.

A small truck-van combo veered dangerously close to Newt's car as he approached a switchback, and he had to pay attention. When he checked for the Mercedes again, he had lost sight of it around one of the curves ahead. He sped up, suddenly finding himself right behind the car. He fell back, hoping that the man hadn't noticed him.

He had thought that the move to France would jump-start his life—fantasizing about new books, a landscape without snow, maybe even a sexy French boyfriend. He'd long harbored a secret desire to retire to the French Riviera. He had studied French in high school, and then for his thirtieth birthday, he had taken a European bus tour with his mother that passed through Nice. The combination of sunshine and handsome men in skimpy bikinis had ignited his fantasies, and he'd sworn he'd go back one day.

But instead the move had simply reinforced the despair of his situation. He was too fat to live in a hot climate. He had to concentrate so much on speaking French that when he tried to sit down and write, he had no English in his brain. And what sexy Frenchman would give a second look to a sweaty blond pig like him?

But this chance encounter might be what he needed to start over. If that was indeed Freddie Venus ahead of him, he'd been able to start over. How had he managed it? Could Newt learn anything from his example?

While unicorn sex paid pretty well, it wasn't enough to buy him that oceanfront condo he'd been dreaming of. He had spent a couple of weeks in Nice, shopping for apartments along the Riviera from the Italian border to as far southwest as St. Tropez, and couldn't find anything decent he could afford. He had to settle for a six-month lease on a two-bedroom apartment across from the train station.

In the three months since then, he'd hunkered down in his apartment, desperate for inspiration. Newt forced himself to stay at the computer for hours each day, but Fledglis had left the building. Instead, Newt spent hours looking out the window at young backpackers arriving on the overnight train from Paris, leaving in the evening for destinations unknown. He walked along the ocean, looking at the men, young and old, in their tiny bikinis. He jerked off to online porn. But no matter what he did, the words wouldn't flow. It seemed like Newt had left his imagination back in New Jersey.

But now God or his muse or whoever had brought him Freddie Venus. Freddie would inspire him; he was sure. Watching Freddie go about his business would be the spur Newt needed to write again. Otherwise his money would run out, and he'd be on a plane back to the States, tail between his legs, even more of a failure than he'd been before.

With no other cars around them, Newt had to hold back, but he got lucky when Freddie signaled a left and turned into a curving driveway between two tall cypress trees.

Newt had watched enough spy movies to know what to do next. He kept going, pulling the smart car into a tiny lay-by a few hundred feet ahead. He struggled out of the car, reminding himself once again that he had to keep losing weight. At least one good thing about all that walking he'd done was that the pounds had begun to melt off. His triple-XL T-shirt had begun to feel loose, and he'd begun cinching his belt one notch tighter. He was still entrenched on the obesity scale, though.

He walked back down the road to the driveway, staying in the shelter of a row of trees. The air was hot and dry, but sweat began to pool under his arms and his man boobs, and he wiped his hand against his brow. When he reached a good vantage point, he saw Freddie carry his groceries into an old stone and stucco farmhouse, closing the heavy wood front door behind him.

Now what? How could he be sure that the man was indeed

Freddie Venus? He had no idea how to check property records in France. He looked around. The house was isolated up a slight hill, with no close neighbors. No one to ask about Freddie—but then again, no one to notice if he did a little more snooping.

He climbed the rise, keeping to the line of trees, huffing for breath. His thighs chafed against his jeans, and his dick stiffened. His mind was filled with images of Freddie Venus naked, his body being worshipped by some equally hot stud. Freddie leaning forward, his hands pressed against a rough brick wall as a blond twink plowed his ass.

By the time Newt got to the top of the rise he was panting for breath like a horse that had just won the Kentucky Derby. He slumped to the ground beneath a twisted olive tree and let his heart rate return to normal. From that angle, the old farmhouse was quite charming, a single story with a red tile roof. The entire rear wall of the house had been replaced with glass.

Because the land in front of the house sloped steeply, too, the man inside had an unobstructed view toward the Mediterranean. Small farmhouses dotted the landscape, giving way to apartment buildings painted in brilliant shades of pink, red, and orange. Farther below Newt saw the cityscape of Nice, gleaming towers of glass and steel up against the narrow alleys and ancient buildings of the old city. If he turned his head, he could see a stretch of blue-green water and the edge of the famous gooseneck of Saint-Jean-Cap-Ferrat.

Once he had his breath back, he crept closer to the house, staying close to the ground. The room at the nearest end appeared to be an office, with a row of computer monitors and a large screen mounted on the wall.

As he watched, the man Newt had seen at the hypermarché entered the room, and Newt was certain that he had found Freddie Venus. Freddie had shucked his long-sleeved T-shirt, and Newt got a clear view of his impressively muscled chest. When he turned to the side, Newt saw that familiar tattoo of angel wings.

Freddie was naked except for a pair of neon green workout shorts. He sat down at one of the computers with his back to the window and began to type, and quickly a movie started to play on the big TV screen facing Newt.

A young blond guy in a bright orange ball cap danced on a stage, wearing only a tiny bikini. He was slim but muscular and very limber. He gyrated sexily, sticking his hand in his bikini and rubbing his dick.

Newt got hard and began to rub his own dick through his baggy jeans. He stood in a patch of lavender, and the scent was intoxicating, like lathering in a shower with a bar of scented soap.

The blond on screen was joined by a dark-haired dancer of about his age wearing boxer briefs. The blond moved toward him, then turned his back and began twerking, rubbing his sexy ass against the dark-haired boy's crotch.

Newt couldn't help himself. He opened the fly of his jeans and pulled out his dick. He rubbed himself into a frenzy and came in a geyser that shot out into the lavender in a milky white arc, yelping as he did.

From behind the wall of glass, Freddie Venus looked outside

and locked eyes with Newt. Mortified, Newt stuffed his dick into his pants and rushed back down the hill toward his car.

3 – Peeping Tom

Freddie Venus jumped up from his desk and stalked over to the glass wall. He said "What the fuck!" as he watched a fat, blond asshole in T-shirt and jeans stumbling down the hillside away from the house.

He couldn't believe it. A Peeping Tom, way out there in the countryside. Was it the same guy who'd been watching him on the Promenade des Anglais? He couldn't say, because he hadn't actually seen anyone, just felt a presence.

He had noticed the bright red smart car following him up the hill but thought nothing of it. Was the fat fuck in that tiny car? Did he think switching from the Fiat sedan of the day before would make a difference?

He shook his head and went back to the computer. He couldn't waste time obsessing about anonymous voyeurs. He'd meditate later—wipe away whatever negative energy the man had left behind. But now, he had a video to edit.

At fifty, Freddie counted himself lucky to have escaped the AIDS crisis, though he'd had many opportunities to contract the virus: barebacking on screen, having sex high on meth, in anonymous back rooms of clubs. He'd spent years in front of the camera doing everything humanly possible with his mouth, his ass, his dick, and every other body part. Most of that time he'd been drunk or stoned, in a spiral that led to a burnout when he couldn't stand to be touched by anyone, not even a doctor or nurse.

By the time he crashed, he was an empty container. Heavy doses of antidepressants and a long retreat at a Buddhist monastery had brought him back to some semblance of humanity. He had pissed away most of the money he'd made in porn, though, and needed a job, preferably one that allowed him to lock himself up in a room by himself. Fortunately, he had bought this house years before, back when he was flush, keeping it as the hidey-hole he must have known even then that he'd need eventually.

Editing porn had become his salvation. The drugs he took to stay on an even keel had removed all sexual desire, but he had an eye for extracting sexual excitement from even the most mundane footage. He had a regular contract with a worldwide porn distributor who sent him hours of raw video. His specialty was choosing the absolute hottest scene to use as a teaser, encouraging customers to purchase the whole film as a download.

It paid well and meant he didn't have to deal with the talent, the directors, or any of the myriad of hangers-on. He had plenty of time left over for workouts and meditation.

He prided himself on having retained his figure and his looks. In the past, when he was active in the business, he'd met other former stars who had let themselves go—losing their hair, getting fat, developing jowls and wrinkles. Guys in porn often had prodigious appetites—for sex, drugs, alcohol, and then, when they no longer had to maintain a figure, for food. No way was anybody going to catch Freddie Venus in a caftan.

He went back to editing. The blond, Justin Johnson, spent way too much time twerking on the other guy, a beefy brown-haired dude named Colt Breaker. Freddie reviewed the footage, looking for places to cut, choosing close-ups to intersperse. One of the trends he hated in porn was the quick jump from a sexy teaser to full-on sex. He took the opposite approach. He kept the footage of Colt easing Justin's red bikini down, Justin's big dick jumping out and banging against his flat abs.

A close-up of Colt's mouth closing around Justin's dick, the way his rosebud lips suctioned around the shaft. Freddie watched that for a minute, then switched to a wider angle shot where he could see the way Colt's meaty hand pressed on Justin's smooth ass, his fingers splayed out.

If you knew what you were doing, you could pull a lot of sexiness out of tiny moments like that, the way Colt's index finger toyed with the very top of Justin's ass crack. Then a different angle, this one on Colt's face, his mouth hanging open and a glazed look in his eyes.

Way back when, this would have been the time when Freddie would take a break. He'd almost always had a hard-on and regularly needed relief. But now there was nothing stirring down there, and he kept on working. Colt was one of an interchangeable series of cute, sexy boys who were willing to bare all for a chance at porn stardom. Even his name was unimaginative—Colt Breaker. Meant to remind people of cowboys, though whenever Freddie looked at him, he thought "electrician."

Justin Johnson was something different. There was an animal intensity in his eyes betraying a real person behind them, and in him Freddie noted a star quality that reminded him of himself. Not only in the definition of his muscles or the girth of his dick. He moved as if he was comfortable in his body, filled with joy at sharing what he had with the world.

Freddie was determined to edit this movie to show off Justin and do his best to make him a star. Of course, porn stardom was a double-edged sword, and in doing so he might destroy the very beauty he sought to celebrate. But he wasn't Justin's fairy godfather, there to help and protect him; it was Freddie's job to create and sell a product.

He switched to a close-up of Justin's face, the way he gazed at Colt as he sucked Colt's dick, the motion of his right hand moving up and down Colt's slickened shaft while his left strayed through a forest of pubic hair, his index finger toying with Colt's root. Then a jump back to Colt's almost vacant face, so the viewer could see how much he was enjoying this action.

Justin finally pulled off the dick and began jerking it rapidly, holding it toward his face so that when the spunk erupted, it sprayed across his face. He had a beatific look in his eyes, as if this ejaculation was all he wanted in life.

While many producers would immediately jump to the next scene, Freddie liked to linger for a moment on that afterglow, and the director knew that, so he'd filmed a few minutes of Colt nestling down next to Justin, the two of them cuddling. Colt wet an index finger and wiped some come off Justin's jaw, then put it into his own mouth and sucked.

That was a money shot, Freddie thought. Yeah, there were guys who watched porn to get off, closing down the browser or turning off the TV as soon as they shot their load. But there were others who longed for the intimacy of a relationship, who cherished those small moments when an on-screen couple appeared to be more than casual fucks who'd go their own ways as soon as the director said, "Cut."

Freddie had been one of those guys once. Somewhere in the middle of his career he had started thinking about having a real boyfriend, somebody from outside the business who would love him for more than his big dick and his ability to fuck. But like his childhood fantasy of owning a jetpack that would fly him all around the world, that idea had been discarded in the trash heap of reality.

He worked for another four hours, until it was time for his evening meditation. One of the reasons he'd chosen France was the prevalence of Buddhist retreat centers—there were over two hundred in the country. He had visited several, sometimes for weeks at a time, and decorated one room of his home with Buddhist *tankas*— elaborate tapestries meant to induce a meditative state.

That evening, though, he was heading to a special lecture by a visiting *Rinpoche*, or Tibetan Buddhist teacher. The announcement had promised a dynamic, spontaneous, and intimate teaching style and an atmosphere that inspired inner wisdom, and Freddie could use all of that he could get.

Driving to the retreat center, he kept thinking back to the

Peeping Tom. The nerve of that guy, to invade his privacy. Where had he come from anyway? Did he know who Freddie was, or had he just stumbled on the house?

The evening was a waste. The Rinpoche was clearly a good teacher, but the teacher cannot help if the student is not ready. And no matter how hard he tried, Freddie could not clear his mind enough to focus.

He sat in the lotus position, his hands cupped open to receive the wisdom of the universe, and he thought about finding the fat man, tying him down, whipping him with a cat-o'-nine-tails until he begged for mercy, then prying open the meaty globes of his ass and fucking him with the biggest dildo he owned.

He realized, with a start, that he had an erection. How embarrassing—in the middle of a meditation. And how unusual—despite the hours of porn he watched every day, this was the first time he'd gotten a hard-on in ages.

It was so not what he needed. He wanted a release from the world, from earthly diversions and stresses. He no longer believed in romance, and all sex had ever brought him before was trouble and pain. He'd sworn off men since the last time his heart had been broken, and he wasn't about to let some fat fuck of a Peeping Tom change his mind.

He struggled to control his thoughts and emotions, listening to the Rinpoche chant, and eventually he achieved a sort of peace. But then, driving back home and thinking of the Peeping Tom, his dick betrayed him once again, stiffening up and even leaking precome as he thought of everything he'd do to that fat fuck if he ever saw him again.

He was so disconcerted that he hardly noticed the car coming at him on the narrow mountain road. It looked like the car was trying to force him off the road, and it was only by a lucky turn of the wheel that Freddie escaped danger.

That was it, he thought. Was it the fat fuck again, now coming after him? He couldn't take this shit anymore. He was going to hire someone to take care of this problem.

4 – Taking the Job

Sitting in the conference room across from the man Aidan had said was a porn star, Liam was amused. "You're sure you need bodyguards?" he asked.

Freddie Venus looked insulted. "Would I be here if I didn't? Last night I was driving home, and the asshole tried to run me off the road."

"Did you get a look at the driver? Was it the same guy?"

Freddie shook his head. "The headlights were blinding me. But who else would it be? The guy's crazy obsessed, and I need someone to keep him away from me."

Liam looked at Aidan. His partner seemed to know the guy's work, and that was interesting. Liam wasn't much of a fan of porn; he had used it when he had to, before he met Aidan. Since then, though, he'd had his hands full with his partner's desire, and he was occasionally surprised to catch Aidan watching some porn clip or reading some sexy book on his Kindle.

His partner had sex on the brain, he thought. Maybe it wasn't a good idea for them to take this case, because it could give Aidan ideas.

But he'd never been able to resist what Aidan wanted, and from what he saw in his partner's eyes, he knew that Aidan wanted very much to take on this job. "We have nothing else on the calendar," Liam said. "We can start today, if you like."

"I have some errands to run in Nice," Freddie said. "Can you meet me at my house late this afternoon?"

"Do you want us to stay with you until the threat is resolved?" Liam asked.

Freddie nodded. "I have a couple of guest rooms, though I never have guests. I assume you'll want the one with the king-size bed?"

Liam hated the way that some gay men could look at him, or him and Aidan, and immediately realize that their relationship was a sexual as well as professional one. Aidan called it gaydar; Liam called it annoying.

"That will be fine," Aidan said. "Say five o'clock?"

Freddie agreed, and Aidan wrote down the directions to the house.

"Do you like dogs?" Aidan asked.

"Aidan," Liam said. "We can leave Hayam with Madame Serroli." She was the concierge at their apartment building and often watched their small mixed-breed dog when they were on assignment.

"Just asking," Aidan said.

"You guys have a dog?" Freddie asked. "Like a guard dog?"

"Not quite," Aidan said. He described Hayam.

"Sure, bring her along," Freddie said. "Maybe we can sic her on the stalker." He stood. "Thank you. I feel better knowing that I have you guys on my team."

"It's our pleasure," Aidan said and shook the man's hand. Liam repressed a desire to kick his partner under the table.

Liam closed the conference-room door after Freddie. Through

the window, Liam could see that he had stopped at Victoire's desk to fill out the required paperwork as well as leave a check as a retainer.

"What do you think?" Liam asked. "Real threat or a drama queen?"

"As far as I know, Freddie Venus dropped out of sight a few years ago. Maybe this stalker is a photographer trying to get a story."

"And jerking off instead of taking pictures?" Liam asked. "Not very plausible."

"Then he's probably just a deranged fan," Aidan said. "The news is full of those these days. People who think they're married to some movie star and keep trying to break into their houses."

By the time they left the office, Freddie Venus had already departed. "So this guy," Liam said as they walked back through the narrow streets toward their apartment. "You've watched a bunch of his movies?"

Aidan shrugged. "I guess. I mean, you know my taste in men." They stepped off the curb to pass a pair of tall, leggy blondes gossiping in rapid French.

"Are you comparing me to that over-the-hill lothario back there?"

"Are you jealous?" Aidan asked, his eyes dancing with laughter. "I like my men big and muscular. Freddie Venus was all that and more, back in the day. Very different from Blake, for sure."

"Did you and Blake watch his movies together?"

"Blake disdained porn," Aidan said. "He used to say things like 'I don't even want to see you naked, much less some stranger on the

TV screen.'"

"That Blake," Liam said. "A real charmer. Sometimes I wonder why you spent eleven years with him."

"He wasn't all bad," Aidan said.

Liam was never quite comfortable talking about Aidan's ex with him. The guy sounded like a class-A jerk, and the one time they'd met, albeit briefly, Blake had done nothing to dispel that impression. For a long time, Liam had doubted that Aidan would stay with him, because he was so different from the wealthy, snobbish lawyer Aidan had been in love with back in Philadelphia.

He had gotten over that, eventually, as he realized the depth of Aidan's love for him and his own love for his partner. The more he lived away from the United States, the more he realized that he had some very puritanical views about sex, formed, he was sure, by his parents, who rarely showed each other any physical affection. Growing up around a relentless negativity about gay men had been part of it too.

He and Aidan stopped at a red light, and a tide of sunburned American tourists in cruise-ship T-shirts came toward them. It was high summer, and Nice was a port on both the eastern and western Mediterranean routes. The tourists reminded him of the last time he and Aidan had been back to New Jersey. He had felt like a stranger, even though he still had the local roads tattooed on his brain.

Where did he belong? Would he ever be able to be as relaxed and open about sex as Aidan was, as so many Europeans were? Or would he always be stuck between the two cultures?

The tourists passed, and Liam shook off his doubts and focused on the case ahead. "I'll organize what we need to take with us. You can do some quick research on the client and then pack everything." He looked over at his partner. "And quick research does not mean watching the guy's videos. Find out if that's his real name, what kind of property he owns, how long he's been in France."

"I know the drill, Liam," Aidan said. They passed a Frenchman with a Gauloise hanging from his lip, and Aidan waved away the cloud of smoke.

"Don't get prissy," Liam said. "It was a joke."

"Uh-huh," Aidan said as they reached the front door of their apartment building. Aidan opened it with a flourish and waved his hand. "After you, master."

Liam swallowed a snappy comeback. He didn't need Aidan in a mood before they'd even started with the client, who was sure to be even more dramatic in his home than he'd been at the office.

Aidan and Liam rented a one-bedroom apartment on the ground floor of a modern apartment building in the center of Nice, with a concierge at the front desk and tall French doors that opened to a small courtyard where Hayam could play.

Once inside, Aidan sat down at the laptop while Liam let Hayam out into the courtyard. She was always so happy to see them, even when they'd only been gone for a few minutes. Kind of like the way Aidan had reacted to Freddie Venus.

Liam cleaned his gun and Aidan's, assembled ammunition, flashlights, a long-handled mirror for checking underneath cars. He made sure all their electronics were charged, that the first-aid kit was stocked. When he finished, he went out to the living room. "Find anything?" he asked.

"I e-mailed Richard for a financial workup," Aidan said. Richard was a British hacker they used for electronic snooping. "And I also dug up some old articles on Freddie Venus. His birth name was Ventura, and he changed it legally a few years after he started work in porn."

"Any ideas why he left the porn business?"

"He hasn't," Aidan said. "He stopped acting but now he edits porn movies."

"Sounds like a good life. Until somebody tries to kill you."

"I couldn't find anyone online who appears obsessed enough with Freddie to come to France and track him down," Aidan said. "But I'll keep looking once we get to his house and see if he can give me any leads."

Aidan sat back in his chair. "What do you think we're going to do for food? I looked his place up on the map, and there aren't a whole lot of restaurants in the area for takeout."

"Pack up what we've got in the house."

"All right. We don't have much, so we'll have to go shopping at some point." He stood up and leaned toward Liam for a kiss, but Liam hadn't anticipated that, and he had already slid into the chair, leaving Aidan kissing air.

"I'll take over computer duties for a while. You can get your cute butt into the bedroom and pack everything I've laid out."

Aidan sashayed toward the bedroom, making sure that Liam saw the way his cute butt could move. Liam shook his head. Aidan was dramatic enough without the influence of a real drama queen with screen credits. It was going to be an interesting assignment.

5 – Scurvy Traitor

Driving home after he ran away from Freddie's house Sunday afternoon, Newt was appalled at what he'd done. He wasn't some horny teenager, jerking off to fantasies of a classmate. He'd done all that and thought he'd long since outgrown it. But as he stumbled down the hill, he had realized he hadn't come very far at all. He was still the lonely outcast, observing the world instead of participating in it.

He was sure that Freddie Venus had seen him, so there was no chance that he could casually walk up to the guy somewhere, introduce himself as a fan, and then see where things led. He'd ruined even a glimmer of that possibility.

Who was he kidding? He was five-ten and three hundred pounds. The hair was thinning on his head and sprouting out of his ears. Before he'd left Jersey, he'd been struggling to find anyone even willing to let him provide a blowjob. He didn't think he'd been naked with another man for at least ten years.

Teased for everything from his weight to his salamander-like name, Newt had had few friends and hated school. His only refuge was in fantasy novels, and as a teenager he began to write his own, about wizards and dragons and magical lands.

He'd always known he was gay, but had no chance to act on those feelings because he wasn't comfortable in bars, and no one would give him a second look. With the rise of the Internet, he started having anonymous sex with guys who then wouldn't return his calls or e-mails. In his forties he began bringing gay characters and hot sex into his fantasy writing, building a reputation in discussion groups and then self-publishing his books.

And where had it all led him? To a level of desperation he'd never thought he could sink to.

He trudged the last few steps to his car, got in, and started to drive back down the winding mountain road lined with red-roofed stucco buildings right up against the street, garbage cans out for collection, random wildflowers blossoming along the road. It was beautiful, and that made Newt even more depressed. He'd never live in a house like these with a man like Freddie. His life was a disaster.

By the time he reached a road he thought would take him back to his apartment, he realized that he was crying, and he pulled into the parking lot of a big home-repair store. He shut the engine off and leaned against the steering wheel.

How could he fuck everything up so royally? No matter what he tried, he always ended up a failure. And now, he couldn't even write. He should have stayed in Jersey. He should have slit his wrists and given up.

Eventually he roused himself from his pity party and drove the rest of the way home. There were a few parking spaces in a dark garage below the building, and he pulled into the one reserved for his apartment. He sat there in the car for a while, watching a relentless drip along the wall in front of him. He closed his eyes and remembered Freddie Venus at work. His dick stiffened and his pulse raced, and he jumped out of the car and hurried upstairs.

He sat down at his computer and opened a new document. Fledglis had always been a loner, like his creator. Most of the time he remained in his unicorn form, though for the right man he could shed his hooves and assume the form of a man with pale skin and long, flowing white hair.

Fledglis had lots of sex—sometimes even with men he found attractive. But he had never found anyone to stay with. Now, though, another character appeared in the sky beside Fledglis as the unicorn soared above a cloud. A half man, half angel with wings on his back, he introduced himself as Ulric and smiled at Fledglis.

The two of them flew together for a while, but no matter what he did, Newt couldn't make them land or talk to each other. He finally gave up and went to sleep.

Newt had fevered dreams of sex with angels that night. They enfolded him in their feathery wings, and he felt as light as air. They nipped at his body with their teeth, and they stroked his dick to orgasm. When he woke, the sheets were sticky and wet, and he was pretty sure the moisture on his pillow was from tears.

He tried to write again, but was stymied. He had never felt particularly superstitious about his ability to put words on the page, but now he believed that he'd only been able to start the night before, after such a long dry spell, because of his encounter with Freddie Venus. And now, no matter how much it might shame him, he had to return to that hilltop farmhouse for another glimpse of his idol.

He thought about going for a walk along the Mediterranean.

Walking was good exercise, and he knew he had to keep up his regular routine. But it wasn't the serenity of the ocean he needed.

As if he was in a trance, he walked down to the garage and got into his car. It was a warm, sunny day, and he put the air conditioning on high, which stressed the tiny engine, so he drove slowly up into the hills, surprised that he could find his way so easily. He pulled his car into the same spot beyond Freddie's home and shut the engine off.

Maybe he could stay there, he thought, and daydream about Freddie. Those broad shoulders, that narrow waist, that sexy butt dotted with silky black hair. He rolled down the windows and let the fresh air blow in, and then opened his fly and pulled out his half-hard dick.

He began rubbing it with his eyes closed, daydreaming of Freddie Venus. He was nearing orgasm when a harsh voice disrupted his reverie. "I could shoot your dick off right now," it said.

His eyes popped open. Beside his car window stood Freddie Venus, holding a handgun that was aimed at Newt's crotch. He wore a pair of loose workout shorts and a low-cut tank top that exposed his biceps and his impressive pecs.

"Please, no! I can explain," Newt said.

Freddie backed away, still aiming his gun at Newt. The man didn't have to be a good shot, Newt thought grimly, considering he was as big as a barn.

"Get out of the car."

Newt complied, then fumbled to stick his dick back in his shorts as Freddie spoke. "What the fuck do you think you're doing?"

Newt babbled, unable to find the right words. He said something about the hypermarché and the angel tattoo and then about how Freddie was his idol, he was so sexy, Newt couldn't help himself.

Finally Freddie held up his hand. "Enough." He motioned with the gun toward the farmhouse. "Start climbing."

Newt was paralyzed with fear. What was the man going to do to him? Shoot him and roll his fat carcass into the woods where no one would ever find him?

"Come on, asshole, I haven't got all day," Freddie said.

Newt started climbing the hillside, with Freddie behind him. The sun was high in the sky, and there was no shade along the driveway, and Newt felt sweat pouring down him.

"Jesus, you're a fat pig, aren't you?" Freddie said. "How do you let yourself look like that?"

Newt started to protest, but Freddie shut him up. "Keep climbing."

He reached the front door of the farmhouse, and Freddie said, "Inside and to the left."

Newt noticed, as he walked inside, how beautiful the house was. He passed the living room, with its own set of big glass windows looking out to the hills. Then he was in the computer room. He stopped.

"Peeping Tom," Freddie said. "You got a name?"

"Newt. Newton. Newton Camilleri."

"Newt," Freddie repeated, nodding his head. "Sounds like nude. Let's see what Newt looks like nude."

Newt was appalled at the thought of stripping naked before this gorgeous god of a man. How much more embarrassed could he get?

"Go on, Newtie. Get nudie."

Freddie was still holding the gun, so Newt complied. He kicked off his sandals and pulled his triple-XL T-shirt over his head, revealing his man boobs and his big belly. He fumbled with his baggy shorts but got them open and dropped them to the floor, then stepped out of them.

Newt was left in his boxers. At least they were a conservative plaid, not like some of the ones he owned. He was embarrassed at the way his belly fell over the waistband and at the way his dick was harder than it had ever been before. "Please. Let me go. I promise I'll never come back."

Freddie waved the gun at him. "Big hands, big feet. Let's see if the old saying is true."

"Please," Newt said, but Freddie ignored him.

He dropped the gun on his desk and grabbed a pair of scissors. He pulled at the waistband of Freddie's boxers and snipped through it. He was so close to Newt that Newt could smell Freddie's lemon aftershave. His heart felt like it was going to burst out of his chest like that alien in the long-ago movie.

Freddie grabbed the fabric, the rough skin of his knuckles grazing against Newt's flesh. Flexing his impressive arms, Freddie ripped the fabric. As soon as he released the tatters, they fell to the floor, leaving Newt naked.

Newt thought he would die of shame.

Then Freddie said, "Not bad."

"What do you mean?"

"Your body is a hot mess, but you've got a decent dick. Not as big as mine, of course, but few men are."

For the first time, Newt looked down at Freddie's groin. The head of his sizable prick was poking against the shimmery fabric of his workout shorts.

Freddie saw where he was looking. "Doesn't work anymore, but it's still a big sucker." He put the scissors down and appraised Newt. "Now, what do we do with you? You've got to be punished. And I've got to deal with you before my bodyguards get here. Won't need them now. You, I can handle."

Newt had no idea what the man was talking about. Punished? For being a Peeping Tom? But wouldn't that involve calling the police? What was that about bodyguards?

Freddie turned to the side and opened a closet. He pulled out a black rubber whip with a bunch of tentacles at the end. "What is that?" Newt asked.

"A cat-o'-nine-tails," Freddie said. "Pirates used them to punish scurvy traitors. How about you, Newt? Are you a scurvy traitor?"

The thought of those rubber tentacles caressing his skin made Newt's dick, already hard, start to ooze precome. He hung his head and said, "Yes, sir."

"Against the wall," Freddie said. "Put your palms flat and spread your legs."

Newt did what he was told, nervous with anticipation. The first touch of the cat was a caress from his shoulders down to his ass, the tentacles trailing down his crack, and he shivered with pleasure.

Whack!

The second pass was a snap that made the skin of his back tingle.

Then another, and another, slapping across his back and his ass until pain stung from every pore. Tears began to leak from his eyes, and he whimpered when the rubber hit his flesh. This was his punishment, and it was supposed to hurt.

But his dick stayed stiff and quivered every time he was slapped. Eventually he couldn't hold back, and without ever touching himself, he gasped as an orgasm wracked his body, and he spurted sticky white come onto the gray marble floor.

"That's not good," Freddie said. "I didn't tell you that you could come."

"I'm sorry, sir," Newt stammered. "I couldn't help myself."

"You're a horny fuck, aren't you?" Freddie put the cat down and moved close to Newt, the fabric of his tank top pressing against Newt's tender back, his breath hot on Newt's neck. He reached around and took hold of Newt's nipples and began to pinch and twist them.

Newt couldn't help himself. He writhed in pleasure and pain, pushing back against Freddie. His ass stung as he felt Freddie's stiff dick press against him.

"Oh, Jesus," Freddie said, and Newt felt a hot spurt against his ass.

Holy crap. I made Freddie Venus come.

6 – Home at Last

Freddie stumbled backward, away from Newt's bulk. What had just happened? He hadn't had a freaking orgasm in years, at least not one like that. He was stunned.

"Get out of here," he said.

"But..." Newt said.

"I said get out of here. Now."

The big tub of lard grabbed his shirt, his shorts, and his sandals and scurried for the front door. "Get dressed before you go outside," Freddie yelled. "I've got neighbors, you know!"

He heard the front door slam and then collapsed into a chair. His dick hurt, and his crotch was clammy with sweat and semen. He closed his eyes and leaned his head back. He knew he ought to get up, clean himself and the floor, throw away the boxers, and get back to work.

When was the last time he'd had an orgasm like that? Not for years. Maybe not even since Rodney.

He'd met Rodney Wang on a porn shoot when a director paired them up. Rodney insisted that was his real name, and Freddie had never asked for a birth certificate. He remembered their first scene together clearly.

Rodney played a virginal Chinese student who came to meet with a college tutor, Freddie. He wore geeky glasses and baggy clothes and begged for a better grade on an exam. When Freddie opened his pants and pointed down at his dick, Rodney rebelled. "I don't, I've never…" he said.

"There's always a first time," Freddie said. "You get down on your knees and open your mouth, and you figure it out from there."

Rodney had coal-black hair, black eyes, and skin as smooth as silk. His aura of innocence gradually transformed during that scene into a voracious sexuality. It was as if Freddie's dick had unleashed the tiger inside Rodney. They were supposed to stop at a blowjob, but the director, a jaded old queen, told them to keep going, to improvise.

Before Freddie could shoot his load, he pulled back from Rodney's hot mouth. He leaned back against his chair and began stroking himself as he demanded that Rodney strip, gradually revealing the impressive body beneath his preppy polo shirt and neatly pressed khakis.

When Rodney was naked, Freddie motioned him close and wrapped his lips around Rodney's throbbing rod. He sucked the long, slim dick for a while, teasing Rodney behind his balls, and all that Chinese inscrutability disappeared into a portrait of a man desperate to shoot his load.

Freddie wasn't finished with him, though. He stood up and wrapped his arms around Rodney's hairless back, and the two of them began to sway together in an erotic frottage as they kissed. Rodney was a world-class kisser. He could do things with his lips that few men could, sucking and nibbling in a way that pushed all of Freddie's buttons.

The cameraman zoomed in on their crotches as Rodney shot off into Freddie's pubes. Then Rodney grabbed Freddie's dick with his long, sensitive fingers and worked their magic, and Freddie erupted in a massive orgasm that made him throw his head back and howl like a wolf in heat.

When they'd finished, the director told them it was one of the hottest scenes he'd ever filmed.

Freddie had fallen hard for Rodney that day. After they had fucked, they'd gone out for Chinese food, which Rodney had ordered in fluent Mandarin. He said he was twenty-five, born in San Francisco's Chinatown to immigrant parents. He'd said he'd never acted in porn before, that Freddie had made it all seem so easy.

Within a couple of months, Rodney had moved in with Freddie, bringing with him an awesome appetite for cocaine and a lack of interest in sex when the camera wasn't running. They worked hard and played hard. Rodney loved to travel, and he had introduced Freddie to the French Riviera.

They both hated the pebbled beach, but they loved to hike through the hills. One day they had driven up the Rue de Canta Galet, parked their rental car, and begun to climb. They had stumbled upon a run-down farmhouse with a sale sign out front and gotten nosy.

The front door hung loosely on its hinges. They walked inside and discovered that the stone walls kept the place cool even in the summer heat. The walls were covered in stained, torn paper in a hideous floral print. Cracked linoleum tile, spiderwebs, broken glass in the few small windows.

Rodney hated it. He turned on his heel and walked out, but Freddie was curious. The only bedroom was small and dingy, the bathroom primitive. A rusted hot plate and ancient refrigerator against one wall of the living room. Part of the roof had fallen in, and birds nested in the exposed beams of the ceiling.

He walked out the back door and fell in love. He saw the sweep of the landscape, the hills dropping down toward the sea, a swath of sparkling blue-green Mediterranean. It was peaceful there too, so different from the hustle of LA.

Freddie had money to burn back then. Before they left Nice, he called the real-estate agent and made an offer. A couple of months later, the house was his. He hired a contractor the agent recommended to fix the roof and secure the property.

Back in LA, he began to learn that almost everything Rodney said was a lie. He wasn't twenty-five, he was thirty. He had been whoring himself out since he was a fifteen-year-old in the New York suburbs, sucking dick at turnpike rest stops, bus stations, and X-rated bookstores for cash and drugs. A man he met at nineteen took him to Amsterdam, and Rodney stayed there long after the man died, making porn and developing a taste for hashish. And contracting HIV as well.

Rodney had pissed off everyone he worked with in Europe, so he had come to LA to reinvent himself. It had worked for a while, but soon enough Freddie had discovered that Rodney was stealing from him, and everyone else the guy knew, to support his habit.

He didn't often let himself think of Rodney, because their

relationship had been so confusing, so damaging. It made him angry that Newt had brought those memories up when Freddie had put so much effort and pain into quashing them.

The way he'd pushed those thoughts aside in the past was through work, so he turned on the computer and brought up the scene between Justin Johnson and Colt Breaker. Justin was still naked, on his hands and knees on the bed, looking over his shoulder at Colt, who was stroking himself prior to entry.

Justin had a tramp stamp on his lower back, an arrow pointing down and the words *This way in*. Freddie hoped that was a temporary tattoo, the kind that could be removed with liberal applications of soap and water. Otherwise the boy would be stereotyped as a bottom, and that was a shame, because Freddie could see real potential in him.

It was hard to find a porn actor without body ink. In his experience, either a guy got one small tattoo somewhere and then stopped, or considered his whole body a canvas. Colt Breaker had a small lightning bolt above his right breast, which for Freddie served to continue the electrician motif. He wondered if Colt's pants would hang down, revealing his crack, when he was dressed and bent over.

Colt also had a barbed-wire tattoo around each bicep and the phrase *Love Conquers All* in a fancy script across his abdomen. It was an odd combination; was he trying to be a tough guy or a Romeo?

Freddie's approach to tattoos had been to commemorate special events. The rising sun on his abdomen was a souvenir of his first visit to Japan, early in his career. It was the first place where he had been treated like a king, with fans clamoring to touch him, to get his autograph, to whisper Japanese words in his ear.

Just below his waistline he had the words *Further Up and Further In* in cursive script. It was a kind of litmus test for him. Most guys believed it was a sex thing—fuck me harder and deeper. Only a select few recognized the source of the quotation. The full quote, from the last of the Narnia books, was "I have come home at last! This is my real country! I belong here. This is the land I have been looking for all my life, though I never knew it till now... Come further up, come further in!"

He'd loved those books as a young teenager, the chance to immerse himself in a distant world, and the end of the last book, when the true believers were reunited, had blown him away. He'd been looking for that mythical country ever since.

With a sigh, he went back to editing. There were only so many ways that male body parts could fit together, so to him the art of making porn was in the way you focused on the action to develop emotion. The first time Colt penetrated Justin, Freddie focused on Justin's face, the mixed play of pleasure and pain that flitted across his handsome features.

He switched to a close-up of Justin's ass as Colt's dick slid slowly inside, then was pulled back. The tempo increased as Colt began riding Justin, waving his right arm like a bronc buster in what had become his signature move. With his left hand, he slapped Justin's blond butt.

Justin bucked back like the good little horsey that he was, and occasionally Freddie switched to a shot of his face, showing that he was enjoying himself as much as Colt was.

It was all about the fantasy, of course, but bits of reality couldn't help but intrude. You had to show that Colt was wearing a condom—not just to prove that the shot had been a "safe" one but because porn producers had eventually come to understand that they had a role in promoting safe sex. After all, if every gay man caught the virus and died, where would their business model be?

He looked at the clock. The bodyguards should be there soon. What was he going to tell them—that he'd fucked the stalker into submission and didn't need their services anymore? Wouldn't that make him look like the biggest drama queen ever?

He could lie, of course, and pretend that the threat was still real. Keep them at the house for a couple of days, and then when nothing else happened, he could let them go. He didn't care about the money he'd have to spend.

But did he want other people in the house when he was so confused? He'd have to do a lot of meditation to understand what had happened that afternoon. How had a man who didn't fit his ideas of handsome or sexy been able to turn him on so much? Was it the need for revenge against this guy who'd violated his privacy?

He brought up an image of Newt's naked body. His floppy man boobs, the way his belly hung over his groin, almost hiding that meaty dick. He felt his own dick begin to rise. How strange. He could watch videos of gorgeous guys fuck all day long and feel nothing, and yet a mere memory of that big tub turned him on.

Was he desperate for human contact? He couldn't remember the last man who'd touched his naked body, the last skin-to-skin contact he'd had. It must have been in LA.

Thinking of LA brought back those memories of Rodney. Freddie had been living in a Santa Monica high-rise when they'd met, with a wide balcony and a distant view of the Pacific. Rodney loved that balcony and often talked about Freddie's angel tattoo and how if he had wings like Freddie's, he could fly. When he took a header off the balcony and crash-landed on the pavement twenty floors down, Freddie believed he was trying to fly, not commit suicide.

Rodney's death was the end of Freddie's career as a performer, in part because he couldn't be sure that he wasn't HIV positive himself until he'd had a few years of tests. He fell into a spiral of drugs and alcohol and a friend convinced him to go into rehab. He'd discovered Buddhism then, and antidepressants, and the rest was history.

Ancient history, he reminded himself. A story that needed to be as dead and buried as Rodney Wang was.

7 – Losing Track

The back of the Jeep was jammed with clothes, gear, and food. They had no idea how long they'd have to stay with Freddie Venus, though Aidan had a feeling the job would be pretty quick once they intercepted the stalker and convinced him to go on his way. "You know, where Freddie lives isn't far from Louis and Hassan's place," Aidan said as they climbed into the foothills of the Alps.

Their friends Louis and Hassan had gotten married a few months earlier, as soon as it became legal for two men to wed in France and once the State Department, Louis's nominal employer, began recognizing same-sex marriages. Hassan was an architect, and he had found them a small farmhouse in poor condition and renovated it.

"We've been here in Nice for two years, and we're planning to stay," Aidan continued. "Why keep renting when we could buy something?"

"A house is a big pile of trouble. What's wrong with staying where we are?"

"Seriously, Liam. You've seen how much space they have. And we could have a real yard for Hayam."

"A real yard for Hayam is not high on my list of priorities right now." The little dog heard her name and nosed forward from the backseat. Aidan reached back to pet her.

Why was Liam so resistant to something that seemed so obvious? Aidan wondered. It was what couples did once they were settled—buy a house. Why keep pouring money into a rental without building up any equity?

His own parents had bought their house soon after they married, and by the time Aidan arrived they were well situated in a good neighborhood with excellent schools, close to their families.

Was that it? Did Liam resist buying a house because it would make them more like their parents? Liam's father was a raging alcoholic, his mother a foul-mouthed enabler. One of Aidan's sisters was twice divorced, while the other had gone in the other direction, becoming a suburban supermom.

"Focus, Aidan," Liam said, and Aidan looked over at him. "We have a case, remember. Where do I turn?"

"Should be ahead on the left. See that big plastic trash bin? Turn in there."

The driveway was steeply sloped upward. Liam stopped in front of a stone and stucco farmhouse, and Aidan thought it was a beautiful place. How much would a house like that cost? Could they afford to buy something similar? Probably not. They made a good living as bodyguards and had money stashed away, but a place this nice had to cost serious bucks.

"I'll get the bags; you take the dog," Liam said. He stepped out of the Jeep as the front door opened, and Freddie Venus came outside.

Hayam jumped out of the Jeep and rushed up to Freddie. "Hey, you're a little sweetheart," Freddie said. He reached down to pet her.

He looked up. "You know, I'm glad you're here. I'm usually

pretty good about being on my own, but I feel pretty shaken up, and I think it will be good to have you guys around for a day or two. Keep me from obsessing about things."

There was something in Freddie's demeanor that made Aidan think that there were more "things" going on than Freddie was letting on, but it wasn't the time to pry. The presence of a threat, and bodyguards, had a way of forcing to surface what had been long repressed, and Freddie looked like a guy who had a lot of issues in his past, if not his present.

Hayam abandoned Freddie to run over to a patch of grass and pee. Aidan and Liam unloaded the Jeep and carried everything inside. Freddie showed them to the guest room, then said, "I've still got some work to do. Should be finished by six."

After Freddie left, Liam said, "People who are afraid they're being stalked shouldn't open up their house and walk out until they see who's arrived."

"You can tell him that," Aidan said. "Liam, do you think there's something more going on here that Freddie isn't letting on?"

"We haven't had a client yet who's told us the whole truth at the start." Liam hoisted the duffle onto the king-size bed and began to unpack guns and flashlights. "Why should a washed-up porn star be any different?"

"You're not jealous of him, are you?" Aidan asked.

Liam snorted. "Jealous? Of what?"

"If you don't know, then I'm not going to tell you," Aidan said.

"You know, sometimes you can be infuriatingly dramatic." Liam turned to him. "If you have something to say, say it."

"Fine. I'll say it. We haven't had sex in weeks."

"You have got to be kidding me. Are you keeping track? Marking up your orgasms on a little pocket calendar?"

"*Little* being the operative word," Aidan said. "I'm taking these groceries out to the kitchen. You can stay in here and play with your guns."

"Play with my…" Liam sputtered, but before he could finish the sentence, Aidan had left the room with Hayam following.

He carried the bag of food down the hall, trying to remember exactly when the last time was they'd had sex. They had spent the past two weeks on one of the mundane assignments that paid the bills—waiting around outside hotel rooms and offices while their client, a Canadian multimillionaire, carried out negotiations with an Arab sheikh. The Canadian owned an oil distribution business and had the sheikh over a barrel, so to speak. He was worried that the sheikh would do something shady to reverse the advantage and had hired Aidan and Liam ostensibly as bodyguards but also to keep an eye on the sheikh.

It was tedious work, enlivened only when Aidan was at a urinal in the hotel men's room and the sheikh stood next to him. Out of the corner of his eye, Aidan saw the man hike up his *thobe* to his waist, and Aidan realized that he was naked beneath the white robe.

The man sighed happily as he peed, shook his dick vigorously when he finished, and then walked out of the bathroom without washing his hands. Aidan was first turned on, then turned off.

He and Liam had both been tired when they'd returned home at the end of each long day. Before that? If he had to hazard a guess, Aidan would have said his last intimate contact with Liam had been at least another week or two before.

Liam often accused him of being a horndog because he liked sex. But who could blame him, living with Liam, who was a walking wet dream with those impressive biceps and pecs, that narrow waist, that sweet, sexy ass.

Freddie could give him a run for his money, Aidan thought. There was a louche quality about the former porn star, a sense that here was a man who not only had the goods the way Liam did but had a range of experience that the longtime closeted Liam didn't.

Not that Aidan was complaining. Liam was a generous lover, and if he wasn't the most inventive guy in bed, he was usually willing to follow Aidan's lead. In the early days of their relationship, they'd had sex in the desert, in a steam bath, in bedrooms and bathrooms and kitchens and lots of other places too. But after their relocation to Nice, their sexual relationship had tapered down to an infrequent series of encounters.

Could he ask Freddie for advice? He put the perishables in the refrigerator and the dry goods in a cabinet, trying to frame the question.

"Three weeks ago," Liam said from behind him.

Aidan turned around.

"When we got home from dinner with Hassan and Louis," Liam continued. "You were horny, and I took care of you."

"It was a hand job, Liam," Aidan said. "And you weren't into it. You kept looking at your phone while you were jerking me."

They heard a cough behind them and turned to see Freddie Venus standing in the kitchen doorway. "Don't let me interrupt. Sounds like a fascinating discussion. But I was wondering what we were going to do for dinner. I don't have much food."

"I could put together a stir-fry," Aidan said. "I brought a lot of fresh vegetables, and I saw you have a box of rice in your cabinet."

"In the immortal words of Jean-Luc Picard, *make it so*. I'll be back in the editing room." Freddie turned and began to walk away, then stopped and looked back. "Here's a piece of unsolicited advice. Unless you're into phone sex, put your electronics away when you fuck and pay attention to each other."

He disappeared down the hallway. "Just what I need," Liam grumbled. "Sex advice from a former porn star."

"Who better?" Aidan asked.

"I'm going for a run. Give me an hour before you start making dinner." He left Aidan in the kitchen, with Hayam sitting on the floor, eager for a treat. Aidan tossed her a biscuit and then looked around the kitchen. The appliances were only a few years old and top-of-the-line; the counters were stone, the big table sturdy oak. If only he and Liam could have a place like this.

He finished unpacking the food and then went back into the guest bedroom to set up his laptop. He wanted to see if Richard's report had come through yet or if there was anything else he could discover about Freddie online. But there was nothing from their hacker friend, and Aidan couldn't find anything new about Freddie on his own.

At six they reconvened in the big farmhouse kitchen. "I'd cook all day if I lived here," Aidan said. He and Liam sat across from each other, with Freddie at one end. Hayam curled beside Aidan's chair, knowing he was the soft mark when it came to food.

"I don't cook as much as I would like," Freddie said. "The single life, you know. I get so caught up in my work that I lose track of time and forget to eat."

"Aidan never has that problem," Liam said.

Aidan kicked him under the table, and Liam grinned at him. Liam had a killer smile, one that lit up his face, and in Aidan's opinion he didn't smile enough.

"Listen, there's something I need to tell you," Freddie said. "My stalker? While I was waiting for you this afternoon, I went out for a run and saw his car. I came back to the house, got my gun, and went out to confront him."

"It was a stupid idea to confront a stalker right after hiring bodyguards to protect you," Liam said. "What happened?"

"It's all worked out," Freddie said.

Liam put down his fork and looked straight at Freddie. "What did you do to him? Where is he now? You didn't hurt him, did you?"

Freddie looked down at his plate.

Crap, Aidan thought. What if Freddie had killed the man and was expecting Aidan and Liam to help dispose of the body?

"I didn't kill him, if that's what you're asking," Freddie said. "He went home. I told you, it's all taken care of."

"What exactly do you mean by that?" Aidan asked. "Did he agree not to bother you again? Because you know, when somebody gets obsessed, they're likely to say anything to get out of trouble."

"I'd rather not go into it," Freddie said.

"But what if he comes back?" Liam asked. "And he escalates the situation? You only have to read the papers to see what can happen."

"We fucked, all right?" Freddie said. "Yeah, I know I said the guy was big and fat and disgusting, but I couldn't help myself."

Aidan's mouth gaped. This guy, this hunky former porn star, couldn't help himself when confronted with a man who was big, fat, and disgusting? Something didn't make sense.

Freddie shifted uncomfortably in his seat. "Look, I've had some bad shit happen in my life. Kind of put me off sex, if you know what I mean. And when Newt showed up, something started to work down there, something that hasn't worked in a while. I was pretty surprised myself."

Aidan could tell that Liam was as uncomfortable with this topic as Freddie was, so he tried to shift the conversation. "The bad shit," he said. "Any chance that someone from your past is here? Maybe putting this Newt guy up to this?"

Freddie laughed harshly. "If you saw Newt, you'd never think he'd be good dick bait," he said. "And as for my past? I put all that shit behind me. I've been hunkered down here for five years. Nobody from my past would know where to find me. I don't publicize where I live."

"Then how did this guy find you?" Liam asked.

"He saw me in the supermarket," Freddie said, and he smiled. "Recognized my back tattoo and followed me home."

"Do you have his full name?" Aidan asked. "We can check him out for you."

"Don't worry. When he left here, he had no intention of coming back."

Aidan wondered what Freddie Venus could have done to the guy that wouldn't have him eager as hell to come back. He'd seen the movies; he knew the kind of skills Freddie had back then, and he was sure you didn't lose everything, even if it didn't work for a while.

Freddie stood up. "I've got some editing to finish up this evening, and then I want to meditate for a while. I'll see you guys in the morning."

With Hayam underfoot, Liam cleared the table, and Aidan rinsed the dishes and slotted them into the dishwasher. "What do you think about what Freddie said?" Aidan asked. "You believe him?"

"Like we said earlier today, he's not giving us the whole story. He seems like the kind of guy who dribbles out bits of information. Give him some time. He'll tell us more. In the meantime, we'll hang out but keep our eyes open."

"Not a problem for me. I love this house," Aidan said. "If we found something older, maybe run-down, you think we could afford it? Fix it up as we go along?"

"You planning on a career as a porn star to finance it?" Liam asked. "Because as much as I love you, sweetheart, I think you're a little old for a career change."

"I still have some moves," Aidan protested. He didn't like the way that Liam had shifted the conversation so quickly, but he wasn't going to argue, at least not while they were on a job.

"I never said you don't. I'll take Hayam out for a walk, and then I want to do a little research on Mr. Venus."

"I've already looked," Aidan said. "There's nothing out there to find."

Liam leaned down to pick up the little dog. "How's Daddy's girl?" he asked and let her lick his face. "You want to go see what this new neighborhood is like?"

He carried the dog out of the room, talking to her, and Aidan realized he was slamming the dishes into the dishwasher. Oops. Didn't want to break any of the client's appliances on the first day.

What was Liam's problem? They'd been together for almost six years, and usually he could read Liam's moods and anticipate his requests. But lately Liam had been so distant.

Aidan realized that Liam's distance had been going on for a while, maybe back as far as Louis and Hassan's wedding. Aidan had asked what he thought was a simple question: did Liam ever want to get married?

It wasn't a proposal, or a request. There was no deep subtext. Aidan just wanted to get Liam's opinion on the issue now that same-sex marriage rights were gaining ground around the world.

Liam had taken it the wrong way. First he'd gotten upset; then he'd proposed, even though his heart clearly wasn't in it.

Aidan had been stunned by the surprise proposal, and he'd stumbled to find the right words to say that while he liked the idea of being able to get married, it wasn't on his agenda at that time. That he loved Liam and always wanted to be with him and didn't need a piece of paper or government approval to prove that.

Liam had accepted the information easily, and they hadn't talked about it since. But now that Aidan looked back over the past few months, he wondered if Liam's ease had masked something deeper. But Aidan couldn't ask without opening what could be a very dangerous, difficult subject once again.

By the time he finished in the kitchen and went into the bedroom, he was very confused. He tried to shake the fog by unpacking what Liam hadn't. He was clearing a space on the bureau to put out some toiletries when he discovered a DVD of one of Freddie's early films, *Don't Ask, Do Tell.*

He remembered that movie. Freddie was a drill sergeant, initiating a bunch of new recruits. It had been pretty hot. Maybe a little porn action in the bedroom would be the ticket to get Liam's attention. He slid the DVD into the player next to the TV in the console across from the bed and hit Play.

He fast-forwarded through the credits until he saw Freddie, nicely filling out a khaki uniform, standing in a desert landscape with six young recruits facing him. Freddie was barking out orders to them, and one guy with close-cropped blond hair stepped forward, then knelt at Freddie's feet.

Freddie assumed a wide stance, and the blond reached up and

unzipped Freddie's khaki slacks. Freddie's prodigious dick popped out, already half-hard, and the recruit began licking it in long slurps.

"What are you watching?" Liam asked as he came into the bedroom holding their laptop open.

Aidan quickly hit the Stop button on the remote. "Just an old movie," he said. Suddenly he was embarrassed to be discovered watching porn by himself. Whenever Liam had caught him doing that in the past, Liam had been irritated.

Liam raised his eyebrows. "An old movie starring our host?"

"Yeah. I thought it would be good for us to get familiar with his background."

Liam laughed out loud. "You can call it that if you want." He came over and sat beside Aidan on the bed. "Richard came through with the report we asked for. Our client is very well-fixed, which makes him a target for blackmail or extortion."

"But what could someone blackmail him about? He's never hidden anything."

"As far as you know," Liam said. He looked down at the screen of the laptop. "Frederick Ventura, Jr. was born in Omaha, Nebraska. Oldest son of Fred Senior and Muriel. Two younger brothers, Gerald and Earl. Graduated from high school in Omaha, then dropped out of sight."

He flipped to the next screen. "He was nineteen for his first film as Freddie Venus."

"Big deal," Aidan said. "As long as he was over eighteen, right?"

"That's not the problem. He had a pretty long career for a porn star, not that I'm as familiar as you are. Last film he acted in was five years ago. Director credits for a few years after that, then he drops out of the picture again."

"Is that the problem?" Aidan asked. "That he dropped out of the business?"

Liam shook his head. "The problem is that his youngest brother Earl is a candidate for the United States Senate on one of those family-values platforms."

"And having a big-brother porn star could trash his campaign," Aidan said.

8 – STUPID AND FREAKY

One good thing about this couple, Freddie thought, was that at least the smaller one could cook. The stir-fry was great, and Freddie had done his best to be an entertaining host, which helped him ignore what had happened that afternoon.

He hadn't had any interest in another man for years. The images on his computer screen had numbed him to any stimulation. And living in this small town hadn't exposed him to any romantic possibilities.

This wasn't a romance—just a stupid, freaky encounter with a guy who shouldn't have floated his boat, based on looks. And after whipping the guy, he'd certainly chased him away.

He couldn't help himself. He walked over to where Newt's torn boxers still rested on the floor. He picked them up and brought them to his nose. He inhaled deeply, and his lungs filled with the scent of the big man's crotch. He felt a peculiar twitching in his gut, one that had often accompanied arousal.

But his dick wasn't cooperating. Maybe that orgasm earlier had been the last of his career, a valedictory note reminding him of all he'd lost.

Or was it? The only way to tell was to see if he could recreate the experience. But who the fuck was that guy? What was his name? Newt. Nudie Newt. But he'd said his last name too, hadn't he? Something Italian. Camiliere? Cavalier?

He brought up a search program. He hunted and hunted. The sun set over the hills, and he kept on looking. Finally he got a hit he thought might be a lead. It was a piece of gay fan fiction on a message board by someone named Newt Camilleri.

He read it through. The writing was better than average, and the sex was hot. The best character was a half man, half unicorn called Fledglis.

But there were no links at the end of the story, and nothing else published by that author. On a whim, he searched for Fledglis and discovered that there were three novels about the character written by someone named Newton Cale.

It had to be the same guy. He looked online for a photo of the author, but there was nothing. By then he was obsessed with the hunt. This guy wasn't going to slip away from him so easily. Eventually he found a fan page for the Fledglis books on Facebook.

There were dozens of posts by raving fans of the series, and the author periodically answered questions about the future of the series or supporting characters.

The owner of the page had removed the opportunity to send private messages to the author; all fans could do was make public posts on the page.

Freddie debated leaving a post. But what could he say? *Sorry I whipped you; come back for more?* Something sappy, like *Let me soothe your sore back?*

He settled for "Angel wings seeks unicorn. Please come back."

He hit the key to post and then closed down the computer. He hadn't meditated all day, and he felt the need for some real centering. He sat down and closed his eyes, but all that happened was that he remembered the past.

Soon after he met Rodney, the guy had moved into his penthouse in Marina del Rey with him. He was rolling in cash, driving a new Jaguar, eating in the finest restaurants, and snorting the finest coke.

After Rodney's death, he took a break from acting, though directors kept calling him. By the time he'd decided to take up an offer to return to the screen in *Maxx Menn 3*, he had gotten out of shape. When he showed up for work, the director looked at him, red-eyed and jittery, with fat where his six-pack abs had once been, and canned him on the spot.

He went on a binge that lasted a couple of months until he'd been evicted from the penthouse, had the Jag repossessed, and emptied out his money-market fund. The only asset that remained was the house in France, but in his drug-induced state he'd forgotten about it.

He still had a few friends, so when his next birthday rolled around he went out on a binge with them. He had a vague memory of the bar, a seedy dive in West Hollywood where the beer was cheap and the men were cheaper. He remembered waking up the next morning in a cheap rental apartment in the San Fernando Valley, miles from his past success. It was hot and steamy outside and the window air conditioner was broken, so he'd woken drenched in sweat, hungover from the pre-birthday celebration the night before.

The sheer despair of that morning was a wake-up call, and he forced himself to tighten up his abs and cut back on his drinking and drugs. By then he was in his late thirties, and every director he spoke to told him he was too old, washed up, yesterday's rotten tuna salad. "There's no market for daddies these days," one had told him, and Freddie had been appalled to think of himself in that category.

One of his so-called "friends" had suggested he go back to Omaha, lean on his family, and get a fresh start. Maybe real estate sales, the last vestige of the down and out willing to work on commission.

Another "friend" had suggested that Freddie pimp himself out. That there were plenty of rich gay men who'd get off on fucking a former porn star, even one past his prime.

Freddie had slugged him and stalked out. But after another couple of months of no income, he'd put an ad online, accompanied by a picture from his better days and a list of his film credits.

Sex had always been a transaction to him, so he didn't mind collecting cash right away instead of waiting for royalty checks. His first couple of calls had been eye-openers. The guys were fans, so they didn't complain, but Freddie could see in their eyes that he wasn't the man they were expecting.

He'd had new pictures taken, reinventing himself as a butch older version of the hot young stud he'd once been. For the next year, he made enough money to keep body and soul together and spent the rest of the time in a haze.

Then one evening he got a call around six from a businessman named Randall with a small house on a back street in Santa Monica. From the way the guy described himself, Freddie expected some vanilla sex, hoping to get Randall off quickly and then use the cash for bender.

He had expected that the client would be wearing normal business clothes—pressed white shirt, expensive slacks, and so on. But instead he was dressed head to toe in black silicone rubber.

The evening had gone downhill from there, ending with Freddie beaten up and beaten down. He'd known he needed medical attention. He'd stumbled into Randall's yard, still naked, and called the one number he'd been resisting dialing for months, the last ace he had. *"Mario?"* he'd said, his voice cracking. *"I need help."*

9 – ALMOST HUMAN

Newt's back was cramped by the time he finished writing, and he had to twist and turn to loosen the muscles. He looked out the window at the orange glow over the train station and realized that he'd written all the way through sunrise. He thought he'd never written such darkly erotic material—it made all his past work seem almost PG.

The agony began as he ran away from Freddie's house. His back and ass were red and sore, and he couldn't find a position in the car that didn't sting. He stopped at a pharmacy and bought a bottle of soothing body cream, but it was hard to reach all the places by himself. He couldn't sleep on his stomach, even after he took a pill.

He kept thinking about the experience at Freddie's house. He'd never been whipped like that, never fantasized about it, never even thought it was something that would excite him. It wasn't bad enough that it had hurt while it happened, but now he couldn't get comfortable, and he wondered how long it would take for his skin to heal.

Around three o'clock in the morning, he gave up on sleep and opened his laptop to write the raging fantasy that wouldn't give his brain a break. He couldn't sit, and he nearly cried in frustration, until he set his computer on the kitchen counter and stood there to type, his shoulders hunched as a half man, half angel named Ulric began to come to life on his screen.

He wore a black garment that resembled a wrestler's singlet—tiny straps over his shoulders, a scooped front that was open all the way down to below his belly button, and a pouch covering his dick and balls. The stretchy fabric continued around his sides and cupped his ass, which was exposed to the air though covered with a silky flow of that same brilliant silver hair as on his head. The singlet was studded with tiny diamonds, like stars against a night sky.

The words flowed through Newt's fingertips, almost like he was taking dictation from a higher power. Fledglis found a young man who needed to be rescued from some baseball-bat-wielding hillbillies, and Ulric helped him take his vengeance against the gay bashers.

By the time he finished that scene, he was exhausted but at least his brain had calmed. He made sure his file was saved to his hard disk as well as his cloud account, then went back to bed and managed to find a semi-comfortable position on his right side. When he woke, he was still obsessed and went back to writing. Newt's fingers danced across the keyboard, barely keeping up with the flow of his thoughts as he put Fledglis and Ulric together in a sex scene that was so hot, he was left sweating and horny by the time he finished.

When his back ached too much to continue, he stood under a pounding hot shower. The water stung his skin, but the pain felt good, cleansing almost. He closed his eyes and thought of Freddie pressing against his ass, of the way the handsome stud had sagged after ejaculating. He rubbed some soap in his right hand and stroked himself, holding on to the shower wall with his left.

He remembered Freddie's hot breath against his neck, the way he'd moaned as he came, almost like a small hiccup. Newt's orgasm wasn't as powerful as the one at Freddie's, but it was good enough.

He dried off, massaged some more cream into the places he could reach, then put on his loosest clothing, unwilling to have any fabric chafe against his back. It was gloomy and overcast outside with a threat of rain in the air, but Newt didn't mind. He walked down toward the beach, dodging pack-laden travelers, clueless texters, and skinny women waving Gauloise cigarettes.

The ocean surged at the shore in frothy waves. The pebbled beach was nearly deserted, only a few hardy vacationers desperate for time by the water. The African men who sold wooden carvings on carpets were busy packing up before the rain, as was the violinist who played for spare change across from the beaux-arts pile that was the Hotel Negresco.

Newt understood that he owed this boost of creativity to Freddie Venus. But how much clearer could the man have been—that Newt needed to be punished for his voyeurism and then chased from the house? Could Newt control himself enough not to go back? Maybe he should leave the area entirely. He only had two months left on his lease. He could lose the money and move on.

But where would he go? He'd fallen in love with this corner of France, with the landscape of hills and ocean, the handsome, nearly naked men on the beach. Who the fuck was Freddie Venus to chase him away from all that?

The rain began spattering the pavement of the Promenade des Anglais, and Newt darted across the street to the shelter of a café. He desperately wanted something sweet, a pretty little pastry or a flaky chocolate croissant. But he steeled his resolve, ordered a mineral water and a green salad, and watched the rain slant down on the passing traffic.

When the shower passed, the sun glistened on the wet pavement in bright shards. Newt finished his salad and walked back to his apartment. By the time he climbed the three flights, he was mentally and physically exhausted. He stripped down and looked at his back and ass in the mirror. They were a paler shade of red, and he applied the lotion again.

He had to prove to himself that he could write without Freddie's inspiration, so he went back to the computer. He had ended the sex scene between Fledglis and Ulric on the floor of a bar, the two of them naked and surrounded by sawdust and peanut shells.

Fuck that angel, Newt thought. Fledglis had done fine without him, and he'd manage on his own again. Ulric would be a one-time visitor to the Fledglis saga.

Fledglis was still in human form after his barroom romp with Ulric. Newt wrote him out of the bar, into the sunlight, where Fledglis opened his arms and transformed back into the white unicorn with the rainbow-colored mane. He galloped down the street, darting between cars, and then took off, free once again.

Even as he wrote those words, though, Newt knew that neither he nor Fledglis was truly free, at least not yet.

10 – MILITARY MAN

Liam leaned back against the pillows of the king-size bed. "Let's see what Freddie Venus looked like when he was making movies," he said.

Aidan picked up the remote and pressed Play. Liam watched for a few minutes. "This is what I hate about porn," he said. "It's so fake."

"What do you mean?" Aidan protested. "It looks pretty real to me."

"The uniforms are all wrong," Liam said. "They're costumes, and no military outfit dresses like that. None of those guys look like they've even arrived at basic training, much less completed it."

"I can't imagine that everyone in the military was as butch as you."

"It's not about being butch." Liam took the remote and paused the video. He pointed at one twink. "That guy couldn't pass the basic requirements—be able to run a mile and a half, do two pull-ups and forty-four sit-ups."

"You could, of course."

"I could when I was seventeen, and I can today. Way more than that." He pointed to another guy. "His hair is too long. Recruits get shaved almost bald when they first arrive at basic training. If he was still in training, he'd have nothing more than stubble there."

He pointed at the third guy. "And there's no way this wimp can even hoist a forty-five–pound pack on his back, much less carry it over rough terrain."

Aidan crossed his arms over his chest. "Great. Now you have completely ruined this movie for me."

Liam reached over and caressed the bulge in Aidan's slacks. "Not quite ruined," he said. "There's still some interest down there. Would you like me to demonstrate what sex with a real military man is like?"

Aidan smiled at him. "I would like that very much."

"Well, first of all, a soldier has to be able to do push-ups." Liam rolled on top of Aidan and assumed the push-up position. Up and down he went, rubbed his body against Aidan's, kissed him as he went down.

He remembered doing push-ups in basic training at RTC Great Lakes, though there had been nothing erotic about the exercise. The seven-week training had been nonstop academics, athletics, and military drill. During the day, they studied marksmanship, seamanship, and water survival, among other things, and at night they were too exhausted to even think about sex.

"I like this," Aidan said, bringing Liam out of his reverie. "But aren't we wearing too much clothing?"

"That is absolutely correct." Liam sat up and pulled his black polo shirt over his head. The cool air rippled against his skin, and he felt like a well-toned animal, all flesh and hunger. He looked down at Aidan and growled.

Aidan wriggled out of his matching polo, revealing the hairy chest that camouflaged his muscular development. The two pink nubs of his tits made Liam want to lean down and suck them, but they still had more clothes to get rid of.

Liam rolled off Aidan and quickly shucked his pants and jockstrap. He'd begun wearing a jock as a high school athlete and never lost the habit, or the erotic attraction. He knew that his jock turned Aidan on, bringing back pubescent memories, but he was too eager to get to the main event to waste time on preliminaries.

Maybe Aidan was right, he thought, as his partner stripped down. It had been too long since they'd had fun like this. What in the world had kept them from it?

Liam resumed his push-up position, but Aidan slid down the bed so that his mouth was even with Liam's dick. There was nothing like that warm, wet embrace, he thought. He could feel the rasp of Aidan's tongue, the gentle scrape of his partner's teeth.

Liam began a steady rhythm, moving up and down, his dick riding in and out of Aidan's mouth. He loved the way his inguinal ligaments and his adductor muscles flexed in their intricate dance, his butt rising and falling, his heart rate increasing, all those powerful endorphins racing into his blood.

When his arousal rose, he slipped out. "A good soldier has to be able to do squats and sit-ups too." He positioned himself over Aidan's stiff dick, his own dick sticking out at an angle and dripping precome and saliva onto Aidan's belly.

In small increments, he lowered himself on Aidan's dick, using his partner's precome for lubrication. He focused on opening his ass to the intrusion, absorbing the momentary sensation of pain that jittered through him. Then Aidan was inside him, and Liam felt that satisfying sensation of fullness, that visceral connection to the man he loved.

He kept moving down until his ass was resting on Aidan's hairy thighs. Then, with Aidan still impaling him, he clasped his hands behind his head and began his routine of sit-ups.

He had done his exercise that morning in the courtyard, but an extra workout was always good, especially when it involved Aidan. The rocking motion made Aidan's dick move inside Liam's chute, pressing sideways and then forward, hitting Liam's prostate and sending waves of pleasure through him.

He lost himself in the routine until he felt Aidan squirming beneath him, breathing heavily, and realized that his partner was ready to come. Liam stilled himself, looking down at Aidan, who stared back up with a raptured grin. "I'm so close," Aidan groaned. "Liam, you're torturing me."

"I'm showing you the way a real military man makes love," Liam said, holding his position, though his thighs screamed with effort. When he finally felt Aidan relaxing, he pressed down on his partner's chest with his hands and raised his ass in the air. He began bucking like a horse, fucking Aidan's dick while moving up and down.

Aidan took a deep, gulping breath, which ended in a strangled cry as he shot his load up Liam's ass. That look on Aidan's face, that scream—they were enough to send Liam over the edge himself, and he was surprised when he ejaculated over Aidan's chest without even touching himself.

"You must have been one hot dude when you were in the SEALs," Aidan said as Liam levered himself up and then slumped beside his partner.

"I am still one hot dude," Liam said, and yawned. Then he was asleep, his body sweaty and sticky and feeling very well used.

When Liam awoke the next morning, Aidan was already up somewhere else in the house. He reached down to his belly and felt the scratch of dried semen in his pubic hairs and on his chest. He did a quick wash in the bathroom and then pulled on his workout gear.

His thighs were tight, and his ass ached with a pleasant reminder of the previous night's exertions. Couldn't let himself get out of shape for anything, he thought as he walked out to the kitchen. Aidan was right, as usual; they needed to fuck more often.

Aidan was at the stove with two frying pans going—hash browns in one, a nearly finished omelet in the other. Liam walked over and kissed him on the lips, tasting fresh orange juice. Aidan neatly flipped the omelet onto a plate and ladled hash browns to the side. He added an orange slice, then delivered the plate to Freddie at the oak table.

"I could get accustomed to this kind of service," Freddie said as he picked up his fork. "Freshly cooked breakfast and eye candy for dessert."

"I can have another omelet ready in a minute," Aidan said to Liam.

Liam shook his head. "I'm going for a run. I'll eat an energy bar when I get back." He watched Aidan as he moved so easily around the large, well-appointed kitchen, preparing an omelet for himself. This was undoubtedly the kind of house Aidan wanted, where he belonged. Too bad Liam doubted he could ever provide it on the money they made in close protection.

"You're lucky," he said to Freddie. "Aidan's a gourmet chef. Studied all different kinds of cooking back in Philadelphia."

"This is delicious," Freddie said, his fork poised in the air. "Anytime the bodyguard business doesn't work out, you can come and cook for me."

Liam felt a burst of jealousy. Was there a subtext to what Freddie had said? Was he really saying if Aidan got tired of Liam, he could join Freddie up here in this beautiful house, which Aidan had already said he loved?

Hold on, tiger, he said to himself. He was beginning to think like Aidan, looking for drama in the most ordinary situations. Freddie was a single guy without anybody to cook for or eat with. And Aidan's food was mouthwatering.

As Aidan plated his own eggs and potatoes and sat at the table across from the client, Liam leaned back against the wall and stretched, aware he was showing off his muscles. He asked Freddie, "What's on your agenda for today?"

"Work. I've been distracted these last couple of days, and I need to finish this editing project."

That was good, Liam thought. Maybe Freddie would get his head out of his ass about this stalker and agree to lie low until he and

Aidan had a chance to scope things out.

"When I get back from my run, mind if I use your backyard to work out?"

"Just watch out for the lavender," Freddie said. "Might still be sticky."

Liam chose not to think about that. He walked out of the kitchen, and stopped at the front door to survey the area for potential trouble. Finding none, he took off down the hilly driveway, then cleared his mind as he focused on the feel of the pavement beneath his running shoes, the warmth of the early-morning sun, the smell of lavender and automobile exhaust in the air.

The sex the night before had been a good release, and Aidan had enjoyed it too. Maybe they'd be able to get hold of more of Freddie's work on DVD to watch when they got back home.

There was little traffic on the road, and to the west of Freddie's house the land sloped upward so that his neighbor's property looked down on his. Liam kept going until he had conquered the first steep switchback. Most of the running he did in Nice was on flat ground along the ocean; it was good to change things up, challenge different muscles.

He turned around and sprinted back down to Freddie's house, slowing to a cooldown trot as he jogged up the driveway.

Then he saw the poster stuck under the windshield wiper of the Jeep. It was about twenty-four by thirty-six inches, a promotional piece for a movie called *Dark Desires*, starring Freddie Venus. There was no mistaking a younger Freddie in the center of the image, butch and shirtless. Nor was it easy to miss the red circular target hand-drawn on his chest.

11 – Target Acquired

Seeing the target drawn on Freddie's poster pushed Liam into full alert, and he began a systematic survey of the area around him. Everything was still except for a bird with a high-pitched call, singing from one of the cypress trees by the street. He walked slowly toward the Jeep, checking for any disturbance on the ground that might indicate a trip wire or the presence of explosives.

When he was confident it was safe, he moved in close. He didn't want to touch it; the sweat on his hands would make his fingerprints stick and perhaps cover up evidence. But leaning forward, he could see that the poster had crease marks where it had been folded. The red circle had been drawn with a thick marker, the color washing out where the circle was connected.

The obvious conclusion was that Freddie's stalker was not willing to go away peacefully, but Liam didn't like to make rush judgments. Perhaps this was just the stalker's way of saying good-bye. If that was the case, it was a threatening sort of au revoir.

In any case, Freddie needed to know that his safety was not as assured as he believed. Liam stepped around the Jeep and walked into the house. Aidan and Freddie were still in the kitchen, talking and laughing as Aidan loaded dishes and cookware into the dishwasher. "Thought you were going to work out," Aidan said.

"You guys need to come out front," Liam said.

Freddie started to ask questions, but Liam held his hand up.

"You have any rubber gloves?"

"There are some under the sink," Freddie said.

As Aidan slotted a frying pan into the machine and closed it, Liam retrieved a box of thin rubber cleaning gloves. Liam led the way outside with Freddie and Aidan following.

Liam pointed at the poster on the windshield. "Look familiar?" he asked Freddie.

"Jesus Christ," Freddie said. "That was a lousy picture. What's the poster doing there?"

"I doubt whoever drew the target over you was a film critic," Liam said. He tried to get one of the gloves over his right hand, but it was meant for a woman with a daintier hand than his, and it tore.

"Let me," Aidan said. His hands were slimmer than Liam's, and he slipped a glove on easily. He carefully lifted the windshield wiper that was holding the poster in place. He removed the poster and folded it into quarters along the creases, then slipped it into a zip-locked bag Liam held.

"You think your stalker could have put this there?" Liam asked Freddie.

"Jesus," Freddie said again. He began to shake, and wrapped his arms around his chest. "I have no idea."

Aidan took Freddie's arm with the hand that wasn't holding the zippered bag. "Come back in the house," he said. "I saw a bottle of prosecco in your refrigerator. How about if we have some mimosas while Liam continues his workout." To Liam he said, "We might want to call the police in at this point. This is a pretty clear threat."

Freddie shook his head. "No police. Not unless we have to. That's why I hired you guys."

He and Aidan walked back into the house. The driveway, paved in a pebbled light brown, revealed no clues. Neither did the landscaping on the slope down to the street—a combination of sandy dirt and thin grasses. Liam looked around the base of each tree and shrub, but nothing had been disturbed. Then he began a careful circuit of the property, checking each window and door for signs of attempted entry, for footprints in the dirt.

It was obvious that Freddie let the landscaping around his house grow naturally—there were no manicured lawns, no pretty beds of flowers. The lavender Freddie had mentioned grew in random patches, and the stems in one area had been trampled, most likely by the stalker Freddie had spotted jerking off there.

When he was confident there were no present dangers and no clues as to who had left the poster, Liam assumed the first position of the sun salutations, using the yoga to warm up as he often did. He centered himself, stilled his breathing, put his palms together.

When he had achieved normal resting breathing, he inhaled, arched his back, and raised his arms above his head. His movements flowed smoothly, following the pattern of exhale and inhale as he bent, stretched, and then returned to the first position.

Liam had begun learning yoga during his stint as a SEAL, at the suggestion of one of his teammates. He found that the repetitive movements allowed him to let his subconscious mind rise to the surface, giving him insights that might have remained hidden.

The poster had to be a threat. Perhaps the stalker resented Freddie's confrontation and was determined to regain the upper hand. Freddie had said he and the stalker had sex too. So maybe the man had gotten a taste of Freddie's awesome sexual power and couldn't walk away.

Liam was inclined to discount that theory almost immediately. He loved Aidan and enjoyed having sex with him, but if one day Aidan decided to walk away, Liam wouldn't run after him like a lovesick puppy or threaten him with harm unless he returned. Sex was just sex, after all.

Unbidden, a line from a song rose in his brain. "One pair of arms is like another; it's all the same."

What was that from? One of Aidan's movie musicals?

There was no way Liam was going to burst into song in Freddie's backyard. He finished his tenth salutation and then went into his regular routine of jumping jacks, sit-ups, and push-ups. No thinking required.

He finished with a cooldown routine, then pulled his T-shirt off and mopped his brow. When he looked up, he realized that Aidan and Freddie were watching him through the wide glass windows. Well, Aidan always accused him of being an exhibitionist. At least this time he'd stayed clothed. He gave them a wide bow, and they applauded.

After a shower, he joined them in the kitchen. Hayam was sitting up on her hind legs beside Aidan, who was feeding her bits of leftover scrambled egg.

"We've been talking about Freddie's brothers," Aidan said.

"We've been estranged, to put it nicely," Freddie said. "Haven't spoken to Earl or Gerald in a long time."

"Is your brother Earl as homophobic in private as he is in public?" Liam asked. "We've read some of his campaign statements about family values." He put air quotes around those words—something he'd never have done before he met Aidan. First he was hearing musical songs in his head; then he was using air quotes. Christ, he really was gay, wasn't he? And not just because he liked to suck dick.

Freddie shrugged. "I wasn't out when I lived at home. Didn't even know what 'out' was, or what 'gay' was. I knew that I had these feelings that other boys didn't seem to have, and I took off for LA as soon as I could to explore them."

This was the kind of client background that made Liam uncomfortable. He felt that sexuality was a private thing and couldn't understand why some people made such a big thing out of it. A football player was gay. Big deal. A movie star had been caught in a compromising position with a transvestite hooker. So what?

He hated the trend of making a big deal out of everyone who came out of the closet. Just shut up and make your movies, sing your songs, play your sports. Get over yourself.

"I told my family that I was working in the movie business," Freddie said. "I kind of embroidered stories that made it sound like I was some low-level gofer-assistant to the assistant director, that kind of thing. Nobody pressed me, and we got along fine. My parents were well-off, and they were disappointed that I didn't go to college, but Earl and Gerald filled that void. Both of them got married and provided the required grandkids, so I was off the hook there too."

He sat back in his chair. Liam noticed that Freddie didn't seem to be a clotheshorse; he wore a faded T-shirt that stretched over his chest and a pair of baggy board shorts.

"By the time my dad died, I was done acting, but I was directing porn, and I was fierce," Freddie continued. "Wasn't going to hide anything. Had a big dustup with my brothers after the funeral, and I walked away with no intention of ever going back."

"That must have been tough," Aidan said.

"Nah. I'd long since given up on those people. My mom kept in touch, though. I talked to her almost every week until suddenly she wasn't answering her phone."

Freddie choked up, and Aidan handed him a napkin, which he used to blow his nose. "I wasn't talking to my brothers, so I called the neighbors. Most of the ones I knew were already dead, but finally one lady told me that my mother had fallen in the house and broken her hip, that she was in the hospital. My bastard brothers never called me. I called around and found out what hospital she was in, found out she had caught an infection and was dying. I flew to Omaha right away, took a cab to the hospital. It was after dinner by then, and Earl and Gerald were both there. Earl tried to keep me from coming into her room, saying he didn't want her upset. But I pushed him out of the way."

He began crying outright. Liam hated it when clients got

emotional, because he never knew what to say. That was Aidan's department.

"Take your time, Freddie," Aidan said. He put his hand on Freddie's lower arm. "We're right here."

Freddie sniffled, then blew his nose again. "She was so much skinnier than I remembered, and her hair was uncombed, which I knew she hated. She used to go to the beauty parlor every other week to have her hair done. I took a comb out of my pocket, and I started to fix her hair the way she liked, and she opened her eyes and smiled."

This story was not going to have a happy ending, Liam thought. Deathbed visits never did.

"I held my mom's hand and kissed her cheek," Freddie said. "She looked up into my eyes and said, 'My baby boy. You came to see me.' Then she smiled again and closed her eyes, and I was crying so hard that it took me a minute to realize she was gone."

He stifled a deep sob. "I'm supposed to be the big tough guy, huh? But that killed me, the way it was like she was waiting for me to come to her. I lit into Gerald first, broke two of his ribs. Then Earl stepped in, and I broke his nose. The nurse had to call the cops and have me hauled away."

That topped his own dysfunctional family, Liam thought, though not by much.

"Wow," Aidan said.

"Yeah. Wow. Earl was a big shot even then, and he got everything hushed up, got the charges dropped provided I never set foot in Nebraska again. That was fine by me."

"Have you had any contact with either of them recently?" Liam asked.

Freddie stared into space for a moment. "Yeah, a couple of weeks ago. My father had bought some land in Sioux County, northwest part of the state, and when he died he left it to the three of us. I'd forgotten all about it until I got a certified letter from an attorney back in Omaha, frat brother of Earl's. He wanted me to sign off so we could lease the land to some oil exploration company for fracking."

"Did you sign it?" Aidan asked.

"No fucking way," Freddie said. "You know what fracking does to the land? To the people who live around there?"

"Do you think one of your brothers could have sent someone to put that poster up?" Liam asked. "Threaten you to get you to sign those papers?"

"Seems like a big reach," Freddie said. "I mean, how am I to know that's what they want from that poster?"

"You'd probably be an embarrassment to your brother's Senate campaign if word got out about you," Liam said. "You think he could have hired someone to run you off the road night before last?"

"Earl? Christ. I mean, he's a bastard, but try to kill me?" Freddie thought for a moment. "I don't know. I haven't said more than a couple of sentences to him since I was eighteen years old. Who knows what he's turned into?"

"We need to find out who put that poster on the Jeep and make sure that this stalker you've befriended isn't part of some larger conspiracy. Can you get back in touch with your stalker?" Liam asked. "See what his intentions are?"

"I'm trying," Freddie said. "As soon as I hear back from him I'll let you know."

12 – Bait Bus

As soon as he could get away from the bodyguards, Freddie went to his office, opened his laptop, and checked the Facebook page for Newton Cale. No response from the author to his post, though several fans had tagged his message with stupid shit about angels and unicorns.

Freddie tried to keep from obsessing. Odds were the author wasn't even the guy he'd met and that this Cale guy would ignore the message. And even if he was the right guy, if Cale had put that poster on the Jeep's windshield, then he was somebody to stay away from.

Freddie locked himself in the editing studio, trying to finish the video he'd been working on, but he was too distracted thinking of his brothers, of Newt, wondering who could be carrying a grudge against him.

Sure, he had pissed off some people back in LA. But all that was years behind him, and he couldn't imagine anyone tracking him down. He tried to meditate, but he couldn't focus. He kept thinking about the incident that had finally forced his hand, made him give up on LA and get the hell out of there.

* * *

Mario Dellarosa was the first director who ever hired Freddie, the one who gave him the name Freddie Venus. Freddie had avoided calling Mario once he started to fall, because he was embarrassed.

But Mario came through. He picked Freddie up at Randall's and took him to the emergency room, where he was diagnosed with a broken lightbulb up his ass.

The subsequent hospitalization gave Freddie the impetus to start over again. Mario paid his medical bills and gave him a place to stay for a while, then hired Freddie as a production assistant on his latest film. Quickly Freddie taught himself editing on Mario's Mac, and within six months he was living on his own, staying away from booze and drugs and bad influences. He began to make money because he was fast and had a good eye for what was sexy enough to get a guy off.

He caught up with the back taxes on the property in Nice and socked as much cash as he could into investments. Then Mario picked up viral encephalitis on a trip to Mexico and had to be hospitalized himself.

Mario called Freddie to his bedside. His face was ashen, his cheeks sunken, his once luxurious dark hair now thin and graying. He pulled the oxygen mask off his face and said, "I need you to finish the movie I'm working on. It's called *Straight Suckers*, and I think it could be big."

"You'll be out of here in no time, Mario. You can finish it yourself."

Mario wheezed and put the mask back on his face for a minute. When he pulled it off again, he said, "I'll be tied to this bed for a while. And I've got a deadline. Please, Freddie?"

How could he say no when Mario had been there for him? He got all the information from Mario and showed up at the shoot the next day.

Mario had this idea that most straight guys would be willing to fuck another guy if the money was right and if they could pretend they didn't know what they were getting into. Mario had hired a big-busted girl named Holly to cruise hardware stores for straight-looking guys, then entice them into coming to the studio. Holly would get them hot and bothered, then convince them to let a guy take over—for extra cash, of course.

Mario had filmed five sequences already, and Freddie watched the rough cut of each one with a critical eye. One of the guys agreed too readily to get a blowjob from a guy, while another was such a skank that Freddie wouldn't have touched his dick for love or money.

The best scene was with a sweet-looking guy who said his name was Brent. He was six-two with a wholesome, corn-fed look. He swore he'd never done porn before, and Freddie believed him. He said that he'd been out of work for months and was desperate to take care of his wife and baby son.

Brent had such an expressive face that Freddie could see every emotion played out. His reluctance to cheat on his wife balanced with the cold, hard cash that could put food on their table. The way his face lit up when Holly offered to double his money if he was interested in something different. The momentary revulsion when she asked if he'd ever had sex with another guy.

Freddie almost wished he'd been on the set that day so he could have walked over to Brent, handed him a wad of cash, and sent him on his way. That kind of innocence was rare in porn, and it ought to be protected.

Holly said, "You wouldn't be cheating on your wife if you have sex with another guy, right?" She reached down and stroked Brent's crotch, and the poor guy took that first step down what Freddie knew was a very slippery slope. He said, "I guess you're right."

Holly called in a paunchy middle-aged guy with wild eyebrows, and he got down on his knees in front of Brent. He tried to unzip Brent's pants, but the guy stopped him. "I'm not sure about this," he said.

Holly took over. She opened Brent's pants, popped his half-hard dick out of his tighty-whities, and began to stroke him. "See, it's all good," she said.

Brent leaned back and closed his eyes, and the middle-aged guy began to suck him. As long as his eyes were closed, Brent seemed to be okay; when he opened them, though, you could see the unhappiness wash across his face.

The cocksucker was clearly a master, and after a while Brent was smiling even with his eyes open.

Then Holly leaned in. "You ever fuck a girl's ass?" she asked.

Brent blushed, and Freddie knew that was the kind of emotion you just couldn't fake. "Tell me about it," Holly said.

"We were in high school," Brent said. "I was on the football team, and she was a cheerleader. The only place in town where you could buy rubbers was the drugstore where her father worked."

Oh, man, Freddie thought. This was pure gold.

"She said I could do her from behind, and that way she couldn't get pregnant," Brent continued.

"Did you like it?" Holly cooed.

Brent's eyes were glazed over—either from the blowjob or the memory. "Yeah," he said. "She was so tight, and her ass was so smooth. My wife, you know, she doesn't like to shave her bush, and it's scratchy sometimes. That ass, though. That was so sweet. Like fucking velvet."

"Javier's ass is like that," Holly said. "Smooth and tight."

"Javier?" Brent looked down at the man sucking him. "That's his name?"

"Nah, that's Ed," Holly said. "Javier, come out here."

Javier was a Mexican kid who looked no older than seventeen. He had olive skin and a slight slant to his eyes, and he was buck naked, his dick soft, and his pubes shaved smooth.

"Oh, hell to the no," Brent said. He tried to get up, but Holly put her hand on his shoulder.

From off camera, Mario offered to double Brent's money again if he'd fuck Javier's ass.

The look on Brent's face said it all. He recognized that he had become a whore, that he was willing to do anything for money. "Can I keep my eyes closed?" he asked.

"Sure," Holly said.

Ed got up and walked away. Holly tugged at Brent's pants. "Come on, handsome," she said. "Let the camera see it all."

Brent stood up. He kicked off his shoes and awkwardly shucked his jeans. His plaid shirt hung open, the pearlized buttons glinting in the camera light. Holly slipped the shirt off, and Brent stood there for a moment, his slick dick hanging out over the waistband of his briefs. He had a great chest, light hairs between his pecs, decent abs, a narrow waist.

Holly tugged down his briefs, and the mix of shame and lust on Brent's face was such a turn-on Freddie had to stop and jerk himself a few times. Even for a hardened porn viewer like him, this was hot stuff.

Javier turned his back to the camera. He had an arrow-shaped tramp stamp above his crack, and he wiggled his butt, looking over his shoulder with a grin.

Holly opened a condom and slid it onto Brent's dick, and he sat back down on the sofa and closed his eyes. His dick had started to wilt, and Holly stroked him until he was hard again.

Javier climbed onto the sofa and positioned his ass over Brent's dick. Holly rubbed some lube on the outside of the condom, and the cameraman moved in close as Javier's ass slid down onto Brent's dick.

Javier had impressive control of his ass muscles. Very quickly, despite Brent's earlier reservations, the poor schmuck was getting into it, smiling and moaning.

Freddie fast-forwarded to the end of the scene where Javier stood up and Holly took the condom off Brent's dick. Javier grabbed the dick and jerked it a couple of times, and Brent shot his load over his stomach.

"See, that was kind of fun," Holly said to him. She leaned in and kissed him, her big tits bouncing off his chest.

But all Brent said was, "Where's my money?"

Mario needed one more sequence to make the movie long enough for distribution. One afternoon a couple of days later, Freddie drove over to the warehouse Mario had been using as a studio, where he met Javier and Ed. They were waiting for Holly to return with her latest conquest.

When they heard Holly's old beater pull up outside, Freddie picked up the digital movie camera, and Javier and Ed went behind a makeshift divider to wait. Holly walked in and introduced him. "This is Freddie. He's the director. Freddie, this is Carl."

Carl was a skinny-looking tough guy. From his skittish manner, Freddie thought he might be on meth. But that didn't matter to him; if Carl needed the cash to get his next hit, he'd do almost anything.

Holly sat down beside Carl on the leopard-print sofa and popped one of her breasts out of her blouse. Carl leaned down to take it in his mouth and suck. Freddie hated that kind of footage, but it was what Mario wanted to establish Carl's bona fides as a straight dude.

Freddie zoomed in on Holly's tit, and then back out as she began stroking Carl through his faded jeans. Then she reached over for a blindfold.

"I don't get into that shit," Carl said, batting her hand away.

"Oh, come on, baby," she said. "You never got a blowjob blindfolded, didja? It makes all your senses, you know, more."

Holly was a real Rhodes scholar, Freddie thought.

"You're gonna come like you never did before," Holly said. She stroked his dick with one hand, his chest with the other.

He agreed, and she tied the blindfold around his head. Then Ed crept out quietly as Holly unzipped Carl's jeans and popped his boner out. Ed was wearing a wig that looked like Holly's shoulder-length blonde hair. His face had been shaven smooth, and with some makeup he might have passed for a drag queen from the shoulders up.

Ed knelt down in front of Carl and took the dick in his mouth. Carl said, "Oh yeah, you're right. That is awesome."

Ed had very expressive eyes, which was great for the camera, since Carl was blindfolded and Freddie was focused in on the dick, watching it go in and out of Ed's mouth.

Carl reached down and stroked Ed's hair, and the wig passed the test.

At a signal from Freddie, Ed backed off Carl's dick and Holly leaned in to him. "Want to fuck my ass, baby?"

"You bet," Carl said. He reached up to untie the blindfold, but Holly stopped him.

"It turns me on when the guy can't see me," she whispered into his ear.

"All right."

Javier stepped onto the set naked with a pink dildo up his butt. He walked over to Carl and pushed the dildo out, then sat down onto Carl's dick.

Something must have felt wrong to Carl, though, because

without warning he pulled the blindfold off. "What the fuck!" he said. "I ain't no faggot."

He punched Javier in the gut, and the Mexican boy fell backward to the floor, hitting his head. Carl jumped up and saw Ed going to help Javier. "Did you blow me, you asshole?" he asked. He began flailing at Ed and then Holly when she stepped in to pull him off.

Freddie captured the first bit on film, but when he noticed Javier wasn't moving, he jumped into the fray. He was way more ripped than Carl, and he got the dude in an armlock and muscled him out of the studio, his pants hanging open and his dick wagging.

Freddie locked the door and turned back to his crew. Holly was crying on the phone to the 911 operator, and Ed kept saying, "He needs CPR, but I don't know how to do it. Anybody know CPR?"

* * *

Looking back now, Freddie knew instinctively that was when everything turned to shit. But how could something that had happened years before matter now?

13 – Inspiration

When Newt woke on Tuesday morning, he felt almost human again. He took a long, hot bath, and then awkwardly rubbed more body lotion on his back. As he did, he noticed himself in the mirror.

He tried not to check out his reflection, especially not naked, because he was repulsed by how he looked. But it appeared that he had lost some weight, and he understood why some of his clothes had started feeling looser. All that walking, and his determination to avoid sweets, must have been working.

He poured himself a tall glass of water and sat down gingerly at his desk chair. It wasn't too bad, so he opened up the document that he'd been working on and reviewed it.

Perhaps Fledglis and his angel lover could have a holiday on the gorgeous Riviera? They could romp on the beach, make love on top of Mont Boron, the hill that overlooked the port. Fly out over the Mediterranean, chasing sailboats. It could be a gorgeous story, because the beach at Nice was so beautiful. The deep blue water, the gray stones, the dark green of the hillsides in the distance. The colorful umbrellas, chairs, and towels, a mix of stripes and patterns. The way the sun sparkled on the light waves.

He remembered the way the beach vendors cried, "Cola-cola, *gini, bieri,* Schweppes" against a background of traffic noise, with the faintest sound of waves hitting the beach. He began to type furiously, bringing all that in, the skinny, gap-toothed North African men, the white-haired elderly women clutching patent leather pocketbooks, the cute young men in their tight bikinis, strutting like proud peacocks.

He began a scene in which Fledglis and Ulric flew down from the foothills of the Alps and swooped arabesques over the ocean, an aerial dance between angel and unicorn. They landed on the sand of a secluded cove, gnarled trees rooted in the steep stone. Ulric positioned himself at Fledglis's horsy ass and fucked him in gentle, smooth movements.

Fledglis neighed, and Ulric flapped his broad white wings. Ulric stroked Fledglis's colorful mane and called him a good pony. But then Newt stopped writing.

He knew that when he was writing a sex scene, if he wasn't getting a boner, then something was wrong. And that was the problem with this scene. It was too happy. Nobody got beaten up or fucked into oblivion.

He pushed back from his desk, and his back zinged with pain. Was this the inspiration that Freddie Venus had provided? To turn Fledglis from a daring avenger to a lovesick horse who needed to get bruised to get off?

His mind was too cluttered to keep writing, so he decided to go for a long walk along the ocean. Maybe he would get a pedometer, he thought, to track his miles. And he could do a better job of keeping track of his calories.

He walked down toward the Promenade des Anglais, careful to stay out of the way of grungy backpackers and busy French men and women on their cell phones. Once he had crossed the big highway that ran beside the ocean and was safe on the walkway, he let his mind wander.

Fledglis had been born out of anger, and Newt's righteous indignation had fueled the unicorn through three books. Newt loved the chance to exact literary revenge on every tormentor, every Bible-thumping hypocrite, every weasel politician who promised equality but then didn't have the balls to follow through. Maybe his experience with Freddie was his body's way of taking things further.

He stopped to listen to a saxophonist play a mournful melody, which was so at odds with the beauty of sea and sky. Then from behind him, Newt heard someone say, "*Voilà l'éléphant*," and laugh. When he turned around, he realized that two of the bikini boys were giggling and pointing at him. "*Ces Américains*," one of the boys said.

Newt was mortified, and he crossed the street against traffic, horns blaring, brakes screeching, so eager to get away. Yes, it was a bright, sunny landscape, but there was darkness there too. It seemed that he couldn't get away from that pain—perhaps because it was so deep inside him that nothing could fully exorcise it.

His head was full of unicorns and angels as he walked back up the hill toward the train station and his apartment across the street from it. He was sweaty and tired, but his brain was fevered. He sat down at his laptop, ignoring the shimmering pain in his back, and began to revise the story he'd written earlier. He closed his eyes and remembered the way those two bikini boys looked and wrote a scene that began with them tormenting another boy because of his weight.

Newt's fingers danced over the keyboard as Fledglis and Ulric swooped in to give those two bullies what they deserved. He imagined those two boys laid flat on the pavement, their tiny bikinis pulled to their ankles, as Fledglis and Ulric fucked them into submission.

Then they took off for that secluded cove, the romantic interlude their reward for good deeds. By the time he closed the document, his dick was hard and his brain was clear.

He realized it had been a couple of days since he'd gone online to answer e-mails and do some social networking. When he checked, he saw that the Newton Cale Facebook page had gotten a lot of hits, and he scanned through the messages, looking for anything he ought to answer.

Angel wings seeks unicorn. Please come back.

Holy crap. Was that a message from Freddie Venus? How had he tracked Newt down? He was sure he hadn't given the man the Newton Cale name or ever said that he was any kind of writer. He'd told Freddie his real name, but he hadn't used that for writing for years, not since he'd begun to break out of fan fiction.

Freddie must have hunted him down. That was impressive. So was the message to come back to the farmhouse.

Did he want to? Go back for more whipping, more debasing? Who knew what else Freddie Venus was capable of doing to him?

Who was he kidding? A real-life porn star had fucked him and then asked him to come back for more. Of course he'd return.

Did what they'd done really constitute fucking, though? Newt had come from being whipped, and Freddie had spurted after rubbing his clothed groin against Newt's ass. Not exactly the stuff of romance. No hearts or flowers. The guy hadn't even bought him a drink.

Yet it was the most intimate contact Newt had had with another man for years. That was sad, he thought. That he could be treated the way Fledglis did his victims, and enjoy it, and then turn sappy over it. Was that all he'd have for the rest of his life? Was he giving up on that dream of meeting a nice guy, settling down, growing old together in rocking chairs on a wooden porch?

He clicked on the post to reply. If Freddie was serious, would he be willing to do some of the chasing? Newt typed, *In front of the Negresco Hotel. Tonight at 6.* Then before he could change his mind, he hit Enter.

What if Freddie wasn't online? It was almost noon. What if he didn't read the message in time? If, if, if. His grandmother used to say, *"If the cow had balls, she'd be a bull."* If he was meant to see Freddie Venus again, he would, no matter how desperately he wanted to. In the meantime, he had to make sure that money kept flowing into his bank account, and that meant answering fans, posting teaser excerpts, replying to the questions provided by a blogger. He got so busy that he didn't notice time passing until he looked down at the clock display in his taskbar and realized that he had to get moving if he was going to make it to the Hotel Negresco in time.

14 – FOLLOWING

Freddie had thought it would be weird having the bodyguards there in the house with him, but they managed fine on their own. He wondered how often they fucked. The big one, Liam, looked like a sex machine, the kind that Freddie himself had been when he was younger. Had either of them ever considered porn?

Not that Freddie was eager to get back into the business of making movies. He was perfectly content with editing. After a rough morning, he finally got absorbed in work on Tuesday afternoon, and it wasn't until nearly four o'clock that he read the request that Newton Cale had sent.

Holy shit, he thought. He would have to scramble to get into Nice in time to meet. That is, if the bodyguards were willing to let him go. He stood up and went in search of them.

Aidan was sitting on the couch in the living room, reading his Kindle, and Liam was on the floor playing with their little dog. It was such a sweet domestic scene that it pierced him. Would he ever have that? Did he even want it?

"Sorry to disturb you, but I heard back from Newt," Freddie said.

"That's the stalker?" Liam asked.

"I wish you wouldn't call him that." Freddie held up his hand. "I know, I'm the one who started it. But I'm going on instinct here. I need to spend some time with him, see what he's up to."

He didn't add that he was still trying to figure out why he'd been able to come with Newt when he hadn't been able to for so long. That wasn't anybody's business but his own. "He wants to meet me at six on the Promenade des Anglais, in front of the Hotel Negresco."

"Absolutely not," Liam said.

"Hold on, Liam," Aidan said. "It's a public place. You and I can stake out a defensive position and be ready to intervene if we have to."

"You won't have to," Freddie said. "This is just a hookup. Nothing more."

"You have a full name on this guy?" Liam asked. "Address? Anything?"

"He's a writer," Freddie said. "His pen name is Newton Cale. But his real last name is Camilleri."

"Spell it, please," Aidan said.

Freddie had to think for a minute, and even then he wasn't sure if there were two m's or two l's.

Aidan wrote the name down a couple of different ways. "We'll do some research before we go. That all right with you?"

Freddie nodded. "But make it quick. We have to get moving soon if we're going to make the meeting in time."

While the bodyguards went online, Freddie hurried into his bedroom to get dressed. Instead of his usual disguise of sunglasses, ball cap, and baggy clothes that covered his tats, he threw on a spaghetti-strap tank top that let his pecs and nipples poke through and exposed the broad expanse of his back and the angel wings there. It was almost like those wings were pushing him forward.

When he walked back out to the living room, he noticed Aidan trying not to salivate, and smiled to himself. He still had it.

Liam insisted on driving them in the Jeep. Freddie preferred to have his own wheels, but he was willing to compromise if they could get down into the city in a hurry. He sat in the front seat, and Aidan climbed into the back. The whole way down the hill into the city, Freddie felt stupid, like a teenage boy on his first date. And yet here he was, a weathered ex-porn star with a limp dick that only popped from whipping a fat, naked Peeping Tom. What a strange old world it was.

Liam parked in a public lot a few blocks from the beach, and the three of them hurried down a narrow street toward the ocean. The buildings leaned in close and shadowed the pavement, so it was a surprise when they exited into the full brilliance of the setting sun, with the ocean sparkling ahead of them.

There was a lot of eye candy around, both male and female. Freddie had never had a desire for pussy, but he could recognize a pretty woman. The women on their way to or from the beach were tanned and slim, with an aura of chic so common to the French. A few had saggy tits or hair tinted a shade too brassy, but they carried themselves well.

The men were just as sexy. Slim young guys in tiny bikinis, showing off their flat stomachs and tight booties. Dark-skinned Tunisian and Moroccan men who moved with catlike grace. Even the white-haired older dudes had sex appeal.

Not a bad place for a gay man to choose for a rendezvous, Freddie thought. He'd never have considered such a public place; he usually had no desire to be recognized. And yet, the one time a man had identified him and come after him, he'd gotten so excited he'd creamed his shorts.

"We'll have you in visual all the time," Liam said. "But try to think with your big head, please, not the little one. Don't get into a car with him. Don't go into any dark alleys."

"But those are the most fun places," Freddie said. Liam frowned, and Freddie laughed at him. Yeah, someone might be trying to kill him. But he was pretty sure it wasn't Newt.

A breeze blew in from the Mediterranean, bringing the scent of salt water and coconut suntan lotion, and Freddie had a fleeting memory of the beach at Santa Monica, the way it had looked from his apartment balcony.

The same balcony Rodney had jumped from.

He pushed the memory aside and focused on the present. He moved quickly along the pedestrian walkway between beach and street. Most of the people around him were leaving the beach, carrying towels and portable chairs. Rush-hour traffic zoomed past on the Promenade, cars honking and motorcycles revving.

He kept the round dome of the Hotel Negresco in sight, occasionally looking around to see if Newt was approaching. Ahead of him the sky was lit with a reddish glow, and streetlights popped on one at a time, like pearls being added to a string.

He stopped on the pavement across from the hotel. It was a beautiful old pile, with a central tower at the corner and a gold-topped dome. He'd been inside a few times to the cavernous lobby decorated with huge oil paintings. Maybe he'd take Newt over there, rent them a room with a view of the ocean, order a bottle of champagne. Freddie Venus knew how to treat a man.

But where was that man? It was a few minutes before six, and he'd expected Newt to be waiting for him. Had he misunderstood the date or the time or the location? He wished he'd printed something out, but he had dashed out of the house so quickly he hadn't thought to do so.

He turned around in a complete circle, scanning the area. No Newt.

Fuck. The asshole was playing with him, getting back at him for the whipping. Freddie had no interest in playing head games; he'd had enough of that with Rodney. He was about to give up and head back to where he and the bodyguards had parked when he heard someone behind him, panting, his footsteps heavy on the pavement as he ran-walked.

Freddie turned to see Newt. "Don't give yourself a heart attack," he said.

"I didn't think you'd come." Newt was short of breath, his big chest rising and falling.

"I didn't think I could come," Freddie said, smiling. "Until you made me cream my shorts."

Newt had a nice face, open and smiling. Deep, soulful brown

eyes, full lips that looked like they were made for French kissing.

The rest of him was a shambles, though. Freddie couldn't imagine how he had been attracted to such a doughy lump of flesh. He was a fucking porn star, for Christ's sake. In his time, he could have had any piece of ass he wanted. Even today, he could walk into a gay bar anywhere in the world, flash his tats and be recognized, and have men falling over themselves to offer their dicks and asses.

But instead of all those men, he had Newt Camilleri in front of him. Newt's arms were fat. His legs were fat. Even his fingers were fat. He was like a big white marshmallow man. Freddie had always disliked marshmallows.

Newt's dick was pretty fat too, Freddie remembered. "Do you want to look the way you do?" Freddie asked him.

"Hello to you too," Newt said. "And yes, my back and ass still hurt after the whipping you gave me. There are places I can't even reach to put on cream."

"I can take care of that for you," Freddie said. "But you didn't answer my question. Do you want to be a fat fuck, or do you want to get in shape?"

"What are you now, a personal trainer?"

"I asked you a simple question." Freddie scowled at him—a look that by itself had cowed many guys who thought they were tops into bottoming for him. But the fat fuck seemed impervious.

"Oh, Christ," Freddie said. "I give up. You live around here?"

"Why?"

"Because if you take me home with you, I can put cream on

those places you can't reach."

"Is that all?"

"What the fuck do you want from me, asshole? Because you're really starting to piss me off. First you come snooping around my house, jerking off in my yard. Then when I try to show you what a douchebag you are, you make me shoot a load. I haven't come like that in ten years or more. So what do I do? I follow my damn dick, something I swore I'd never do again. I hunt you down on the Internet like a crazy person. I travel miles in traffic to meet you. I swear, I don't know if I want to kiss you or fuck your ass with the biggest dildo I can find."

"Can we start with kissing?"

The guy looked so much like one of those sad basset hounds that Freddie couldn't contain himself anymore. He stepped up and pressed his chest against all that flab, then reached around behind the guy's head to pull it forward. And then he kissed him.

Freddie Venus prided himself on his oral skills. He could suck like a vacuum cleaner, lick like a happy puppy, and kiss a man hard enough to make him swoon. He pressed his lips against Newt's, feeling their moistness. He exhaled gently through his mouth, and his warm breath flowed into Newt's.

He pressed his tongue forward, let it roam inside Newt's mouth, all the while maintaining the pressure of his lips. He had one hand on the back of Newt's head, the other at the guy's waist, and he could feel the moment when Newt gave in, when he kissed Freddie back with the same passion.

Freddie pulled back, leaving Newt gasping for air once again. "Now, before we get arrested for public indecency," Freddie said. "You have a place near here?"

Newt nodded dumbly and turned to lead the way.

Freddie shook his head. This was twenty-five different kinds of wrong. The bodyguards were going to have a fit. Newt was humongous, had no social skills, and didn't seem to care that Freddie Venus was a goddamned porn star. But Freddie's dick didn't mind any of that. For the first time in years it was standing up and demanding to be paid attention to.

He was intrigued, not just by his own reactions to Newt but by Newt himself. The guy had to be insecure, looking the way he did, and yet he was feisty too. He was creative enough to come up with a flying gay unicorn, and his eyes revealed a sensitive soul struggling to get out from under all that lard.

Freddie had to know more, about himself and about Newt. So he fell into step with Newt as they walked along the Promenade, passing all that eye candy that didn't move him half as much as the man beside him.

15 – Rendezvous

From the shelter of a stand of tall palms beside the hotel's art nouveau entrance, Aidan watched Freddie Venus lean forward and kiss Newt. Not behavior between a stalker and victim. How sweet, in fact.

"How did we get such a stupid client?" Liam asked.

"I think it's romantic," Aidan said.

"I think you have no clue."

That was Liam. He assumed bad motives and disdained sweetness as a kind of weakness. And yet he could be so kind to Aidan sometimes, so loving. The night before had been almost like the past, the two of them joking around, then having sex. He'd felt close to Liam again for the first time in a while.

Nearly an hour had passed by then, with Liam and Aidan hanging out by the beach across from the Negresco, where a lithe woman with a lined face performed acrobatics on a mat along the pavement. Each time a crowd gathered to watch her, they had to adjust their position to keep their client in view.

After some discussion, the two men turned and began walking back down the Promenade toward where Liam had parked the Jeep. Liam started toward the traffic light at the corner, and Aidan hurried behind him. It was clear that Liam intended to cross the highway and intercept Freddie and Newt.

"Leave them be, Liam," Aidan said. "Let's just watch them."

"I'm telling you, something is wrong here."

"This is a public place, so there isn't much that the stalker can do. We'll do what we said, keep them in visual contact. If we see any danger, we'll intervene."

Liam grumbled, but they kept pace with Freddie and Newt. "What did you find out about this guy?" he asked as they walked.

"Newton Camilleri, aka Newton Cale. Born in Trenton in the same hospital where I was, though years before."

"What a charming piece of trivia," Liam said, and Aidan elbowed him.

"Worked for the state of New Jersey until last year, a bureaucrat in a benefits office Published his first book under the Cale pseudonym three years ago."

"You ever heard of him before?"

Aidan shook his head. "It's not the kind of stuff I read. Weird gay fantasy sex stuff. Unicorns with giant penises."

Liam laughed. "Really? People write that? And other people buy it?"

"You'd be surprised," Aidan said. "A lot of straight women get into M/M romance, and they like the sex explicit."

Liam looked over at him. "How do you know that?"

"I read an article. Anyway, Cale's books weren't big sellers until the last one came out about nine months ago. Got some good reviews from bloggers, and sales took off. Four months ago he left his job, sold his house, and moved to France."

"Could you find any connections between him and Freddie?"

Aidan shook his head. "Just started searching. I e-mailed Richard what I knew, and he's going to get some more background."

Ahead of them, they saw Freddie and Newt stopped at a traffic light at the Avenue Auber, getting ready to cross and head inland. "That street goes up toward the train station, doesn't it?" Liam asked.

"Yeah. You think they're going to get on a train and go somewhere?"

"No idea. But we have to be suspicious of this guy's motives until proven otherwise."

They lagged and watched the two men cross the street and begin climbing the gentle hill. They kept to the opposite side of the street so that they wouldn't be too obvious, and watched body language, trying to be sure that Freddie wasn't being forced to go along.

It was early evening. Stores were rolling down their metal shutters, and the streets were filled with working people hurrying home. The traffic on the Avenue Auber was steady, and Aidan knew that Liam was constantly considering how best to cross if it appeared the client was in danger.

A hundred feet before the Avenue Thiers, which ran past the mansard-roofed train station, the two men stopped, and it looked like Newt was fishing in his pocket for something.

"Let's go," Liam said. He darted across the street between cars stopped at the traffic light, with Aidan right behind.

"Time to call it quits," Liam said to Freddie. "You had your rendezvous. We need to get you out of here now."

"I can take care of myself," Freddie said.

At the same time, Newt said, "Who are you?"

"We're Mr. Venus's bodyguards," Aidan said.

Newt's eyes opened wide. "You have bodyguards?" he asked Freddie.

"Well, I thought I had a stalker," Freddie said. He turned to Liam and Aidan. "You're fired. Now fuck off."

Aidan noted the way that Liam set his jaw, which meant he was priming for action with a difficult client. Aidan put his hand on his partner's arm. "Remember, we drove you here," Aidan said to Freddie. "We can wait for you."

"I can drive you home," Newt said to Freddie.

"In that little clown car of yours? Not likely." Freddie looked from Aidan and Liam back to Newt. "Could be a while," he said.

"We'll wait," Aidan said. "You have our cell numbers, right? Call when you want us to pick you up."

"Fine." Freddie nodded to Newt, who opened the tall wrought-iron door with a big skeleton key. They walked inside, and Freddie closed the door with a clang behind them.

"We are not a taxi service," Liam said through gritted teeth.

"But we're not prison guards either," Aidan said. "You've said it to me a hundred times. Clients need to go about their daily lives, or else they start to resist their protection."

"You know what they're going to do," Liam said.

"I have a pretty good idea. Does that bother you? Or turn you on?"

Liam laughed harshly. "Sometimes you are completely clueless, you know that, Aidan?"

I'm not the one who's clueless, Aidan thought. But again he wasn't going to get into an argument in the middle of a job. "I know that restaurant across the street," he said. "Le Poissonnier. We can get dinner while we wait."

Liam allowed himself to be led across the street and into the restaurant, which was obviously quite popular with backpackers and other travelers. The walls were papered with local photographs, from scenes of fishing boats to mountain vistas. The tables were small and close together. The hostess-cashier motioned them to a table at the back, and they threaded their way between piles of luggage and aluminum-framed backpacks.

"The clientele here could use a bath," Liam muttered as they sat down. He took the chair that faced the street so he could keep an eye on Newt's doorway.

"Relax, sweetheart. Enjoy your meal." A harried waitress dropped them a pair of plastic-coated menus. Aidan looked over at the diners around them and decided that the food looked and smelled delicious. He was going to have a dinner that he didn't have to cook or clean up after, and that was celebration enough.

Liam's mood improved with the first course, garlic-butter stuffed mussels. By the time their main courses arrived, swordfish for Liam and sea bream for Aidan, he was almost happy.

Then he noticed Freddie and Newt leaving the apartment building across the street. He jumped up. "I'll follow them. You pay the bill and catch up with me."

At that moment Aidan's cell rang. "It's Freddie," he said, holding up a hand to keep Liam there.

"Newt and I are going to get some dinner," Freddie said. "There's a fish place across from his apartment."

"We're already there," Aidan said. "A good bodyguard anticipates the movement of the client and is prepared."

Liam's mouth gaped and Aidan smiled.

16 – ROUND ONE

That was what a kiss was like, Newt thought as he led Freddie toward his apartment. Jesus Christ, that was a kiss. Newt had only been kissed on the mouth a few times in his life, and it had never felt like that before. His face was electrified and his whole body was humming. He wanted more, more, more.

He was glad he'd arranged to meet Freddie Venus near his apartment, because he doubted he could walk too far, the way his body was reacting. With a shaking hand, he pulled out the big iron key that opened the front door.

Suddenly there were two guys on them. He watched as Freddie dispatched them and then motioned him to open the front door.

"Nice building," Freddie said.

"I'm renting for six months," Newt said. "In season it's more than I can afford. Who were those guys, really?"

"I told you. Bodyguards. I had a couple of incidents, including a stalker jerking off in my backyard, and I hired them. I'm letting them go tomorrow."

The elevator door opened. Newt didn't say anything. "Aren't we going in?" Freddie asked. He nudged Newt, who stepped into the car.

"What do you do, anyway?" Freddie asked, as they rose. "Just write those unicorn books?"

"You know about them?"

"I found your freaking Facebook page, remember?"

"Oh, yeah, right. Um. I used to be a government worker back in New Jersey. I'm trying to see if I can make a living from Fledglis." From the blank look on Freddie's face, Newt could tell Freddie hadn't actually read anything. "That's my character's name. He's half man, half unicorn."

"And all gay, right?"

The elevator door slid open. "Yup. Just like me." Newt led Freddie down the hall to his apartment. He opened the door and ushered Freddie in before him.

"Not bad," Freddie said. "Though you could have gotten a better view than the train station."

"I don't know how to do this," Newt said.

Freddie turned to face him. "Do what?"

Newt waved his hand around. "This. You. Me. Here." He felt like he was going to cry. For the first time in his life, he had a hot man in his home who clearly wanted something from him. But Newt didn't know what, and he didn't know how many more whippings or beatings or whatever he could take in the name of—what was this? Not love, surely.

"Come here," Freddie said, and he wrapped his arms around Newt. Nobody had ever done that. No guy ever liked to get that close to him.

Freddie kissed him, gently at first, and then with passion, the way they'd kissed outside. Newt's brain was rushing a mile a minute, worrying what to do next. When he'd met someone online for sex, there had always been an initial moment, no matter how quick, when the guy appeared revolted by Newt's bulk. Then there had been a matter-of-fact "let's get this done" attitude.

Sometimes the guy didn't even want to strip. He'd whip his dick out of his pants and motion for Newt to get down and suck him. Newt had so little experience with sex that either the guy came too quickly or too slowly. Most of the time the guy didn't even offer to get Newt off, just closed his pants, said good-bye, and walked out. He'd come to expect that all sexual experiences outside of fiction were like that.

But Freddie had other ideas. He put his hands up under Newt's shirt, feeling around for his fleshy man boobs. How Newt hated them! He almost never took his shirt off anywhere because he was so embarrassed by them.

Freddie began caressing Newt's nipples with his thumbs while kissing Newt's jaw. They were about the same height, so when Newt leaned forward he found he was kissing Freddie's ear. He'd never done anything like that before, and he was bashful about it. But when he curled up his tongue and stuck it into Freddie's ear, Freddie shivered with pleasure.

Freddie pulled and tugged on Newt's nipples until they were taut and radiating a direct line of pleasure to his groin. Then he began to massage Newt's massive belly, eventually sticking one hand beneath the waistband of Newt's shorts. "You want to get naked?" Freddie breathed into Newt's ear.

He was so eager to comply that he elbowed Freddie in the chest as he tried to shuck his T-shirt. "Hold on, cowboy," Freddie said. "This rodeo's in no hurry to start. Here, let me take care of things for you."

Newt hadn't been undressed by anyone else since he was a small child, and he marveled at how erotic it felt. Freddie grasped the bottom of Newt's T-shirt and lifted it, and Newt lowered his head obediently. "I don't get it," Freddie mumbled. "You shouldn't turn me on, but you do."

Newt didn't say anything, scared of breaking the spell. Freddie untied the drawstring of Newt's shorts and then tugged them down over his ample hips. Hoping desperately for a moment like this, Newt had put on what he considered his sexiest underwear, a jockstrap with a blue waistband and a giant red pouch. "Sexy," Freddie murmured as he ran his hand up and down over Newt's erection.

Freddie backed away for a moment, then shed his shirt, shorts, and shoes with careless abandon. He hadn't worn any underwear, so he was completely naked in a matter of seconds.

Freddie dropped to his knees on the carpet. He reached out to Newt's balls and caressed them. Then he took Newt's dick in his mouth.

"Oh God," Newt said. "The mouth that launched a thousand dicks."

Freddie pulled off long enough to say, "Just don't call me Helen," and then he was sucking again.

Newt had gotten a couple of blowjobs in his life, when he was younger and rooms were dark. But he'd never felt anything like this.

Freddie's hands, mouth, and tongue seemed to be working in synch with one goal in mind: to get Newt off.

He looked down at the top of Freddie's close-cropped head and saw that Freddie had a small balding spot at the crown. He was filled with a wave of love at that, as if this minor imperfection in Freddie made him all the more human.

Freddie sucked dick like an orchestra conductor, Newt thought. He maintained a masterful rhythm, pulling back when he sensed Newt was close to coming, then picking up again when Newt's body slowed. He caressed Newt's perineum, and Newt felt ripples of pleasure roll through his body.

Newt was sweating and his heart was pounding and he felt wobbly. He grabbed the edge of the desk for support, and Freddie redoubled his efforts. Newt felt his orgasm rising, and he began moaning and thrashing around, losing control of everything, focused only on the pleasure.

He shot off down Freddie's throat, and before Newt could apologize, Freddie looked up at him and smiled, then wiped his mouth. "Haven't done that in a while." When he stood up, Newt heard his knees creak. "Christ, I'm getting old."

"Thank you," Newt said in a small voice. He wasn't sure what the proper etiquette was, but he'd always appreciated being thanked when he'd blown a trick.

"Don't thank me yet. We're nowhere near finished," Freddie said. "Where's that ointment?"

"In the bathroom."

"Don't move," Freddie said. A moment later, he was back with the tube of ointment in his hand. He squeezed some into one palm and began massaging it gently into Newt's tender skin.

Newt groaned. "That feels so good."

"Just you wait," Freddie murmured. "You don't know what good feels like."

He pushed aside the thong and parted Newt's ass cheeks, rubbing the cream into them, then in slow circles around his hole. It was hard to get in there because of all the flab, but he was determined. "First thing we're going to do," he said, "is put you on a diet."

"The first thing?" Newt panted.

"Well, maybe not the first," Freddie said. "You have any rubbers?"

"In the top drawer of my bureau."

Freddie headed for the bedroom. Newt stood there for a moment without moving, but then touched his left nipple with his right hand, trying to duplicate what Freddie had done. It wasn't as good as feeling Freddie's rough fingers grazing over the nipple, but it wasn't bad either.

"You're a naughty boy," Freddie said when he returned from the bedroom. In addition to a couple of condoms, he had a bottle of lube and a realistic-looking dildo with a rubbery head and veins running down its length.

Newt gulped. He'd bought the dildo in Nice but hadn't been able to get it into his ass. Either he was too tight or it was too big.

Freddie squirted some lube on the dildo's head and then said, "Assume the position."

Though he'd heard the expression, Newt had no idea what Freddie meant.

When he didn't move, Freddie said, "Bend over, doofus. Jesus, what are you, a virgin?" He suddenly stepped back, then around in front of Newt. "You're not a virgin, are you?"

"I've given blowjobs before," Newt said defiantly. "And I've been blown a couple of times, and jacked off too." Newt felt obliged to add, "And one of the guys was even kind of good-looking."

"Oh, Christ," Freddie said, and Newt was worried he was going to give up and walk away. "You poor, dumb son of a bitch."

Suddenly, the idea of Freddie walking away felt right. "I don't need your pity," Newt said. "I've taken care of myself for fifty years, and I can keep on doing it."

"No, you're not," Freddie said gently. "You're going to let me."

The warmth in Freddie's eyes made Newt want to cry. Instead he turned around and blinked back the tears as he bent over and pried open his ass.

Freddie began to massage Newt's hole with lube. The feeling was warm and pleasurable. With one finger, Freddie's explored Newt's hole. With his other hand, he stroked Newt's perineum, and Newt felt so horny he thought he might explode.

After a couple of minutes, Freddie said, "This is probably going to hurt," and Newt felt something warm and rubbery pressing against his ass. "Take a deep breath," Freddie said, and then the thing was inside him, so big and hard that Newt thought he might pass out.

But Freddie knew what he was doing, and he kept the dildo in place until Newt got accustomed to the feeling. Then he began sliding it in and out, bit by bit, until Newt felt waves of pleasure rushing through his body.

Newt loved it so much he wanted more, but he could feel Freddie's hand on the bottom of the dildo, brushing against his ass, still tender in a few places, and realized that was probably all he could get. Freddie seemed to be having a good time, panting and making small sounds like "oh" and "yeah."

Then he sped up, thrusting the dildo into Newt's ass. He reached around to Newt's stiff dick, pushing it out of the restraining pouch and beginning to fist it. Newt couldn't hold out for long, even though he had come a few minutes before. He felt a sensation rise from his toes, swell into his groin, and then explode out of his dick. It was painful as well as sexy, as if he was drawing down from the very bottom of his reserves to shoot a load.

When Freddie pulled the dildo out, Newt's ass felt painfully empty, and his dick was sore, but he'd never felt better in his whole life. If this was all he ever had of sex, it would be enough.

Freddie turned him around and kissed him again, pressing his sweaty chest against Newt's. "Sorry that's the best I can do right now. Maybe I'll be able to get it up better in round two." He backed away, then squeezed Newt's hand. "You got anything to eat here?" he asked. "I'm going to need food before we try again."

Newt adjusted his dick back into the red pouch. He wanted to take a shower, but he didn't want to seem prissy. He went into the kitchen, and Freddie followed after he pulled on his shorts.

Newt opened his refrigerator. "I have frozen cheeseburgers we can microwave, frozen lasagna, boneless chicken wings…"

Freddie stood up and peered around him. "Jesus, don't you have anything fresh? No wonder you're such a fat pig. You need to eat healthy."

Newt turned to face him. "That hurts my feelings when you call me names like that." He knew he was fat, but he didn't need to have it thrown back in his face all the time.

"Then lose some fucking weight. Tomorrow, I'm going to start you on an exercise routine and a healthy diet."

"Tomorrow?" Newt squeaked. What was going on? Was all this some sort of punishment for his sneaking around outside Freddie's house? But it couldn't be.

"Yes, tomorrow. Now put your clothes on, and let's go get some dinner." Freddie pulled on his T-shirt and his sandals. "Come on, get moving. I'm hungry."

"I'm coming; I'm coming," Newt said. They went back outside, and Freddie pulled out his cell phone. He had a quick conversation, then put the phone away and led Newt to a seafood restaurant across the street. Newt had often passed it, but since he hated fish, he'd never even looked at the menu.

He saw the two bodyguards at a table in the back. So they really did keep an eye on Freddie. What was that all about? Had it just been Newt's obsession? Or was there something more going on that he didn't know about?

Freddie quizzed the waiter about what was fresh and then ordered grilled branzino for both of them, with a side of roasted vegetables. "And I want the salads before the entrée, not after."

"I don't like fish," Newt said when the waiter had gone.

"I don't care. You're going to eat healthy from now on."

"Or what?"

Freddie leaned forward and said very softly, "Or I'll never fuck you again."

Newt felt his face reddening. He'd never gone out with someone after having sex, never had a second date. He had no idea what to expect.

"Not accustomed to that kind of talk?" Freddie said, leaning back in his chair and laughing. "Get used to it, bud."

The waiter brought them each salads. Newt tried to coat his with dressing, but Freddie held his hand back. "Go easy."

Newt didn't like the taste of the salad when it wasn't swimming in dressing, but he was starving, so he ate. The same went for the fish and the vegetables. It wasn't terrible, but he was so hungry he'd have eaten anything. He used a piece of bread to wipe his plate clean and then said, "Dessert?"

"We'll have dessert back at your place," Freddie said, and from the wicked gleam in his eye, Newt had a feeling he wasn't talking about chocolate cake. Freddie paid the check and stood up. "Now we go for a walk."

"A walk?"

"Yes. Got to work off those calories."

"Can't we do that back at my place?"

"Oh, we'll do that too."

They walked outside. "Hold up a minute. Let me talk to my guys." Freddie walked over to the bodyguards and spoke to them, and then Freddie steered him out to the Avenue Thiers.

Freddie forced him to walk nearly a mile before he was willing to turn around. By the time they got back to the apartment, Newt was huffing and puffing and felt like he might be having a heart attack. "I need to sit down," he said, collapsing in a chair. "Just for a minute." He closed his eyes and waited for his breathing to still.

When he woke up, the apartment was dark, and he was alone.

17 – Neighbors

It had been a long time since Freddie had deflowered a virgin. He couldn't remember ever doing that in his professional career, but before he turned pro, there had been at least two or three guys who had surrendered their asses for the first time. He'd done one picture with another actor, also famous as a top, who was allegedly bottoming for the first time. Hardly.

He felt an odd sort of affection for big Newt. He hadn't been able to get it up enough to penetrate the man with his dick, but the dildo had been a good substitute. It wasn't his best effort by a long shot, but given the circumstances, he thought he'd done pretty well. He wasn't sure if it was the sex or the walk after dinner that had worn the poor guy out, but it was clear he needed his stamina built up.

Newt looked so sweet and innocent, snoozing in his living room, worn down by the big, bad porn star. Freddie picked up Newt's phone and copied down the number, then scrawled a note with his own number. He was about to leave it on the counter when he had the sudden urge to mark his territory. He whipped his dick out of his pants and stroked it. It was only half hard, but he was able to get a drop of precome from the tip.

He wiped that drop on the page, then initialed it and let himself out of the apartment with a smile on his face. For the first time in a long time, he'd enjoyed himself with another guy—in and out of bed. It was an interesting turn of events.

When he got downstairs, he looked around for the bodyguards.

They were lurking across the street, and he waved toward them.

"Have a good time?" Aidan asked. His partner just glowered.

"I did," Freddie said. "First time I've been on a date in years. But you know what they say, it's like riding a bicycle."

Freddie remembered a scene in one of his many movies where he'd lain on the ground and pretended to be peddling a bicycle while a guy blew him. That had been fun, he thought. Maybe that was something he could do with Newt.

Freddie had no idea what he was doing, making plans with this guy. Dating was for suckers, for normal guys, not porn actors. Yet he'd had a good time. Newt was funny and sweet and so determined to make a new life for himself. Freddie empathized. When he fled LA for Nice, he'd had that same determination and had burrowed down to work.

Maybe it was time to look up from his video screen for a while, spend some time in the real world. And if he could get Newt in better shape, they might have fun together. But how was he going to monitor Newt's diet and exercise when they lived so far apart? He had work to do, after all. He didn't have hours to spend commuting back and forth into Nice.

By the time he and the bodyguards returned to his house, he was tired and fell into a deep, dreamless sleep. Wednesday morning he was up early and found Liam in the living room, stretching. "I'm about to go for a run," Liam said. "Want to come along?"

"Sure. I love a good run."

Freddie owned nearly an acre of land around his house, much of it hilly. The street that ran past his house was a fairly narrow stretch of flat land with steep slopes to both sides. He knew his closest neighbors by sight, and often while running, he passed them putting out the garbage, walking dogs, or getting into their cars.

His closest neighbor was an elderly Frenchwoman who lived in a converted trailer brought to the site years before by her late husband. She was eccentric but chatty, and sometimes Freddie took a cooldown period in front of her driveway to talk with her.

He and Liam had completed most of their circuit when they approached Madame Banville's driveway, neither of them having said more than a few words to the other. The skinny old woman with wild white hair was waiting at the side of the road for him. He did not intend to stop, but she called to him and waved a piece of paper at him.

He stopped and said, *"Bonjour, Madame."*

"Have you seen this?" she asked him in French, thrusting the paper toward him. "It was in my post yesterday."

Freddie was surprised to see a collage of images of him from his past films. In some he was naked, in others engaged in fucking or sucking. The headline read, VOTRE VOISIN EST UN PERVERS! in angry red script.

"Is this true?" she demanded of him.

Freddie was too astonished to respond. He looked at the pictures and translated the text in his head. Neighbors were warned that Freddie Venus was a pervert, that he acted in pornographic films and victimized young boys.

"Not true," Liam said to the woman in French. "Mr. Venus is a good citizen, and this paper comes from someone who wishes to buy his property cheaply."

Freddie looked at him. There had been no offers on his property.

"Ah," Madame Banville said, and nodded. "I understand."

Liam took the paper from Freddie. "We will alert the authorities," he said to the woman. "Thank you for showing this to us. When did you receive it?"

"This morning," she said. "I know it was not there last night." She smiled and turned back toward her house.

"What the fuck?" Freddie said to Liam.

"We'll talk about it back at your place," Liam said. "Come on, we've still got some running to do."

Freddie struggled to push the flyer out of his head as he ran, but he couldn't. If Madame Banville had gotten one, then so had everyone else on the street. How could he show his face? He had never been embarrassed by his career before, but neither had he proclaimed it to every person he met.

It couldn't have been Newt, he thought. Even if Newt had been the one to leave the poster on the Jeep, which Freddie doubted, he'd have been too tired the night before for any mischief.

"That was smart back there, with Madame Banville," Freddie said. "You can really think on your feet."

"One of the many things I learned as a SEAL," Liam said. "Though Aidan's the brains of our team."

Freddie wasn't a big fan of false modesty. "Yeah, when I was in porn, I tried to make people think I was dumb too. Being underestimated comes in handy sometimes."

Liam looked at him and grinned. "Good to see we're on the same wavelength. How'd you feel about a workout? I find that helps me put things in perspective."

Freddie agreed, and he enjoyed going through his routine of calisthenics with Liam, then led him inside to the back room where he kept his free weights.

"I don't usually lift," Liam said. "But it's good to break up a routine."

Freddie was secretly pleased that he could hoist more weight and do more reps than the big, muscular bodyguard, but he didn't say anything. They finished up and went to their respective bathrooms to shower.

By eight thirty the three of them were sitting at the kitchen table. Freddie had opted for a bowl of granola and a glass of juice instead of a full cooked breakfast. The flyer was on the table in front of them. "Newt couldn't have put these flyers out yesterday," he said. "He and I were together from six o'clock on, and when I left him, he was exhausted."

"He could have had these flyers printed up yesterday before he met with you, and hired someone to distribute them," Liam said. "We can't discount him completely."

He paused and looked uncomfortable. "About last night," Liam continued. "Sorry if I seemed like an asshole. But it's our job to protect you, and we take that very seriously."

"I appreciate it. And I'm sorry if I reacted badly. Now I'm really starting to believe there's someone after me."

"Someone who knows about your past," Aidan said, and Freddie nodded. "Can you think of anyone?"

"I thought I had left all that behind," Freddie said. He sighed. "I'll try and dredge up some names, but it was all so long ago."

"You're still working," Liam said. "You may be far from LA but you're still involved. Make a list of everyone you can remember working with in the past and everyone you work with today. Think about anybody who has a grudge against you, anybody who could be jealous of you."

"Could be a pretty long list," Freddie grumbled.

18 – ALL THE WAY

After Freddie had left for his editing room, Liam picked up the flyer from the table. "I knew there was something fishy going on," he said. "On top of that poster yesterday, I figure somebody has a real hard-on for Freddie. And not in a good way."

"But you don't think that Newt is behind all this, do you?"

"I'm withholding judgment," Liam said. "I'd like to get a look at his apartment, at his computer, see if he's one of those freaks who puts up all kinds of pictures, creates a little shrine. Those are the ones to worry about."

"You're going to break into his place?"

Liam shook his head. "I'm going to start by asking nicely. I know, that's not my strong point. But I need you to stay here with Freddie, keep an eye on things."

"I could go to Newt's," Aidan said.

"I'm meeting Louis later," Liam said. "Before that, I'll stop by this guy's apartment. You can stay here and work your online magic, looking for information."

"Be careful, sweetheart," Aidan said.

As Liam walked outside, he felt the first droplets of rain, and by the time he had made it down Freddie's driveway and onto the Rue de Canta Galet, it was coming down in sheets. He gripped the steering wheel, navigating the switchbacks and curves with precision, but his mind was on Freddie Venus.

Liam had never been a fan of X-rated movies, though he'd seen his share at sleazy adult bookstores while on leave from the Navy. They seemed so phony to him, just a bunch of actors pretending to get excited by dicks and asses. If he were to tell the truth, Liam hadn't even liked sex that much until he met Aidan. It had been a necessary release, nothing more.

Back in high school, his friends had been desperate to "go all the way" with girls. Then in the military, men had often bragged about their sexual conquests or longed for girlfriends back home. Liam didn't get it.

Sure, he'd had crushes on other guys, but that was all they were. He thought he'd never let a man get under his skin. Then Aidan turned his world upside down, beginning with a very hot kiss back in Tunis when they barely knew each other.

But lately, Aidan had been weird. He had become obsessed with getting married, buying a house, settling down like a pair of straight people. Wasn't he happy just being who they were, having the life they had?

Liam had always known that Aidan was way smarter than he was, though Aidan downplayed that. He was a college graduate, had a master's degree. Liam had barely made it out of high school, and he'd gone into the Navy before the ink was dry on his diploma. He'd taken enough college courses for an associate's degree, but then his assignments heated up. He went through the BUD/S training to become a SEAL, and that was it for book learning.

Maybe all this fuss about marriage and home ownership was Aidan's way of saying that if he and Liam weren't on the same page about their future, then they ought to go their own ways. And that was definitely something Liam didn't want.

An old clunker was plodding ahead of him, and Liam had to slow down. Time to get his head back in the game. What was Newt Camilleri's angle? Was he an obsessed fan? A stalker? Or had he been hired by someone else to get close to Freddie?

He was an unlikely decoy, though, not somebody Liam would have hired to seduce an ex-porn star. But then, what did he know about that kind of thing?

He nosed the Jeep into a tight parking spot a few blocks from the train station as the rain began to taper off. He raised the collar of his lightweight jacket, hunched down, and strode ahead. At the apartment building across from the train station, he pressed the button for Newt's unit, and the idiot buzzed him in without even asking who he was.

No way was he letting his client back into this lax security situation. He shook off the rain as he climbed the stairs to the third floor, then knocked on Newt's door.

"Oh," Newt said when he opened it. "You're the bodyguard."

"You always buzz people in without asking who they are?" Liam asked.

Newt shrugged. "Nobody comes to visit me, so I assume they've rung the wrong bell, and I let them in."

Liam sighed. Civilians. "May I come in?"

"Oh, sure. Sorry." Newt stepped back, and Liam entered the apartment, which looked like it belonged to an elderly woman. It was small and dim, the main feature a pair of tall French windows that looked out at the train station. A trestle table faced the windows, with a laptop computer on it.

"I was trying to write," Newt said. "Um. Would you like to sit down?"

Liam sat. He knew that his height could sometimes be intimidating to people, and he didn't want to bully Newt, just find out what his story was. "So, I understand you're from Trenton," he began. "I grew up in New Brunswick, and Aidan's from Lawrenceville."

"It's a small world," Newt said.

Liam hated this kind of meaningless chitchat. Aidan was much better at it than he was. "How long have you been…interested in Freddie?"

"I'm not some deranged lunatic, if that's what you're asking." Newt waved his arm. "Feel free to snoop around the apartment. You aren't going to find any shrine to Freddie Venus. He's a porn star, and I recognized him at the supermarket from the tattoo on his back. But I've watched enough of those movies that I'd probably recognize a dozen guys, at least the ones who had a distinctive look."

Liam tried not to let his distaste show on his face, but he must not have been successful.

"Smirk all you want," Newt said. "If I looked like you, I could have had sex with other guys instead of just my right hand." He leaned forward. "Why are you here? Does Freddie want me to leave him alone? Because he could have asked."

Liam shook his head. "No, he seems to like you and want to keep seeing you. So I figured I'd better come over and check you out."

"That what you do, as a bodyguard? Interview guys who want to have sex with your client? Wouldn't that make you a pimp?"

Liam could have reacted with anger, but then he'd have lost control of the situation—probably what Newt wanted. Instead, he leaned back and opened his posture, spreading his legs and his arms. "I'm trying to keep my client safe. You've got to admit, your showing up at the same time as the poster and the flyers seems pretty coincidental."

"What do you mean, posters and flyers?"

Liam had developed a good sense of whether someone was lying, and he was coming to realize that Newt had no idea what was going on. He was most likely who he said he was—a sad, horny bastard who had somehow managed to find his way into the bed of a washed-up porn star.

"Freddie has experienced some incidents of harassment," Liam said. He explained what he'd been told and what he'd witnessed.

"You think I'm behind all that? Why?"

"You're a creative guy," Liam said. "You write; you come up with ideas. You could have orchestrated this whole thing as a way to get into Freddie's pants."

"Come on, I write about unicorns, for Christ's sake," Newt said. "You really see me creeping up Freddie's driveway in the middle of the night? I'd probably trip over something and fall into a pile of poison ivy."

Liam nodded. "I believe you. But you should know about what's going on. You may want to keep your distance from Freddie for a while, until things settle down."

"You love your partner, don't you?" Newt asked. "I can see it in the way you guys look at each other. I never thought I could have anything like that, that nobody would be able to look beyond this train wreck." He motioned to his body. "But for some crazy reason, Freddie is interested. I'm not walking away from that for fear or money."

Liam stood up. "I hope you won't have to. But if you don't mind, I would like to have a look around."

There were no photos of Freddie Venus on the walls of the bedroom. "I've got nothing to hide," Newt said from behind him. "Go on, open up the closet, look through the drawers. I tossed my porn collection back in Jersey and sold off all my DVDs. Don't need them with everything available on the Internet."

Liam was mildly embarrassed, but he knew what he had to do. As Newt had instructed, he opened the drawers of the big armoire, snooped around in the closet. Nothing there. Nothing incriminating in the bathroom, either, just a large realistic dildo on the counter still glistening from a recent scrubbing.

"Look, I'm not a bad guy," Liam said when he finished. "But my job is to protect my client, and I take that very seriously."

"I understand," Newt said. "I want Freddie to stay alive too."

Liam thanked him and walked down the stairs to the street. He thought about the way Newt could tell he and Aidan loved each other by the way they looked at each other. He hoped that Aidan could tell that too. Their relationship was bound to have its ups and downs, but there was a rock-solid foundation between them, whether they had sex or not.

By the time Liam got outside, the rain had turned into a slow, steady drizzle that slipped in behind the neck of his jacket. No way he was going to walk all the way to the café where he was to meet Louis without getting soaked. He'd have to drive instead.

He was so accustomed to walking around Nice that he had forgotten how difficult it was to park in the central part of the city, especially a vehicle as big as the Jeep. He had to park at an expensive lot and then hustle, trying to stay beneath awnings, to meet Louis at a café in the Zone Piétonne, the pedestrian area along the Rue de France, one long block in from the Mediterranean.

He had known Louis for years, first in Tunis, where Louis's nominal job was as cultural attaché. His real one was as a field agent for the CIA, and in Liam's gigs as a private-duty bodyguard, he and Louis had worked together occasionally. It wasn't until Aidan entered his life, though, that Liam discovered that Louis was gay too, with a partner named Hassan, a Tunisian architect.

The two couples had become friends, and Liam enjoyed having another couple to go out to dinner with, to share the occasional concert or performance. Soon after Liam and Aidan had relocated to Nice to join the Agence, Louis had taken a transfer to the consulate there, and Hassan's firm had opened an office in the city.

Louis was about forty, a bear of a guy with a bulky build who was even hairier than Aidan. His head was shaved, but he had a dark mustache and goatee. He waited under the restaurant's awning, intent on his cell phone in his hand, yet he looked up as soon as Liam got close.

They shook hands. "What's up?" he asked.

"New client," Liam said. "Guy named Freddie Venus."

"Not *the* Freddie Venus?" Louis asked as they sat down at a round iron table sheltered from the rain. "Porn god with angel wings tattooed on his back?"

"I guess you know him."

"Know him? His dick is burned on my retinas. He's one hot dude."

Liam laughed. Louis was so straight acting that before Aidan twigged to him, Liam had never considered he might be gay or a secret porn addict.

They ordered cappuccinos, then Liam said, "Don't tell me you still watch that shit with Hassan right there."

"Hassan is an even bigger size queen than I am. He has every one of Freddie's videos on DVD. Broke his heart when Freddie stopped acting."

"Is the whole world obsessed with gay porn?" Liam asked, as the waitress brought their coffees in big white steaming mugs. Liam blushed and was glad he'd spoken in English rather than French.

"Come on, Liam. Tell me you never jerked off to a movie."

"I can't say that. But I also can't name a single porn star and wouldn't recognize one if he walked in this café naked."

"What's Freddie's problem?" Louis asked. He picked up his coffee and inhaled the aroma. "Overeager fan?"

"That's what it looked like at first," Liam said. He explained once again the things Freddie had experienced. "But I've talked to the fan, and I believe he has nothing do with the harassment."

"What's his name?" Louis asked as he took out a pocket notebook. "I'll check on him anyway."

Liam spelled Newt's name and Freddie's names, both his birth name and his nom de porn. "I'll see what I can find," Louis said. His cell phone rang, and he looked at the display. "Crap. I have to get this." He picked up his coffee and said, "Catch you on the flip side."

Liam watched as Louis deftly answered his phone and continued to speak as he poured his coffee into a paper cup. Liam pulled out his phone and opened a web browser. The screen was tiny, but he was following a hunch; if there was more to research, he'd keep looking at home.

He Googled the terms "organized crime" and "gay porn" and was surprised at how little popped up in the way of search results. He had always assumed that the porn industry was tied in with other criminal enterprises like prostitution and drug dealing and that there were organized groups behind it all.

But that wasn't what showed up. Maybe he had his search terms wrong? Maybe Richard could do a focused search correlating Freddie's name and the names of people he had worked with, or who had backed his films, with known crime figures or syndicates.

It wasn't much, but it was a direction. Whoever was after Freddie had a reason, and a money trail was always a good start. He decided to stop by the Agence office, use the computer there, and see what he could find.

19 – Outsourced

Aidan was sitting at the small desk by the guest-room window with his laptop open when Liam returned from his trip into Nice. Hayam jumped up and ran over to sniff Liam's feet, and he picked the little dog up and kissed her head. "How's my sweetheart?" he asked.

"Hmph," Aidan said. "Replaced in your affection by a dog."

"You're my human sweetheart," Liam said. He came over to Aidan and kissed him on the lips. Then pulled a chair up next to Aidan's, keeping the little dog on his lap. "Discover anything interesting today?"

"I found a website that listed porn actors and the films they'd been in, and I started there," Aidan said. "I built this spreadsheet with the title of the film, the studio, the director, the actors, and the crew."

"He was a busy boy," Liam said. "Lots of movies."

"Those are the ones he acted in. I figured it was going to take a long time to put it all together, and I couldn't see spending days online looking up every single person Freddie ever came in contact with. So I outsourced."

"Richard?"

Aidan shook his head. "Too expensive, and we'd get too much useless data, at least at the start. I went to Fiverr and hired three researchers." In the past, he had used the site, where people listed what they were willing to do for a five-dollar gig, for a variety of projects.

"I assigned each of them a set of films and agreed to pay a premium for quick turnaround. The data started coming in an hour ago, and I just finished combining everything."

Liam looked at the spreadsheet. "Freddie stopped acting a long time ago."

"I was surprised at that, because I didn't even discover his videos, on DVD and online, until after he'd already stopped. But with *Cocks on Call*, he moved over to the production side."

"I'm guessing it wasn't about roosters," Liam said.

"It's about phone-sex operators getting it on with each other while on the phone with clients. This list shows all the movies he worked on, moving up to editing and then directing." He sat back. "It was more interesting than the research I usually do. But more complicated too, because I doubt that any of these actors were born Dick Bigger, Jack Hoff, or Phil Mee." He sighed. "But at least it's a start. If Freddie can identify problems with any of these guys, I can start to dig deeper."

"Deeper and harder," Liam said, with a hint of a smile. Hayam squirmed on his lap. "You want to go outside, puppy?" He put the dog on the floor and stood up. "Come on, let's take a walk."

"What about your day?" Aidan asked once they were outside. "Learn anything interesting?"

"I'm pretty sure that Newt isn't the one behind the threats," Liam said. "Which kind of sucks, because it means there's another crazy guy out there somewhere."

"It doesn't suck. Now he and Freddie can get together. I feel sorry for Newt. I mean, he's finally found somebody who cares about him, and there's all this stuff in the way."

"Am I missing something here?" Liam asked as Hayam stopped to sniff a flowering plant. "Freddie's over the hill to be an actor, but he's still in good shape physically. What's he doing with that whale?"

"Be nice," Aidan said, elbowing him. "My grandmother used to say that every pot has its lid."

"You'd need a jumbo-sized lid for that pot," Liam said. He held up his hands in a gesture of surrender. "Just saying."

"Well, don't say it to Freddie. Besides, you never know what goes on in someone else's bedroom."

"Unless they put out a sex tape," Liam said. "After I left Newt's, I met with Louis and gave him Freddie's real name and his nom de porn, and he promised to do some research for me. Then I went over to the Agence office and used the computer there to do some research of my own."

"On what?"

"I had this idea that the mafia was behind the porn industry, and I wanted to check it out. Did you know that the majority of the porn produced in this country comes from the San Fernando Valley, over the hills from LA?"

"I did not. But it makes sense."

"The mafia got into porn back when it was made with eight-millimeter cameras and shown only in little theaters. Guys from the Colombo family were actually behind *Deep Throat*."

Liam waited while Hayam sniffed a bush. "Eventually, the mafia controlled the labs that printed the movies, then rented them out to theaters. Then once VCRs became common, they moved into making and selling cassettes. But once the Internet came along and everything went digital, they lost control of the business."

"Interesting," Aidan said. "But how does it relate to Freddie?"

"I was wondering if Freddie ever had contact with mafia guys. Maybe he cheated them out of money or stole copies of movies. Now somebody has tracked him down."

"Sounds improbable," Aidan said. "From what I saw, Freddie was still in LA and working in the business long after people started watching porn online. Why would somebody wait so long and work so hard to track him down now?"

Liam shrugged. "Maybe whoever it was spent some time in prison? Just got released recently?"

They walked back into the house and heard muffled voices coming from Freddie's editing room. "Freddie has a great job," Aidan said. "Sitting there watching porn all day. There are guys who would kill for jobs like that."

"Does that turn you on?" Liam asked, reaching down to rub Aidan's dick. "All that porn going on down the hall?"

"Don't need porn when I've got you with me." He leaned up and kissed Liam on the lips. "Freddie's certainly an accommodating host. Did you see the trick towels on the bedside table?"

"Trick towels?"

"For when you bring a trick back to your room and you want to clean him up afterward," Aidan said.

"Sometimes your breadth of knowledge is surprising," Liam said. "Did you and Blake keep those handy?"

"Are you kidding? Blake required a long, hot shower after any sexual activity."

"Whereas you and I are happy to wallow in each other's sweat and semen," Liam said. He looked at his watch. "We've still got an hour or so before Freddie comes out of his editing room looking for dinner." He grabbed Aidan's hand. "Come on. I feel some wallowing coming on."

Aidan opened the door to the guest room and an idea occurred to him. Maybe he and Liam could act out their own little movie. He put his finger to his lips. "We have to be quiet, though," he said. "My friend Freddie doesn't know I've been out at a club, and I don't want him to know I brought a stranger back to his house."

Liam looked at him in confusion for a moment, then caught on. "Role-play," he said. "Very creative."

Aidan nodded. "When I saw you across the room at that club, I knew you'd have a big dick and be a terrific lover."

"I'll have to prove that to you." Liam reached over and pulled Aidan's polo shirt over his head. "Mmm. You have big nipples. I like that in a man." He leaned forward and grasped Aidan's right tit in his teeth and bit down. Aidan groaned.

"Oh, yeah. Twist the other one with your hand. I like that."

Liam obliged. Aidan's pulse raced as his tits sent electric signals to his groin. He rubbed his hand over Liam's close-cropped hair.

Then Liam lifted his head, and they kissed tentatively, the way men who didn't know each other might.

Their lips touched with the slightest pressure. Then Aidan pushed back at Liam, who opened his mouth to Aidan's tongue. The passion grew between them as they kissed lips, chin, earlobe. "I want you to fuck me," Aidan said into Liam's ear. "Are you into that?"

"I'll bet you have a sweet ass," Liam said. "I was watching you dance and thinking about sticking my cock up there."

Aidan was so hot, he was afraid he'd come right there. He scrambled to pull his clothes off, and Liam did the same thing, leaving shirts, pants, Aidan's boxers, and Liam's jock strap in a pile on the carpeted floor.

They tumbled into the bed, as eager for each other as strangers. They kissed and sucked on lips and grappled. Skin met skin in a dozen places, and Aidan remembered that this was Liam, the man he'd loved for years. He knew where Liam liked to be touched, how his body reacted to the stroke of a fingernail along his spine, the way he loved to rub his stiff dick against Aidan's hairy thigh.

"Roll on your side, baby," Liam said in a husky voice. "Let me at that sexy booty of yours."

Aidan did as he was told, hooking one leg over the other so that his ass was exposed. "So sweet," Liam said. "A little rosebud waiting to be plucked."

"Or fucked," Aidan said.

"All good things take time," Liam said. He slid down on the bed so that his mouth was level with Aidan's ass. He brushed his chin against Aidan's globes, the five o'clock shadow sending shivering sensations through the tender flesh. After he pried the cheeks apart and stuck his face in Aidan's ass, his tongue slithered into Aidan's hole like a snake.

Aidan's dick leaked precome, and his body jittered with sensation. Then Liam stuck his index finger into Aidan's ass. He pressed forward, first one digit, then two, then three. Aidan was full but not full enough.

"More," he panted. "I want all of you inside me."

Liam's dick was already slick with precome, and he abandoned all pretense of an anonymous fuck. He knew exactly the way Aidan liked to be fucked, and he charged forward. Aidan felt that momentary starburst of pain, then the delicious sensation of being filled, complete, one with his lover. Liam's dick filled his chute, pressing against the walls, the tip pushing against Aidan's prostate.

Liam's thighs were awesome, and he manipulated the muscles there, pushing forward, pulling out. He and Aidan developed a rhythm that quickly brought them both to the edge of climax.

"You'll never have anyone better than I am," Liam growled as he made one last thrust, and Aidan felt the spurt of semen push up his channel. Liam grabbed Aidan's stiff dick and jerked it for a moment until Aidan could barely breathe, saw stars behind his eyes, and ejaculated all over Liam's belly.

"Where's that trick towel now that we need it?" Liam asked, and they burst into laughter.

20 – BURNING LOVE

Sitting in his editing room late on Wednesday morning, Freddie thought about calling Newt. It was hard to believe that he'd only first seen Newt three days before, jerking off in the backyard. So much had happened since then.

Should he tell him what was going on, that the bodyguards thought someone from his past was after him? Should he forget about Newt until after this was all over? Wait for the big tub of lard to make the next move?

Christ, he had turned back into a teenage boy. When Newt was ready to call, he'd call. And if he never did? Then fuck him.

But what if Freddie had overworked him, and Newt was dying there in his little apartment? Maybe his heart had given out, and he was struggling for breath even as Freddie…

The phone rang, and Freddie jumped for it. But it wasn't Newt; it was some man speaking Spanish. His years in LA had given him a working knowledge of the language, but having lived in France for so long, his brain had been rewired, and it took him a minute to understand the man was asking something about his son.

"*Número incorrecto*," Freddie said and hung up.

He couldn't sit around moping all day, he thought. He had work to do. When he checked his Dropbox, there was more raw footage ready to be downloaded.

Freddie spent the day editing, thinking only occasionally of

Newt. Was he feeling better? Writing? Thinking about Freddie?

He recognized the signs. He was falling for Newt. He'd had occasional crushes, starting when he was a teenager longing for one of the linebackers on the high school football team. But once he'd gotten involved in porn and then become a star, he didn't need to crush on anyone. Guys came to him. There weren't many straight guys in the world of gay porn, so if Freddie wanted someone, he could have him. There was no need for romance and you could jump into bed without preliminaries.

But he still remembered those days when he'd gotten a hard-on just from thinking about the object of his affection, when he longed for a moment of contact in the hallway or the locker room. It was refreshing to realize that he still had feelings.

After he put in his day's work, he went out into the garden behind his house. A couple of zucchini were ripe, along with some cherry tomatoes and tiny squash blossoms. He harvested them, then passed them off to Aidan in the kitchen.

"I spent the day looking into your past," Aidan said as he prepared the zucchini and some chicken breasts for grilling.

"Not something I enjoy doing," Freddie said. "Why bother? The past is in the past, like that song says. I'm never going back." Ironic, he thought, since he'd been forced to think about his personal history, from high school through Rodney and the demise of his acting career.

"But whoever is after you isn't going to let you forget so easily. After dinner, I'd like you to sit down with us and look through the names I've come up with, see if any of them had a grudge against you."

Liam returned then, and the three of them ate dinner. When they were finished, Aidan brought out his laptop. While they waited for it to boot up, Liam said, "I need to ask you a question, Freddie, and I need you to be honest with me. Did you ever work for any organized crime guys? Mafia, triads, anything like that?"

Freddie shook his head. "From everything I saw, the mafia guys stayed away from gay shit. Afraid they'd get contaminated or something. Most of the money for my movies came from production companies, occasionally from some rich, gay dude who wanted to hang around with porn stars. You don't have to worry about the mafia coming after me because I stole money from them or something."

"Steal from anybody else?" Liam asked.

"You're a fucking asshole, you know that?" Freddie said. "Just because I make porn doesn't make me a douchebag."

"He didn't mean to imply that," Aidan said. "But somebody has a motive to come after you, and we have to ask the hard questions."

Freddie glared at them, then laughed. "That would have been a good name for a movie. Hard Questions."

Aidan smiled, though it was hard to crack a smile from his big partner. Aidan turned his laptop so that Freddie could see the spreadsheet he'd put together.

"Christ, that's a lot of names," Freddie said. "I worked with all those guys?"

"So your film credits say," Aidan said. He pointed at the screen. "Are all these Vanguard guys related?"

Freddie shook his head. "There was a big star called Victor Vanguard back in the eighties. Lots of guys took his last name to be associated with him."

"Are any of these real names?" Liam asked.

"You think people in porn use their real names? Sometimes the lower-level guys would even change their names from movie to movie so fans would think they were new meat."

Aidan groaned. "Does that mean this is all mostly useless?"

"Probably. But let me take a look." Freddie pulled out a pair of reading glasses and leaned toward the screen. "Oh, he was a sweetheart," he said, pointing to one name. "And this one here had the dick of death."

"We're looking for people who might have a grudge against you," Liam said.

"Most of these guys are dead by now," Freddie said. "That kind of work, it took its toll on you. If the virus didn't get you, then the coke or the crack or the booze would."

"How did you make it?" Aidan asked.

"Sheer dumb luck," Freddie said. "Along with a strong immune system and a high tolerance for alcohol. Sure, I crashed and burned. But I was fortunate that a friend looked after me, helped me claw my way back to being a human being."

He shook his head. "I can't do this right now. It's too damn depressing."

"We need to start developing some idea of who's got a grudge against you," Liam said. "From your work, from your family. Maybe that fracking deal."

Aidan put his hand on his partner's arm. "We can do this in the morning. Sunshine and a good cup of coffee will make everything easier."

"I doubt it," Freddie said. "But I'm willing to give it a try." Most of the names meant nothing, but the ones that did—those were the ones who tore his heart out. He couldn't handle it. He got up and went back to his bedroom and shut the door.

Those men were gorgeous: some of them sweet, some smart, some dumb as a box of rocks. So many of them dead or destroyed by drugs. It made his heart sore to think about it, so he tried not to. But sometimes he couldn't help himself, particularly when he thought back to that last film he'd worked on before leaving LA.

※ ※ ※

After the cops took Carl away, Javier woke up and the EMTs took him in for a bunch of tests—but of course since he was an illegal with no health insurance they kicked him back quickly. Freddie knuckled down to finish the movie. He used creative angles and interspersed footage of Javier sucking Ed, making it look like he was still blowing Carl.

It was a crap movie, and everybody knew it. Even Javier, who was so new to the business he hadn't gotten a screen credit yet, knew it sucked. But Freddie had an obligation to Mario to finish the film.

He holed up in the studio, working eighteen hours a day to cut the film together.

He kept the door locked in case crazy Carl decided to come back. He told Ed and Javier and Holly that they were done and paid them off. When Javier came to collect his check, he nearly cried, he was so grateful to Freddie for giving him a chance.

"I grow up in Mexico," he said. "My father, he is *muy macho*. I never please him, so I run away when I am fourteen. I want to come to El Norte, be movie star in El Lay. In Tijuana I meet man who help me come across." He looked down shyly. "He was first man I let fuck me. I think maybe he love me little bit, because he give me money for bus fare here."

"What have you been doing since then?" Freddie asked, reaching for a bottle of water.

"I sleep at shelter for first couple weeks, until I met this guy. He say I can live in his guest house if I clean house and let him fuck me when he want."

Freddie shook his head. His world was full of stories like that, young guys taken advantage of in the most awful ways. At least he paid his actors well, never made them do things he wouldn't do himself, tried to let them retain a little dignity when they could.

"How long were you there?" Freddie asked.

"Nearly six weeks," Javier said. "Very bad. But then I meet Mr. Ed and he have me come live by him. From him I meet you, and now I get pay for what I do. Is very good."

"And you've been with Ed all this time?"

"Soon I have money for my own apartment. Maybe two, three more months. I am staying with Mr. Ed now too long, almost three months."

Freddie did the math so quickly he nearly spit out his water. "Six weeks with this other guy and then three months with Ed? How the fuck old are you, anyway? You told me you were nineteen." He had asked the kid for ID and been given something that said he was of legal age. He knew the name was fake, but he'd assumed, because Ed had recommended him, that the kid was legal.

Javier looked down at the floor. "I lie because Mr. Ed tell me to. He say if I am too young, you not hire me." He looked back up. "I will be fifteen next week."

"Oh, Jesus," Freddie said. "You shouldn't be doing this kind of shit, kid. Not at your age. You're supposed to be in junior high, lusting after football players and jerking off in your bedroom. Not to mention I could go to jail for hiring you. That's child porn, and I don't do that shit. Not at all, not ever. I'm going to kill Ed."

"Please don't," Javier said. "I will never tell nobody."

* * *

Freddie had chased him away. He'd gulped handfuls of speed to stay awake and then drank gallons of beer to control his jittery hands. In the end, it was the beer that had saved his life. He'd gotten up from the editing desk one night because he had to take a wicked piss, and while he was in the john, an explosion rocked the building. The walls fell around him like a bad action movie, and he dashed outside and got away from the flames.

The fire investigator later told him that the bomb had been placed right outside where Freddie would have been sitting. He'd been dazed and scared. Fortunately, he had uploaded the most recent edit to off-site storage before he went to the bathroom, so he'd been able to hand in the movie to Mario's distributor, rough edges and all, and hightail it out of town.

He'd taken a break for a couple of months, waiting until the crappy film was released, to be sure that no one was after him for the underage hiring. He'd decided he was done with talent. Leave him alone in his editing room, without any responsibility greater than to string scenes together and make a good movie.

He'd hired a contractor to completely renovate the old farmhouse and rented an apartment in Nice until it was finished. Then he'd moved his state-of-the-art equipment into the editing room and had never looked back.

Until now.

Freddie stripped down and got into bed, but he couldn't sleep. Every time he closed his eyes he saw that building on fire, and even though the air conditioning was turned down low, he felt hot and sweaty.

Around two in the morning, he reached for the phone. Would Newt still be awake? Who the fuck cared? Freddie wanted to talk to him. Needed to talk to him.

That was the flip side of crushing, he thought, this obsessive need to talk to the object of your affection, to be with him, to feel his touch. It took a while for Newt to answer, and when he did his voice was tentative. "Hello?"

"Newt? It's me."

"Oh. Freddie."

"How are you doing? Need some more of that cream rubbed on your back?"

"Your bodyguard came to see me today," Newt said. "He said somebody's stalking you for real."

"It's nothing."

"It doesn't sound like it, Freddie. You could be in real danger."

Freddie flashed back to that burning building. He didn't think he could sleep alone that night. Or any night in the near future. "I want you to come stay with me for a while."

Freddie hadn't even realized he was going to say those words until they popped out of his mouth. "There's some crazy shit going on, and I won't be able to get away from here very easily. If I want to keep seeing you, I need you here." To salvage a bit of his dignity he added, "So I can get you in shape."

"I still have a lease here," Newt said.

"What does that matter? Christ, do you forget that I'm a fucking porn star? And I'm inviting you to come and stay with me? What kind of moron are you?"

"You're an ex-porn star," Newt said.

Freddie opened his mouth in exasperation but couldn't find anything to say. It was true. He was a washed-up has-been. Even a dopey fat slob didn't want anything to do with him. How far had he fallen? "You know what? Do what you want."

He savagely punched the phone button to end the call. Then he turned the phone off and threw it across the room, where it landed with a soft *plop* on a pile of clothes—a sound that reminded him of the way that dildo had come out of Newt's ample ass the night before.

An hour later, he was still awake, turning from side to side, flipping his pillows, kicking the covers away. He heard Newt's silly car pulling into the driveway and bounded up. Crap, he thought. Better tell the bodyguards I invited company. He hurried out into the living room, where he found Liam poised at the front door, a gun in his hand.

"It's only Newt," Freddie said. "I invited him to come up and stay for a while."

"At three in the morning?" Liam asked. Then he shook his head, lowered his gun, and stepped back so Freddie could open the door.

Newt had thrown on an oversize shirt in a hideous plaid and a pair of extra-large polyester track pants. As if he'd ever gone around a track in his life. He was carrying what looked like a gym bag rather than the big suitcase Freddie had expected. "That's all you brought?" Freddie asked.

"I didn't have a lot of time to pack," Newt said.

Freddie looked around for Liam and realized that the big bodyguard had disappeared. It was creepy the way the dude could move so silently.

Freddie was determined to take control of this relationship, whatever it was, before things got out of hand. "Get into my bedroom and get your fucking clothes off before I cut them off."

"Not even a hello?" Newt asked.

Freddie pointed down the hall. "Speak only when you are spoken to."

Newt hurried toward the bedroom, Freddie on his heels. The big guy fumbled through unbuttoning his shirt, his fingers shaking, but Freddie resisted the urge to help him. Then Newt got his fingers tangled in the drawstring for his pants and eventually had to tug them down. They took his big faded boxers with them.

When Newt was naked, Freddie ordered him into the bathroom. "Get up on the scale. I want to see what we're working with."

"I hate to weigh myself," Newt said.

"I'm not surprised." Freddie pointed again, and Newt walked into the bathroom and stepped on the scale. The electronic display scrolled through numbers. "Wow," he said when they stopped. "The last time I weighed myself I was over three hundred."

"Two seventy-five is nothing to brag about," Freddie said with his arms crossed over his chest. "Now. On your back on the bed with your legs in the air. We're going to establish once and for all who's the boss around here."

Newt lumbered over to the bed and put one knee up, then tried to leverage himself up. Freddie got behind him, one palm on each big cheek, and pushed. Christ, the guy was fat. From this angle his butt was like two huge balloons.

Once Newt was poised there like some big elephant, Freddie

reached into his bureau drawer and withdrew a leather strap. "Ever have your balls stretched?" he asked Newt.

"No," Newt said in a small voice.

"No, sir." Freddie reached between Newt's massive thighs and grabbed his balls.

Newt yelped. "No, sir."

"Good boy," Freddie said as he fastened the strap around Newt's balls. "How does that feel?"

"Weird."

Freddie stood back, contemplating his next move. He'd been planning to put clips on the big guy's nipples, then connect them to the ball strap and lead him around the house like a dog. But a man twice the size of a Saint Bernard would probably bang into his furniture and knock shit over. And there were the bodyguards to consider.

He went back to his drawer and looked for the biggest butt plug he owned. It was almost eight inches long, with a pointed tip and a flared bottom. He squirted some lube onto it, rubbed it in with his fingers, then positioned it at Newt's ass.

Jesus, the globes were as big as beach balls. "Pry your ass apart," Freddie said. "You're so fat I can't find your asshole."

Instead of doing as he was told, Newt rolled over onto his back. "I told you, it hurts my feelings when you say that." He sat up. "I don't want to stay here if you're going to treat me that way."

"You never heard of tough love?" Freddie asked.

"I lived it," Newt said. "All my life. My father criticized my weight from the time I was in kindergarten. He wasn't exactly skinny, but at least he was proportional. Me, I was fat. I had to shop in the husky section of the boys' department. When I wore corduroys, my thighs rubbed together and chafed. I had to start wearing boxers when I was twelve because my mother couldn't find briefs big enough for me."

Freddie was determined not to pity the big lug. Pity didn't do anybody a lick of good. But he did feel an uncomfortable sensation in the bottom of his stomach.

"When we stripped down in gym class, all the boys made fun of me. They whipped towels at my ass and called me names. I had to take it then, but I don't have to now."

"Good for you," Freddie said. "I'm a tough, domineering son of a bitch, so you've got to stand up to me if you want to survive." He brandished the butt plug. "Would you please stand up?"

Newt did so, and his big dick pronged ahead of him. Freddie turned him around and pushed the butt plug in between the globes. He could tell he'd hit home when Newt squirmed. "How do you like that?" Freddie said, breathing warm against Newt's back.

"I like it," Newt said. He added, "Sir."

"Good. You're going to have it there for a while, to remind you who's the boss."

"But what if I have to—you know?"

"What? Take a dump? We're both adults here, Newtie boy. Say what you want."

"What do I do when I have to shit?"

"You take it out," Freddie said patiently. "You clean it up, you do your business, you clean yourself, and then you put it back in."

Newt nodded. "Yes, sir."

"I like your attitude," Freddie said. "I think we're going to get along fine."

21 – Running in Circles

Newt felt awkward standing there naked with a boner and a butt plug up his ass. "Come on to bed," Freddie said. "I'm beat."

"You mean there? With you?"

"Where else?"

"Are you sure there's room for me? I'm kinda big."

Freddie laughed. "Kinda big? Buddy, you're the size of a water buffalo." He held up his hand. "My bad. I know you don't like it when I talk that way."

"But it's true."

"Maybe so. But we'll make it work. We might have to cuddle up close though. You have any problem with that?"

Newt's heart raced, and his dick pulsed at the thought of cuddling up against Freddie Venus. He longed to run his hands down Freddie's muscular chest and squeeze his biceps. He wanted touch Freddie's tattoos and see if the skin felt any different due to the ink.

Newt lowered himself gingerly to the bed, worried that at any moment he'd crack the frame. But the bed accommodated him, and he realized that the air was cold, so he slid under the covers on his side, facing away from Freddie.

Freddie turned out the light and got into the bed behind Newt, wrapping his arm around him.

"I've never slept with anyone before," Newt said. "I mean, in the same bed."

"Don't worry, baby," Freddie said, kissing the back of his neck. "I'll take care of you."

Very quickly, it seemed to Newt, Freddie was asleep. Newt stayed awake, though, baffled by the constant shift of Freddie's moods. One moment he was sweet and loving, the next bitter and almost violent. Newt still had the leather strap wrapped around his balls and the plug up his ass. Reminding him of what? That he was bound to this man, this part-time angel with wings tattooed across his back?

When Newt woke the next morning, Freddie was still asleep beside him. He got up, self-conscious of his nakedness, and hurried into the bathroom to pee. As he stood over the toilet, the butt plug came loose, and he had to clench his cheeks tight to keep it in.

When he returned to the bedroom, he found Freddie sitting up in bed. "Put on a T-shirt and some shorts. We're going for a run." Freddie stood up and stretched, his impressive chest expanding and his big dick hanging half-hard.

Newt couldn't help staring, and that made him fumble for words. "I hate running. I feel like a big cow stumbling along."

"Get over yourself. You have sneakers?"

"Yeah."

"Put them on. Don't worry; I'll go easy on you."

"No, you won't," Newt grumbled. "Sir."

Freddie went into the bathroom, standing over the toilet and pissing loudly. Newt hurriedly stuffed his hard-on into a pair of shorts. He pulled on an old T-shirt, surprised that it felt looser than the last time he'd worn it.

After a few hundred meters down the street, Newt was having trouble keeping up with Freddie, who was only walking fast, not even running. "This little lane circles back around," Freddie said, motioning across the street. "We'll do a couple of laps around it."

He took off at top speed, lapping Newt twice in his first circuit. After he'd completed one circle to Freddie's two, Newt stopped and bent over, wheezing. "Can't...can't do...anymore."

"All right. We'll take it easy back up to the house." He put his arm around Newt's shoulder as they walked, and after a few hundred feet, Newt put his arm around Freddie's waist. It felt strangely nice to be walking that way—better than holding hands.

Perspiration was streaming down Newt's body, and after he soaked his shirt, the moisture rubbed off on Freddie, so they were both drenched by the time they made it back to the house.

"Into the shower," Freddie said, turning Newt down the hall toward the bathroom. "When I bought this place there was no indoor plumbing, so I splurged on stone floors, a huge shower, and a claw-footed tub by a picture window for relaxing and staring out at the hills. Haven't had anyone to share it with till now."

"I can't fit in that tub," Newt said.

"We'll be fine in the shower," Freddie said. Because Newt was too exhausted to do it himself, Freddie undressed him, tugging the sopping T-shirt over his head, then kneeling to undo Newt's shoelaces. He slipped the shoes off, then the socks. He leaned down to sniff the rich aroma of Newt's feet, and Newt giggled when

Freddie pried apart his toes to lick between them.

Then he reached up and jerked the waistband of Newt's shorts. They came sliding down along with his boxers. "Don't tear those up," Newt grumbled. "I only have so many pair."

"Trust me, bud. Soon those'll be so loose on you, they'll fall right off your hips."

Freddie stripped and opened the door to the shower stall. He stepped inside and turned on the water, then waited for it to come to a comfortable temperature.

"Come on in," he said to Newt.

"You're sure there's room for me?"

"Don't worry; we'll be getting up close and personal."

Newt stepped daintily into the shower. He was so big that his shoulders were nearly as wide as the stall.

Freddie reached up to the gel dispenser on the wall and lathered his hands. "You relax and let me do all the work, big guy." He began with Newt's shoulders, massaging and kneading the muscles as he soaped them.

"That feels good," Newt said. His eyes were closed, and he was breathing through his mouth.

"It only gets better." Freddie began massaging Newt's huge man boobs in circles, tweaking the nipples as he went, and Newt groaned with pleasure. "Raise your right arm."

Newt did, and Freddie leaned in close for a whiff. Then he soaped his hands up and kept lathering, first one pit and then the other. When Newt's upper body was lathered, Freddie knelt down and began with Newt's right foot, holding it up and soaping it, massaging the sore muscles. Newt leaned back against the wall for support.

Though Newt could hardly believe it, it appeared that Freddie was enjoying himself. "You're really good at this," Newt said.

"Never been that good with intimacy. Even back when I was fucking all the time, the tricks came and went so fast I never had the chance to get to know any of them. I'm doing my best to change those habits."

Newt didn't like being compared to Freddie's past "tricks." Was that all he was to the man with angel wings on his back? Just a trick? He swallowed hard. Well, if that was all it was, he was going to enjoy it while it lasted.

"Turn around and lean against the wall," Freddie said.

Newt obeyed. Freddie opened his ass cheeks and the butt plug slid out. Newt was embarrassed. What if it had poop on it? But Freddie didn't seem to care. He quickly rinsed it under the spray, then set it aside.

He soaped up his hands once more and began massaging Newt's butt cheeks, poking a finger, then two, into his crack. It felt so incredibly good Newt thought he might pass out from the pleasure. He was completely bummed when Freddie stopped and motioned him to turn around.

"Saving the best for last." Freddie said. He undid the leather strap around Newt's balls and tossed it aside.

He poured more gel in his hands and began tickling his way

around Newt's crotch, lathering his way toward the central prize. Newt's dick was big and hard, and Freddie could barely wrap his thumb and index finger around it. "Who's a big boy?" Freddie asked. "And I mean that in only the best way."

Newt moaned as Freddie began jerking him, hand wrapped around the shaft, up and down. He fingered Newt's perineum, and Newt tiny tears welled up at the corners of Newt's eyes. "Oh God, oh God," he moaned.

"You can just call me Freddie."

"Please, Freddie. Sir. I need to…oh man…"

Freddie finished him off, and Newt spurted a white stream of come. "My work here is finished," Freddie said as he stood up.

"You aren't going to…you know?" Newt asked. Freddie's dick was at best half-hard.

"It doesn't work anymore," Freddie said. "The other day with you, that was the first time in a long time." He stepped out of the shower, grabbed a towel, and dried himself off as he walked out of the bathroom.

After Freddie left, Newt stood in the bathroom, wrapped in a huge green towel, and stared at himself in the mirror. What in the world did Freddie Venus see in him that Newt couldn't see himself? He was a fat slob. He'd always been one, and he always would be. Very quickly Freddie would tire of whatever program he had in mind, and he'd toss Newt back to the curb like a used condom.

But in the meantime? Newt was going to take advantage of every bit of pleasure he could.

When he walked out of the bathroom, Freddie was sitting up on one side of the king-size bed. "Butt plug?" Freddie asked.

"Oops. Back in the shower."

He hurried back to the bathroom, retrieved the butt plug from the shower, and used a bottle of hand lotion on the counter to lubricate it. He couldn't reach around to insert it, though, no matter how hard he tried.

He wasn't going to go back out to the bedroom and admit failure, though. He put the toilet seat down and positioned the plug on it. Then he spread his ass cheeks and carefully lowered himself, feeling the tip penetrate him. He couldn't hold himself up much longer, so he sat down hard, causing the toilet to shake and the butt plug to spear into him.

"Everything okay in there?" Freddie called.

"Fine," Newt said. He stood up, the butt plug in place, and looked around. Should he put the damp towel back around his waist? He didn't want to dress in his dirty, sweaty clothes again.

"I'm waiting," Freddie called.

Fuck it, Newt thought. He strode back into the bedroom naked, waiting for Freddie to make another cutting comment. But all he said was, "Get dressed. I'm going to make you breakfast."

The bodyguards were in the kitchen when they walked in. Freddie insisted on making a healthy breakfast for himself and Newt—eggs and toast, oatmeal, granola.

Newt sat across from Aidan and Liam, and they all waited to speak until Freddie had finished preparing the breakfast. "What are your plans for today?" Liam asked Freddie.

"Work," he said. "I have an editing project I need to finish. And I want to get some meditation time in this afternoon." He looked at Newt. "What about you?"

Newt looked down at the table. "I brought my laptop with me. I could write for a while. And I have to keep up my social media stuff."

Freddie looked at Aidan and Liam. "That leaves you."

"Can we get a few minutes with you?" Aidan asked him. "To take another stab at the names on the spreadsheets? If you could give us some guidance, we'd know where to keep looking."

"I suppose," Freddie said.

22 – STRAIGHT SUCKERS

Aidan brought his laptop into the kitchen and opened it up. "I'll get out of your way," Newt said, and he left the room.

"The last film you directed was called *Locker Room Lovers*, wasn't it?" Aidan began.

Freddie shook his head. "That's the last one that went out under my name. But my last job was finishing a film called *Straight Suckers* for a friend of mine."

"I didn't have that one," Aidan said. "Let me look it up real quick."

"I can tell you who worked on it," Freddie said. "This chick named Holly, two gay guys named Ed and Javier. My friend Mario Dellarosa directed and did the camera work for all but the last big scene. I directed and filmed that, and I did all the postproduction."

"Besides Mario, you know their last names?" Aidan asked.

Freddie shook his head. "Holly, Ed, and Javier were their real names, or at least the ones they said were real. They used different names in the film. I think Javier was Valentino Vasquez. I don't remember the last names or the pseudonyms of the others."

"That's okay. I can look them up later. Now. Any of these remind you of anything?"

"They remind me of a shitload," Freddie said. "Nothing I want to remember."

"Come on, Freddie," Liam said. "Somebody is after you, and

they've got to have a reason. Unless you've pissed somebody off here in Nice, the reason stretches back to your family or someone you worked with."

Freddie sighed. "Usually, people were pretty professional on the job. You know, come to work, get fucked, suck a couple of dicks, go home. There was always drama, of course, but rarely did anything carry on offstage."

He pointed at a couple of names. "This guy, and this one. Both of them nuts, and both of them hated me, for different reasons. Probably both dead by now, though."

Aidan noted those two men, and Freddie scrolled down. By the time they were done, he had a list of ten names for further research, though Freddie insisted that whatever beef he'd had with them was long since papered over.

"What about that last film?" Aidan asked. "Any problems with people on that one?"

"That was *Straight Suckers*. It was one of the first 'bait bus' movies—you know, where the producers roped in some supposedly straight guy, baited him with a girl who got him started, then switched for a guy."

"People fall for that?" Liam asked.

Freddie shrugged. "Lots of gay guys get off on seeing a straight guy get turned on to dick," he said. "Holly was the recruiter; she'd go out and look for guys she could convince to make a porno with her. She'd bring a guy back to the studio, get him worked up, then switch off with Javier or Ed. Usually the guys would get mildly pissed off.

But I got lucky."

He laughed dryly. "The straight guy she picked up for the segment I filmed went nuts when he figured out what was going on."

"What do you mean, went nuts?" Liam asked.

"He pulled off his blindfold as he was fucking Javier's ass, and he started flailing around punching people. I had to call *nueve-uno-uno*."

"You have that guy's name?"

"Holly would have had him sign a release before she agreed to hire him. I must have scanned it and uploaded it to Mario's files." He looked up. "Oh, yeah. The real names of those other actors would be there too."

"Can you get them from him?" Aidan asked.

Freddie shook his head. "Mario is a real artist with a camera in his hand, but he's crap when it comes to record keeping. I doubt he could find anything after all this time." He paused. "But you know what? When I worked with him, I kept all the personnel stuff on a bunch of Zip drives. I still have them in a box somewhere, but I don't know that I have any way to read them."

"What's a Zip drive?" Liam asked.

"Mass storage device from the late 1990s," Aidan said. "I used to have one, but it's long since gone. Richard might be able to retrieve the information, though." He looked at Freddie. "Can you find them?"

"I have work to do. I'll show you where the boxes are."

Liam looked like he was going to complain, but Aidan

forestalled him. "No problem. I'll see what I can do." They followed Freddie to a small room next to his studio, stacked with boxes.

"Most of this is household stuff I never got around to unpacking," he said. "The boxes you're looking for should say something like 'business' on them."

He left, and Liam started looking at boxes. "Here's one that says *business*," he said. He ripped open the packing tape. "Oh, Christ."

"What?" Aidan asked.

"Look at these sex toys. Most of them never even opened."

Aidan stood up and peered into the box with him. He pulled out a battery-operated vibrator in the shape of a larger-than-life penis, complete with veins and a mushroom head. Below it was a black rubber cat-o'-nine-tails, a couple of black blindfolds, and more dildos than Aidan had ever seen in one place outside of a sex store, in a rainbow of colors and sizes.

"What's this for?" Liam asked, holding up a curved gadget in black rubber with small nubs on one end.

"An anal stimulator. This part goes in your hole, and this part rubs your perineum."

"You have such a wide range of knowledge. Your parents would be so proud."

"I can take over here," Aidan said, taking the anal stimulator back from Liam. He wondered if Freddie would give them a couple of these toys and thought he might put aside the ones he was interested in. "Why don't you see what you and Richard can find on Freddie's family, and that fracking deal Freddie mentioned?"

"I'm on it," Liam said. He left Aidan in the small room, and Aidan began digging through the rest of the business boxes. He found shrink-wrapped copies of many of Freddie's movies, promotional photos, copies of distribution agreements. The Zip cartridges were in the fourth box. He remembered them—thick gray plastic containers the size of a deck of cards. And then, praise the Lord, at the bottom of the box was an ancient drive that could read them, along with the flat SCSI cable that would connect it to a computer.

In another box, he found a battered old laptop with Windows 95 installed, and after plugging it in to get it charged, he plugged in the Zip drive. The laptop was so old, and filled with programs, that it moved like molasses. He read the contents of the first disk, and realized that Freddie had been using Lotus 1-2-3—a spreadsheet program that was ancient by current standards—to keep track of his data. He'd never learned that program, so he had to find a program online to convert the old files into Excel so he could read and manipulate them.

Freddie appeared briefly with Newt around noon. They argued for a couple of minutes in the kitchen, and Newt reluctantly accepted a couple of granola bars for lunch. Neither of them appeared to notice Aidan at the dining room table, boxes and disks spread around him.

When they went back to work, Newt in the bedroom and Freddie in the editing studio, Liam appeared, and Aidan grabbed them bars and bottles of cold water. "How's it going?" Liam asked.

"Slow and tedious. I'll spare you all the technical details but I retrieved the data, and now I have to get it into a format I can work with. How about you?"

"Following a lot of leads but nothing I can put my finger on yet." After they finished eating, Liam went back to the bedroom with the laptop, and Aidan returned to the material from the Zip drives. It took most of the afternoon to get all the data into a format he could work with.

His first targets were the ten men Freddie had beefs with back in LA. At a free site that let him search Social Security death records, he found that, as Freddie had predicted, eight of the ten men were dead.

That left two, James Bliss and Kamau Black. And either they had given fake names on their employment forms or had fallen completely off the radar, because he wasn't able to find any information that was a clear match to either of them. Rather than waste more time, he e-mailed the information he had on the two of them, including the Social Security numbers they had used on their paperwork, to Richard.

Then he turned to the records for *Straight Suckers*. He figured out that Javier's last name was Echeverria, though he was credited in the film as Valentino Vazquez. Holly's real name was Elizabeth Angstrom, and that meant that Ed was Eustace Cunningham.

Eustace Cunningham was easy to find; he had died in Los Angeles in 1998. He found an Elizabeth Angstrom on LinkedIn, and the profile photo looked enough like the woman in *Straight Suckers* to be a match. She listed her profession as an independent location scout for film, television, and advertising, and she included the names of a number of low-profile movies she had worked on. But the profile hadn't been updated in several years, and when Aidan tried to connect with her, he was told that the e-mail address she had listed was no longer valid.

Javier Echeverria was a common enough name that there were plenty of records, but Aidan couldn't connect any of them to the porn actor. The Social Security number he had used looked funny—all the digits were zeroes and ones, as if it was in binary code. He went online to look for information and discovered that the first three digits were the area number. The numbers on the card, 001, would seem to indicate the card had been issued in New Hampshire—unusual for a kid with a Mexican name.

The next two digits, the group number, were 00, which was a clear indicator that something was wrong, because only numbers from 01 to 99 had been used by the Social Security Administration. Finally, the serial number, the last four digits, was 1111—and that was statistically very unlikely.

That meant Javier Echeverria, if that was his real name, had a fake ID. Not unexpected from a Mexican kid in Los Angeles. And Aidan had the feeling that there hadn't been a whole lot of ID verification in the porn business back then.

There were a bunch of other records in the folder for *Straight Suckers*, and Aidan assumed that they were for the "straight" talent. The last one was Carl Ousterhout. He had to be the guy who'd gone crazy when he discovered he was fucking a guy.

Though Aidan didn't have access to the LAPD database, it was clear that Carl Ousterhout had a very colorful police record. From notes in various newspapers, Aidan could tell the guy had been picked up for a bunch of petty crimes, including breaking and entering and drug possession, before his eventual death in prison several years before.

That meant that Ed and Carl were both dead ends. Holly, aka Elizabeth, was a possibility, but he couldn't find anything recent about her.

Who was after Freddie? Aidan found it hard to believe that a young Mexican kid with a fake ID would have the resources to track Freddie down and come to France to exact vengeance for some slight on a film from years before. Stranger things had happened, though.

23 – FAMILY MATTERS

Liam pushed the laptop away from him. The vitriol that Freddie's brother spewed was too depressing. Earl Ventura blamed Barack Obama for every problem in American society, from health care to immigration to global warming. And he complained that there was a gay cabal in entertainment and media that was poisoning the minds of young people.

Liam had thought things were changing. Same-sex marriage was legal in a bunch of states, the Defense of Marriage Act had been demolished, and the Don't Ask, Don't Tell policy in the military was history. But out in the heartland of America, antigay prejudice was going strong.

Who was he kidding? There was still a lot of antigay sentiment back home. Aidan had outed him to his mother and sisters when they were in the States a few months before, and since then his mother no longer demanded a weekly call. She had abandoned using a video-enabled version of Skype in favor of quick voice check-ins. Liam had always been his mother's pride and joy, and even though she was often a pain in the ass, it hurt that she was pushing him away.

His sister Franny had stopped e-mailing him pictures of his niece and nephew, probably afraid that Liam had revealed himself as a pedophile. And his other sister, Jeannie, who had problems of her own, had shut off all contact—though that was most likely because Liam had beat up her abusive ex-husband during that visit.

All the more reason to stay in Europe. Who needed all that complication anyway?

His e-mail pinged with a message from Richard—the report on Freddie's family attached. Fred Ventura Senior had run a successful insurance business in Omaha for years. When he died, he left the business to his three sons, though Freddie's share had been placed in a trust to be managed by his brothers.

Gerald was the president and chief operating officer. He was married to a former Miss Nebraska, and they had two picture-perfect kids at a private high school.

Earl was the vice president of the business, but it appeared he spent most of his time in the civic and political arena. He had been the president of the local Kiwanis, a member of the Elks and the Knights of Columbus. He had served on the Chamber of Commerce, eventually ascending to the presidency, and used that as a stepping-stone to the Omaha City Council.

Liam pulled up a picture of Earl. He was a younger, fleshier version of Freddie, without the musculature and with no visible tattoos. He had an open, friendly smile. His wife was even prettier than Gerald's, though without the beauty-pageant credentials. They had twin fourteen-year-old sons.

Earl had been a leader of the Republican Party of Nebraska and had floated on a wave of Tea Party support to a seat in the state legislature. He had set his sights on Washington a few months before and was the favored candidate for the Republican ticket.

An openly gay brother shouldn't be much of a problem for him,

Liam thought. Look at Dick Cheney and his lesbian daughter. There were plenty of other local and national politicos with GLBT relatives.

Freddie's background as a porn star would be more troubling, though. And there was no way to spin him as an innocent victim of a corrupt industry; he was too involved for that. But would eliminating a troublesome brother from a political portrait be enough of a motive for murder? Liam picked up the laptop and walked out to the living room to show Aidan what he had found.

He set the laptop down on the table beside the ancient machine Aidan was using. He grabbed another granola bar and looked over Aidan's shoulder. "I'm impressed you got that caveman technology to work," Liam said.

"Wasn't easy. I finally got everything into Excel and started researching some of the guys. All dead ends so far, though." Aidan gobbled the granola bar and washed it down with a swig from a bottle of cold water. "How about you? You find anything?"

"I did some reading about Gerald's political campaigns. He's an asshole. I can see where Freddie gets his blunt personality from."

"But do you think he's enough of an asshole to want his brother killed?"

"Richard says Earl's campaign is backed by big-money conservatives. He's been endorsed by something called the Tea Party." Liam leaned against the table. "Politics back in the US is getting crazy, Aidan. I'm glad to be here. These right-wing conservatives have co-opted the name of those guys from the Revolutionary War, and they're trying to force the Republican Party into a set of very narrow views. Earl has bought into their garbage, and he comes across as a borderline lunatic."

"Most politicians sound crazy to me," Aidan said. "But what do I know? I'm a liberal Jew from the East Coast."

"Earl is not only bringing in a lot of cash from these outside contributors, he and Gerald are rolling in dough. They each own 40 percent of the insurance business, and Freddie has twenty. Earl and Gerald are each worth several million bucks. Freddie's the poor relation, and even he's a millionaire. And not from sucking dick or filming it."

"Good to know he can afford our services," Aidan said.

"I spoke to the boss, too," Liam said. The regional manager of the Agence was a retired French flic named Jean-Luc Derain, based out of Marseille, and they rarely saw him, though they did speak now and then about cases.

"I asked him and Louis to put out some feelers, see if any of their sources have heard of an American trying to hire a local assassin." He opened the laptop and shifted it so that Aidan could see the photos of Freddie's family.

Aidan looked at them for a couple of minutes and then pointed at the photo of Gerald's twins. "And here, ladies and gentlemen, we have an argument for a genetic basis of homosexuality."

"What do you mean?"

The boys were fraternal, rather than identical, though each wore the uniform of the same private school that their cousins attended. "The one on the right?" Aidan said. "Membership."

"Aidan. How can you tell from a picture?"

"Liam. The real question is how come you can't tell? Look at the kid's posture. He looks like he's made of spaghetti. His brother stands up straight."

"Lots of teenagers slouch," Liam said. "That doesn't mean he's gay."

"That's not a slouch, Liam. That's a kid getting ready to assume the posture on the floor of a Greyhound-station men's room." He leaned closer to the screen. "Look at that pukka shell necklace around his neck. The way his shirt is neatly tucked into his perfectly creased slacks. Then compare to his brother."

Liam had to admit that the boys presented very differently. "It still doesn't mean anything," he said.

"If I were Gerald Ventura, I'd be plenty scared that my boy was going to grow up like my brother," Aidan said. "Scared enough to do something about it? That I don't know."

"How would having his brother killed keep Gerald's son from being gay?"

"Might not keep him from being gay, but it would sure keep him in the closet. See what happened to your uncle, boy? You don't want to end up like that."

"We don't even know that someone wants to kill Freddie," Liam said. "So far all we've seen is harassment."

"You know as well as I do that harassment is often the buildup to something deadly," Aidan said.

"Did you find any motives from Freddie's filmography?"

"Nothing much. I tracked down the people he worked with on his last film, and I don't think there are any leads there."

"Leads where?" Freddie asked. He walked into the living room.

"From your last film," Aidan said. "Holly's married with kids, Ed and the nutcase Carl who caused all the problems are both dead, and I can't find anything about Javier, if that was even his real name."

"Then who do you think torched the warehouse where I was working?" Freddie asked.

"Excuse me?" Liam said. "That's a detail you haven't mentioned yet."

Freddie shrugged. "Didn't think it mattered, until now." He sat down across the dining-room table from them. "I told you Mario asked me to finish his film, right?"

Liam and Aidan both nodded.

"I was almost done with postproduction, working long hours at this warehouse on La Cienega that Mario had fitted out as a ministudio. I was living on energy drinks, speed, and beer, which made me piss like a racehorse. Almost every hour. One night, I got up to take a leak, and while I was in the can, the whole building exploded around me. I got lucky because the Molotov cocktail had been thrown right at the wall by the editing desk, and if I hadn't gotten up, I'd have been blown to bits."

"You don't know who did it?" Aidan asked.

Freddie shook his head. "Police and fire department did an 'investigation,' but they didn't find anything. Probably a plus for them to shut down a porn studio."

"Do you have a copy of the police report?" Liam asked.

"Nope. I wanted to forget everything about that movie, and I did, until you guys showed up." He held up his hand. "That's not fair. Whatever is coming down is all on me, not on you guys. I appreciate your help."

Freddie pushed back his chair. "I need a bottle of water, and then I have to go back to editing. If you need to ask me anything, just come back to the studio."

After Freddie left, Liam picked up his phone. "I'm going to see if Louis can pull some strings and get a copy of that report." He walked out to the backyard to make the call.

Louis answered his phone on the fourth ring. Like Liam, he preferred to take calls in private and didn't answer until he could talk. "Hey, Louis," Liam said. "How's life in the new house?"

Liam hated small talk, but Aidan had been pushing him to be more polite, wait a moment until jumping into the reason for a call.

"Precarious," Louis said. "Take my advice, McCullough. Never buy a house with your husband."

"Not sure I'll ever have one of those," Liam said. "A partner's enough for me."

"No real difference between the two except a piece of paper. That and the chance to get US citizenship for Hassan. But you didn't call to chat about domestic drama. You want to know what I dug up about your client."

"You know me too well. Were you able to find anything?"

"Just your garden-variety pornographer," Louis said. "A couple of arrests back in LA for public indecency, driving under the influence, possession of controlled substances. You picked yourself a real winner."

"Anything in France?"

"Nope. Maybe he's turned over a new leaf. But you know what they say about leopards."

"Can you check one more thing for me?" Liam asked. "A warehouse fire in Los Angeles, about five years ago? Somewhere on La Cienega Boulevard."

"Your client was involved?"

"According to him, he was nearly incinerated," Liam said. "Hopefully that will help you narrow down the incident. Don't know if there's a connection to the threats he's getting now, but I'm grasping at straws here."

"I know a guy in the FBI office in LA," Louis said. "I'll see what he can dig up for me. You're going to owe me, you know."

Liam and Louis had been managing a complicated accounting of favors requested and done for years. "What's it going to cost me?"

"Dinner," Louis said. "Hassan wants to inaugurate the new house. Can you make it Saturday?"

"We're still going to be working," Liam said.

"Bring your client. Hassan would love to meet him."

That was an easy trade for the information, Liam thought. Bring the ex-porn star over for show-and-tell. "I'll have to check with him first. And if we come, we'll be four."

"Four? Your client has a boyfriend? French or Moroccan?"

"Neither. American, and probably the most unlikely guy for him to fall in love with, if you consider looks alone."

"Intriguing," Louis said. "I'll check with my FBI guy and get back to you."

Liam was too restless to go back inside, so he climbed the hill behind the house, stopping at a small plateau that gave him a view of Freddie's property. He sat down with his legs crossed under him and considered Freddie Ventura's life.

On the surface, it looked pretty good. He was handsome and sexy, even if he had put a lot of miles on his odometer since he stopped working in porn. He had plenty of money, from his work and his inheritance. And yet there was something fundamentally unhappy about him—something that seemed to be changing as he spent time with Newt.

Love was a strange thing, he thought. He'd never believed in it himself until he met Aidan. Back then, he'd reserved that concept for his feelings for his mom and his sisters, the camaraderie he felt with his team members. The kind of love represented by romance movies and sappy greeting cards was foreign to him.

Aidan had changed all that. From the moment of their first kiss, Liam had felt something different, an odd stirring that had only a little to do with sex and a lot to do with his emotions. The more time they spent together, the more Liam discovered about Aidan, the more he fell in love.

He hoped Freddie would be as lucky with Newt. But for them to have a happily-ever-after ending, Liam and Aidan had to discover who was harassing Freddie and neutralize the threat before it became even more dangerous.

Unfortunately, there were few clues. Newt was a harmless nerd and so unlikely a match for Freddie that the idea he was being manipulated into getting into Freddie's good graces was ludicrous.

Freddie's family seemed, on the surface, to be unlikely suspects as well. Solid Nebraska folks, maybe a little narrow-minded, but the idea of a political candidate hiring an assassin to take out an embarrassing brother was pretty far-fetched. Look at Jimmy Carter. He'd been able to make it to the White House despite having a very colorful brother.

The only other option was someone from Freddie's porn past. The idea of someone holding a grudge for over five years and then tracking Freddie to France seemed equally far-fetched.

Was there someone else with a motive, someone Liam and Aidan had so far overlooked? He looked down the hill at the house, so peaceful in its acre of rough landscape. What other secrets did it hold?

24 – No Accident

Newt pushed back from the computer as the rays of the setting sun began to filter into Freddie's bedroom. His writing was crap, but that's the way it was with first drafts. He was trying to figure out the story. Once he had that out of the way, he'd go back and fill in the details, clean up the bad writing. It was like sculpting with clay, which he'd done as a kid. You took a lump and formed it into something. But first you had to have the lump.

He was surprised that he'd been able to write at Freddie's house. It had taken him weeks in the apartment in Nice before he'd had any inspiration. But opening the laptop here, he'd begun to type almost immediately.

He looked at the clock. He knew that Freddie spent part of his late afternoon in meditation, though Freddie hadn't spoken of it, and Newt was afraid to ask him about it. The bodyguards were out in the living room, and he was shy about going out there.

Freddie had been so sweet that morning—yes, a taskmaster, but it appeared that he was pushing Newt because he cared. The whole experience with Freddie was so far from what he'd been familiar with. He had always assumed that if he was lucky enough to land in a relationship, he would be the lover, not the object of someone's affection. Yet here he was, being pushed and pulled and spoiled and pampered by Freddie Venus.

He was scared to consider the future. Now that he'd seen what it was like to be cared for, he wanted more. But what if Freddie didn't want to continue? Suppose he tired of Newt like a child with a toy, batting him away when he got bored? How could Newt go back to his old lonely life?

There was a light tap on the bedroom door, and when Newt looked up, Freddie was standing in the doorway. "How's the writing going?"

"I think I'm tapped out for today. How about your work?"

"Getting close to finishing. But I need a break and to stretch my legs. You think you can manage another run?"

"I can try," Newt said. "But I don't think I can run with the butt plug in me."

"Then we'll take it out. Come over here."

Newt was embarrassed, even though Freddie had already seen him naked and hadn't been repulsed. But that had been in the middle of sex. What if Freddie was grossed out by Newt's humongous ass?

"Come on, Newtie. Drop your trousers and pop the plug out. Don't make me reach up there and get it."

Newt felt his face reddening. He turned so that he wasn't facing Freddie and didn't have to see his reaction. He pulled down his shorts and his saggy boxers and pushed. With a squelchy noise, the butt plug shot out of his ass, and it slipped past his fingers. "Oh no!" he said.

"I'll get this cleaned up for you," Freddie said. He picked up the butt plug from the floor before Newt could look at it, and then walked into the bathroom.

When Freddie went into the bathroom, Newt quickly put on a clean pair of shorts and a T-shirt, still embarrassed.

Freddie came out of the bathroom naked and walked to the bureau with supreme indifference to Newt's eyes. He pulled on his clothes. "Come on, put your tongue back in your mouth, big guy. You'll get what you're looking for later."

Newt blushed and followed Freddie out to the living room. "We're going for a quick run," Freddie said to the bodyguards.

"We'll come with you," Liam said.

"You need to change?" Freddie asked. They were both wearing polo shirts and khaki shorts.

"I doubt we'll work up much of a sweat," Liam said.

Liam and Freddie took the lead, while Aidan loped along with Newt. "You don't have to stay with me," Newt panted.

"I'll tell you a secret," Aidan said. "Liam pushes pretty hard. It's nice to go at a relaxing pace for a change. You get to see the scenery more."

Newt thought Aidan was being nice, but he didn't argue. And it was pleasant to be going at a pace he could manage with company by his side. Liam and Freddie got farther and farther ahead of them, which was fine because Freddie wouldn't be able to see how hard Newt was laboring.

Out of the corner of his eye, he saw a big jetliner taking off from the Nice airport, heading up over the hills in their direction. Wouldn't it be nice to be on that plane, Newt thought longingly, instead of toiling along this country road? He imagined himself in first class, plenty of room in his seat, a cute steward delivering a mimosa and a plate of nibbles.

"Come on, Newt," Aidan said. "You can do it."

Newt realized that he had stopped, and he began moving forward again.

Up ahead, Liam and Freddie were stopped at an intersection. From a distance, it looked like they were discussing which way to go, Freddie pointing one way, Liam another. Newt saw a big truck slide out of a driveway and head directly toward the intersection. With their backs to it, Liam and Freddie wouldn't see the danger in time. And the airplane noise, growing louder all the time, would mask the sound of the truck.

Newt was paralyzed with fear, but Aidan clearly knew what to do. He left Newt's side, rocketing forward. Newt slumped against a mailbox and watched openmouthed as the truck bore down on Freddie and Liam. It seemed to be accelerating.

Liam looked up and saw the truck approaching. He grabbed Freddie's arm and dove for the side of the road. From Newt's vantage point, the truck missed them by inches.

Ahead of him, the truck continued down the hill toward Aidan. Newt watched the bodyguard jump to the side, out of the truck's way, then pivot back around to watch it disappear. Newt summoned up his reserves and hurried forward. The truck rocketed past him, but the cab was too high, and he couldn't see the driver. He didn't think to turn around for the license plate number until the truck had already turned down a switchback.

By the time he reached the intersection, Liam was on his feet. Freddie sat on the ground looking dazed. "Are you all right?" Newt said to Freddie. He collapsed on the ground beside him and grabbed Freddie's hand.

"I'm okay," Freddie said, though his voice was weak. He shook his head. "Damn, I've never had that close a call when I've been out running on these roads. Those asshole truck drivers."

"That wasn't an accident," Aidan said. "That truck had no markings and no license plate."

"Let's get everybody back to the house before that truck makes a return pass," Liam said. He offered his hand to Freddie, who stood up.

Newt squirmed around, trying to stand, but he was so tired. "You guys go on without me. I'll just sit here for a while."

"No can do," Liam said. "We've got to stick together." He stepped to one side of Newt and put his hand into Newt's armpit. "Aidan, little help here."

"I'll do it," Freddie said. He grabbed Newt's other side, and the two of them lifted him.

"Not quite the same as lifting free weights," Freddie said.

"I'm sorry," Newt said. "I know I'm huge." He couldn't help himself; he began to cry.

"It's all right, babe." Freddie put his arm around Newt's shoulder.

"It's not," Newt said. "You could have gotten killed."

Liam waved them forward. "Come on, we've got to get inside."

Newt took a deep breath. He wasn't Fledglis or Ulric, but he could be strong for Freddie. He started moving forward, and Freddie scrambled to keep up with him. The two bodyguards followed, and he heard them speaking in low voices.

"What's going on, Freddie?" Newt asked. "Who's trying to kill you?"

"I wish I knew, babe," Freddie said. "I wish I knew."

Newt led Freddie into the bedroom, leaving the bodyguards behind. "I stink," Newt said. "I can't help it. I sweat like a pig."

"If I can't say stuff like that to you, you can't say it about yourself," Freddie said. "Take a shower if you want. I need to do some thinking."

The shower stall was a lot roomier when Newt wasn't sharing it with Freddie. He stood under the spray, letting the hot water massage his tired muscles. He loved the lemon scent of Freddie's soap, the richness of his shampoo. By the time he rinsed off, he felt a lot better.

He wrapped a big towel around him and returned to the bedroom. Freddie was sitting on the bed with his head in his hands. It wasn't until Newt sat down beside him that he realized Freddie was crying.

He put his arm around Freddie, the way Freddie had done with him, and Freddie leaned into his shoulder, still crying quietly. "It's okay, babe," Newt said, using the same endearment Freddie had. "Liam and Aidan are going to protect you."

"But for how long?" Freddie looked up, with tears running

down his face. "I can't live like this forever. I came to France to get away from all that shit."

"Was it dangerous for you back in Los Angeles?"

Freddie nodded. "Somebody tried to kill me there too."

Between sobs and sniffles, Freddie told Newt the story of the film he had finished for a friend and then the explosion at the warehouse.

"They never caught anyone?" Newt asked.

"Not that I ever heard."

They sat together for a long time, until Freddie had stopped crying. "You go eat dinner," Freddie said. "I'm going to take some pills and crash."

"I'm not leaving you," Newt said.

"Go on. You're probably starving."

Newt thought for a couple of seconds. Sure, he could eat. But it was more important for him to stay by Freddie's side. "You take your pills. I'll stay here until you fall asleep."

Freddie leaned over and kissed him lightly on the lips. "You're a good guy, Newt. How did you ever find me, anyway?"

"I saw you in the hypermarché when you were shopping. A kid knocked over a display of kitchen tools, and one of the forks caught the shoulder of your T-shirt and pulled it down. I recognized the tip of your tattoo."

"So that's what gave me away? Just the tip? How'd you recognize it?"

Newt looked down at the bed. "I was kind of a fan." He

hesitated, then continued. "Well, more than a fan. I had a whole porn collection back home, and I used to watch my favorites over and over again."

"Really? Which one was your favorite?"

"The one where you played the college janitor," Newt said without hesitation. "And you found that Chinese kid jerking off in one of the library carrels."

"That was Rodney Wang," Freddie said. "He was…my boyfriend for a while."

"I thought he had to be," Newt said. "There was so much chemistry between you. That time when you hung him upside down by his heels in the men's room and made him eat your ass out. That was so hot."

"Yeah, well those days are over. Not hanging anybody upside down anymore."

"Too bad," Newt said. "Though I'd probably hate it. Get a nosebleed or cramps or something."

Freddie laughed. "There are other things we can do, you know."

Newt took a deep breath. "Do you want to, you know, whip me again? I know you got off the last time you did, and you haven't since then, so if that's what it takes to make you happy—"

Freddie cut him off. "Don't you worry about making me happy."

"But I want to," Newt protested. "Is it that I'm losing weight? Would you rather I was fat? I can let you call me names again."

Freddie reached over and took his hand. "That's very sweet of you to offer. The truth is, I don't know why I managed to come that time. I haven't in years. I think it's the medication I take."

"Do you need it to, like, live?" Newt asked.

Freddie laughed. "To live peacefully, yeah," he said. "Though that seems to be a lost cause right now."

Newt knew that he had to do something to shake Freddie out of this depression, and there was only one thing he could think of. Since their first encounter, he'd watched carefully, looking at Freddie's dick in the shower, in bed, watching it lengthen against his running shorts as they ran.

Through it all, though, he noticed that Freddie's dick only hardened occasionally, and the only time he had come was when he rubbed his dick against Newt's ass after whipping him that first time. Was that the secret to Freddie's sexual release?

Newt stood up and walked over to the bureau. He remembered which drawer Freddie kept his toys in, and he opened it and pulled out the tit clamps. "Will you put these on me?" he asked.

"You want me to?" Freddie asked.

"I do," he said. "Please?"

Newt felt the sharp bite when the clamps were fastened to his nipples, but he didn't mind because Freddie had stopped crying. Freddie knelt down and wrapped that leather strap around Newt's balls again, this time attaching some small silver weights to it. His balls felt heavier—a sensation that wasn't all that terrible.

Then Freddie hooked the nipple clamps to the ball stretcher. The weight of his balls pulled on the clamps and tugged them down.

"How's that feel?" Freddie asked.

Newt felt his dick stiffening. "Good," he said.

Then Freddie fastened a mask around his face so that he couldn't see. Somehow that magnified all the sensations in his tits and balls. His dick was already rock hard, and the pulling of the balls made it ache.

"What else do you want?" Freddie asked.

"Whatever makes you feel good."

"I don't want to hurt you, Newt."

"Don't worry about me. I'm strong. You pass on to me whatever pain you can't handle."

Freddie slapped Newt's butt with the flat of his hand, and the noise echoed around the room. "Does that hurt?"

"Only a little. Give me more, Freddie."

Freddie turned away, and for a moment Newt thought he was giving up, that he'd start crying again. But instead he pulled something out of his drawer. From the first slap to Newt's thigh, he recognized the feel of the cat-o'-nine-tails. As Freddie switched from right to left and back again, Newt felt the pain—but it was a good pain, a cleansing one, Newt thought. He imagined that he was taking in Freddie's sadness and hurt.

He went into an almost meditative state, thinking of Fledglis and Ulric, how Fledglis could absorb Ulric's pain and heal him from whatever had hurt him in the past. He hardly noticed as Freddie moved around, sometimes slapping against Newt's skin with his open palm, sometimes with the cat.

He loved the heightened sensation he felt, and he hoped desperately that whatever Freddie did to him might lead to pleasure for Freddie. That was his new mission in life, he decided. He was going to get Freddie off, even if it killed him to do so.

And as long as Freddie didn't get killed first.

25 – Creature of the Night

Freddie couldn't sleep. Newt snored, and the pills Freddie had popped refused to take effect. He got out of bed, naked, and walked out to the living room, where he stood in the moonlight, staring down toward the lights of Nice in the distance. The view reminded him of a house he'd had in LA for a while, up in the hills.

Back then he was a creature of the night. He'd sleep late, work in the afternoon and evening, and then go out and party, returning to his house in the wee hours of the morning. LA had always been lit up with the promise of another day back then.

He picked up his cell phone and opened the sliding doors to the outside. LA was something like nine hours behind France, so he ought to be able to reach Mario Dellarosa somewhere. He stepped out and punched in the number he knew by heart, then listened to the phone ring a thousand miles away. A weird thing, he thought. Back when he was a kid, he never knew anyone who lived more than a few miles from Omaha in any direction.

"Freddie!" Mario's voice boomed through the phone. "How the hell are you?"

Freddie closed the front door behind him. It was warm and humid, and the light breeze felt good against his naked skin. "I've been better. I think somebody's trying to kill me."

"What the hell?" Mario said.

Freddie repeated the incidents—being followed, the car trying to force him off the road, the truck without license plates, the poster on the windshield, and the flyer sent around to his neighbors. He left out the parts that included Newt. He was sure that Newt wasn't responsible for anything bad, and he didn't want to muddy the situation for Mario.

"Who do you think it is?" Mario asked.

"No idea. That's why I called you."

"You think I would send someone to kill you?"

"Of course not," Freddie said. "But I thought you might have an idea who has it in for me."

In a shard of moonlight, he saw a mouse skitter across his yard, and an owl swooped down and snagged the little creature in its claws. There were predators everywhere, Freddie thought.

"Honestly, Freddie, your name is not on a lot of lips these days," Mario said. "Among directors, you've got a good reputation for editing. But that's about it. There have been at least two generations of boys since you left."

"I had to hire a couple of bodyguards, and they're curious about that picture I finished for you," Freddie said. "*Straight Suckers*."

"Ah, the beginning of a very profitable series. I appreciate your taking care of that for me when I got sick."

"And I'm sure you appreciate my being in that warehouse when it blew up instead of you."

"That was so long ago, Freddie."

"Yeah, but the cops never found out who was responsible for that. At the time they figured it was somebody after you, and I was in the wrong place at the wrong time. But maybe they were wrong."

Freddie hiccupped. "Maybe whoever blew up that warehouse was after me, and since I went to ground here in France, it's taken him a long time to find me."

"The police had some crazy ideas back then," Mario said. "Religious nuts, some other porn studio that didn't want competition. They grilled me eight ways to Sunday and still came up empty-handed. Didn't they do the same thing with you?"

"Yeah, they did." He scratched his balls. His dick, which had always been so reliably hard when he worked in porn, hadn't even swelled a bit. "You still in touch with any of the crew from that movie? My guys found out that Ed died a couple of years ago, that Holly went legit as a location scout."

"Holly? That slut? I'd have thought the only location she could sell was her pussy."

"What about that Mexican kid, the one who could suck like a vacuum cleaner?"

"Javier? He jumped around from studio to studio for a while, changing his name every time, trying to make a career. But like all the rest of them, he burned out."

"You know his real name?" Freddie asked. "I think he was using a fake ID."

"Not the sharpest knife in the drawer," Mario said. "His real name was the one he was using, something Spanish."

"Echeverria."

"Yeah, that's it. Poor kid. I felt sorry for him at the end."

"What do you mean, at the end? He died?"

"Yeah, maybe six months ago. Dumb shit kid barebacked too many times, got sick but tried to ignore it. Finally a producer sent him to a clinic to get tested, and he came back positive. The clinic wanted him to go on a set of meds ASAP, but Javier didn't have any money, and he wouldn't ask his family in Mexico for cash. By the time I heard about it, found his family's address with his stuff, and had the clinic get in touch with them, he was too far gone for anything."

"Christ," Freddie said. "In this day and age you'd think he'd have known better."

"If he'd known better, he would have stayed back in Mexico," Mario said. "Listen, it's great to catch up with you, but I've got to get back to work. You lie low, maybe this whole thing will blow over."

"Thanks, Mario."

Freddie hung up and stood silently, staring out at the darkness. He couldn't blame Mario for not wanting to get involved, not volunteering to look into anything for him. He had his own life, his own work. He didn't need Freddie's crap.

26 – Unicorn Sex

Newt dreamed that he was at the hypermarché and he couldn't find the men's room or remember the French word for it. He woke up alone in Freddie's king-size bed with a desperate need to pee. The digital clock display read 2:08, and he stumbled to the bathroom in the dark.

When he finished, he walked out to the living room and through the front window he saw Freddie standing naked, bathed in moonlight. He still couldn't believe his luck, that he had landed here with the porn star who had been turning him on for years.

He watched Freddie for a couple of minutes. It looked like he was talking on the phone. When he ended the call and walked back inside, Newt was waiting for him. "You all right, Freddie?" he asked.

"Yeah, I'm good. Just wanted to talk to an old friend in LA."

"Did he have any idea who would have something against you?" Newt asked.

Freddie shook his head. "Nah. But he told me that one of the guys from my last movie died. This kid. Such a waste. All those guys dead. And I survived. Why, Newt? Why am I still here when all those other guys are gone? Is somebody out there pissed off that I survived?"

Newt took Freddie's arm and led him back into the bedroom. Newt noticed as they walked that Freddie's dick had hardened, and it flapped against his leg.

From his shoulders to his toes, Freddie was a muscular hunk.

The tattoos on his arms, chest, and legs emphasized his toughness. A fringe of hair beneath his pecs, that tattoo on his chest that Newt recognized from one of the Narnia books, his beefy dick sticking out of a bush of pubic hair.

"You're a good person, Freddie," Newt said. "I can tell that about you. Why did you survive when other people didn't? Who knows. Do you believe in God?"

"Even if I did, I doubt he'd believe in me."

"You never know," Newt said. "I was raised Catholic, went to church every week, Sunday school, memorized my catechism and everything. For a long time, I thought that God hated me because I was, you know, gay. That he was punishing me for it by making me fat."

"Oh, Newt," Freddie said.

"But then I found this gay Catholic group online, and I started to realize that I had to take charge of my own life, that I couldn't blame God, or anybody else, for my problems. That's when I started writing about Fledglis. And once I began publishing, I started to get these e-mails from gay kids. They loved that there was this avenging unicorn that was going to make the world better for them."

"That's a terrific thing," Freddie said. "You're a good guy, Newt."

Newt thought of himself as sad rather than good, but he didn't argue. "And I started believing in God again. I thought that God gave me this talent for writing so that I could make things better. And I believe he brought you and me together."

Freddie leaned his head against Newt's shoulder, and Newt put his arm around Freddie. "Liam and Aidan know what they're doing," he said. "They'll keep you safe."

"They can't stay with me forever," Freddie said. He turned to Newt. "Maybe I was wrong, and you should go back to your place. Until whatever this is washes out. I don't want you to get hurt."

"Not unless you do it?" Newt said, and he smirked.

"I don't usually do that. I'm not some freak who gets off on hurting other people. I'm not that kind of guy."

"I don't know what kind of guy I am," Newt said. "I have so little experience that almost anything turns me on. It's kind of sad."

"Come on," Freddie said. "You write that horny unicorn shit. I mean, stuff. I mean, books."

"You ever have sex with a unicorn?" Newt asked.

Freddie looked at him. "Unicorns are imaginary."

"Exactly. So I can imagine whatever I want without worrying that some reader is going to call me on it. Until you, you know, fucked me with that dildo, I never knew what it felt like to have someone else put it up there. It's totally different from doing it myself."

Newt crossed his arms over his chest and leaned back against the pillows. "When I first started writing, I wrote standard male-male stuff. Guy goes in to have his car serviced, ends up servicing the mechanic. That kind of thing. I posted it on these sites where you share stuff you write with others."

"I did a movie like that once," Freddie said. "I was the

mechanic. I think it was called *Getting Greased.*"

"It was. I used the plot from it. But everybody who read it ripped it to shreds, and I was so embarrassed."

Freddie nestled up to him. "You can't listen to critics. I learned that when I started doing porn. They're all wannabes who will eat you alive if you let them."

"They were right," Newt insisted. "I didn't know what I was doing, and I couldn't make stuff up when people knew how the sex was supposed to work. I gave up for a long time, until I came up with Fledglis. I could have him do whatever I wanted, and nobody could complain, because who knows how a unicorn's dick works?"

"You've got a point there," Freddie said.

"So does Fledglis." Newt laughed. Then he reached down to Freddie's dick, which had remained hard during their conversation. "And so do you."

Before Freddie could say anything, Newt had his hand wrapped around Freddie's dick and had begun jerking it. "It doesn't…" Freddie began, but Newt shushed him. Then Newt leaned forward and took Freddie's dick in his mouth.

Newt wasn't the world's best cocksucker, but Freddie's wasn't the first he'd had in his mouth, and he had tried to learn from each of his encounters, however quick. He swallowed the whole thing down, felt it tickle the back of his throat, and resisted the urge to gag.

Then he began a rapid up and down motion, sucking for all he was worth. "You don't have to do this," Freddie said.

Newt was too busy sucking to answer. If Freddie didn't come, at least Newt would have the pleasure, and the experience, of sucking him. He squirmed around so that he could cup Freddie's balls in his hand as he licked up and down his shaft. Freddie's dick was hard, even if he protested otherwise.

"Oh, yeah, play with my balls," Freddie said, and Newt was happy to oblige. He stopped sucking long enough to take each ball in his mouth as Freddie groaned with pleasure. So Freddie could still feel something, Newt thought, even if he couldn't come.

Then it was back to the dick. Newt nibbled at the mushroom cap, stuck his tongue in the slit, wrapped his fist around the shaft and jerked. Freddie had stopped complaining and was breathing hard, running his hands through Newt's hair.

Then Freddie grabbed Newt's head and was pressing his mouth down around Freddie's dick. He grabbed a fistful of Newt's hair and pulled his head up, then pushed him back down again, forcing Newt to swallow him all the way to the root.

Freddie's pubic hair tickled Newt's nose, but he kept on sucking, joining Freddie in the up and down motion. Freddie began whimpering and muttering and Newt was so turned on he was about to come himself. He felt his balls straining against the leather strap around them, and he struggled to keep his butt clenched enough to keep the plug inserted.

Freddie moaned and writhed around beneath Newt, and for a moment Newt worried his bulk was depriving Freddie of air. "Oh, oh, oh!" Freddie said, and then he shot off in Newt's mouth.

Newt kept his lips clamped around the dick until he had

swallowed all of Freddie's come. Then he lifted his head and saw Freddie leaned back against the pillows, his eyes glazed. "Jesus, for a guy who says he doesn't have much experience, you sure know how to suck."

Newt was panting from the exertion, and he realized that he had come on the sheets. He rolled on his side, ignoring the cold, wet spot beneath him. "You were wrong," he said to Freddie. "It does work."

27 – El Serpiente

Aidan was up first on Friday morning, and he slid out of bed, leaving Liam asleep. His partner looked so sweet when his face and body were at rest, and the sight always made Aidan recognize that despite his size and skills, Liam needed protecting too.

He stretched quietly as Hayam danced around his feet, ready for her walk. He and Liam had had sex twice that week—which was the first time that had happened in a long time. He didn't even want to try to remember the last time they'd gotten horizontal together, because he was afraid the result would be too sad, or scary.

He hooked up Hayam's leash, and they crept out through the quiet household. The sun was beginning to rise in the east, and the day felt fresh and new, but Aidan's mind was still on sex.

Had this burst of activity come up because of Freddie's influence or proximity? Aidan had been wanting to try a bit of role-play to spice things up between him and Liam, but he'd been worried Liam would think it was foolish.

Obviously not, he thought, when he remembered how hot the scene had been. But was this a last gasp of a dying sex life? Would they return to being roommates back at their own apartment?

He circled the block, and Hayam did her business behind a bush, shaded from the street. She was a shy girl, and it was tough to find a private enough place for her in the bustling city. Maybe, if things stayed good with Liam, they could find a house somewhere like Louis and Hassan's. A private yard where Hayam could run and Liam could work out.

He didn't realize until he was almost back at the house that he should have been observing the area, looking for anything new that the stalker might have left in his campaign to harass Freddie. He took a quick walk around the house just to be sure. When he got back into the guest bedroom, Liam was sitting up in bed. Hayam rushed over and launched herself up beside him.

"See anything outside?" Liam asked, tickling the dog's belly.

"An ordinary morning." Aidan sat on the bed beside Liam. "What do you think is going on? Who was in that truck last night? Were they really trying to kill Freddie?"

"I'm not sure if the aim was to kill him or scare him more, up the stakes."

The little dog curled between them, relishing the chance to get belly rubs from both her daddies. "Why do you think no one in the truck tried to shoot at Freddie?" Aidan asked.

"Remember, guns aren't as easy to get hold of in France as they are in the US. You and I only have sports shooting licenses and the authorization to own our guns because Jean-Luc pulled some strings. That's why we have to have that *motif légitime* form with us when we're carrying." Liam shook his head. "If the harasser is a foreigner, he wouldn't have easy access to firearms, and even a local would probably need an underworld connection."

Liam picked up the dog and put her on the carpet, then stood up. "And just because he hasn't used a gun yet, that doesn't mean he never will." He nodded toward the door. "Let's go out to the kitchen.

I want to be able to short-circuit any plans Freddie has for today before they get going."

The house was still quiet, the kitchen empty with sunlight streaming in through a multipaned window over the sink. Exactly the kind of kitchen Aidan would love to have in his own house.

He prepared egg-white omelets and granola for himself and Liam, and they ate together quietly. When Freddie and Newt joined them, Aidan thought there was something different about their relationship. Before, they'd appeared a real odd couple, not quite connected. But this morning they seemed together, in a way that made Aidan glad for both of them.

"Can I fix you both breakfast?" Aidan asked. When they agreed, he began working as Freddie and Newt sat at the table with Liam.

"New rules," Liam said. "Freddie doesn't leave the house alone. No more jogging. And Freddie, I want to spend some time with you today going over anyone who might want to harm you."

"I don't want to be a prisoner," Freddie said.

"You won't be," Liam said. "We're just being careful."

Newt put his hand tentatively on Freddie's arm. "You hired them, so you should listen to them. I don't want anything to happen to you."

While the omelets cooked, Aidan brought bowls of granola to the table.

"Fine," Freddie said, though Aidan had the clear sense that Freddie wasn't the kind of animal to stay caged for too long.

"You probably still have editing work, don't you, sweetie?" Newt asked.

"Yeah. It's not like I had plans to see the sights or anything."

Aidan plated the omelets and delivered them, then slid into the seat across from Liam, Freddie, and Newt at the other end of the table. Freddie and Newt both ate for a couple of minutes.

"Listen, I called a guy I know in LA last night," Freddie said. "That Mexican kid? Javier? He was using his real name. And he died a couple of months ago."

"I'll do some research later," Aidan said. "First, I'm going to see if anyone in the neighborhood saw who was driving that truck yesterday. The driver had to hang around somewhere waiting for Freddie."

"I want to work out," Freddie said. "And get Newt some exercise. All right if we use the backyard?"

"I'll work out with you," Liam said.

"Like a personal trainer," Newt said.

Aidan noticed Liam's lip curl up in a half smile. "Not exactly," he said. He stood up. "You guys get dressed and meet me in that flat spot alongside the house. The hedge along the street should give us some privacy."

The three of them left, and Aidan looked at Hayam. "That leaves you and me, sweetheart," he said. He cleaned up the kitchen and then got the dog's leash. "Today is your lucky day, Hayam. You're getting an extra walk."

The morning had warmed up considerably since Aidan had been out earlier, and he was glad he wasn't exercising with the others. It was the perfect kind of day for a stroll out into the countryside with his dog—as long as there were no crazed truck drivers lurking.

He led Hayam down the hill to the street and then across to the fifties-style ranch house across from Freddie's. No one was home. He continued down the street and discovered that for the most part Freddie's neighbors were working folks who were unlikely to be around in the afternoon.

He met a woman named Madame Banville, who thought Hayam was a *petit mignon*, or little cutie. She told him that she had seen nothing out of the ordinary. The only other neighbor at home was an elderly man with a Gauloise hanging out of his mouth, who said he had no interest in foreigners or homosexuals and slammed his door in Aidan's face.

When he climbed the driveway back to the house, he glimpsed Newt slumped on the ground, his face red, his T-shirt and shorts soaked with sweat. Liam and Freddie were doing jumping jacks, and it looked like the two of them were competing to see who could do more.

Aidan shook his head and walked inside. He went back online to look for an obituary for Javier Echeverria, now that he knew the man had died, presumably in LA, in the last few months. He found a notice that had been placed by the funeral home, which said that Javier, a native of Mexico City, was survived by parents Reinaldo and Silvia Echeverria.

He was about to begin a search for them when Freddie, Newt, and Liam came in from their exercise. Newt looked like he was about to have a heart attack, still red-faced and sweating, breathing heavily. Freddie and Liam were arguing.

"I don't want to," Freddie said. "After I broke my brother's nose, I said I was never going back there, never talking to any of them again."

"Forget about that," Liam said. "You need to call them and see if they're still holding a grudge. If somebody back there is behind these threats against you."

"My brothers aren't like that. If they want to fight, they'll do it to my face."

Newt tried to speak, but he was still having trouble catching his breath. "And no guff from you," Freddie said to him. "Or you can go right back to that crappy apartment of yours."

He turned and stalked toward the bedroom. Newt looked about to cry.

"Don't worry," Aidan said. "I'm sure he's just stressed."

"And stupid," Liam said. He went in the opposite direction, toward the guest room.

"Come on, sit down," Aidan said, pulling a chair out for Newt. "Let me get you some water."

"I'll be all right," Newt wheezed. "I need to catch my breath."

"Sit." Aidan walked into the kitchen and returned a moment later with a glass of water, which he handed to Newt.

While Newt drank, Aidan turned back to his laptop and logged in to a database that contained news from Mexican papers, though he doubted Javier Echeverria's obituary would have been placed there.

He was deluged with results—over forty thousand for "Javier Echeverria," many of them about a former president of Mexico. Nothing on the first few pages of search results related to a dead porn actor. He shifted his search to include Javier's parents' names, hoping there might be a connection.

At first, the results were even more overwhelming. But toward the bottom of the first page was a link to an investigative report on a Reinaldo Echeverria from *El Universal*, a Spanish-language newspaper in Mexico City. His Spanish was very limited, mostly based on his knowledge of French and all the years he'd lived in Philadelphia and taught Spanish-speaking students, but in the preview, he recognized the terms "*esposa* Silvia" and "*hijo* Javier."

That sounded like the right guy, with a wife and son of the names he'd read in the LA obituary. He clicked on the report, and while waiting for it to load, he looked up at Newt. "Do you think Freddie's a bad person?" Newt asked.

Newt's face wasn't so red anymore, and he was breathing more regularly. "Why?" Aidan asked.

"Because, you know. He acted in porn."

Aidan shook his head. "I don't judge people that way. I look at the way they treat others. And Freddie has been kind to you, hasn't he?"

From the way Newt looked down at the table, he thought perhaps what went on behind closed doors was different from the way the two men interacted in public. But Newt was an adult, older than Aidan by at least ten years, and he ought to be able to take care of himself.

"He wants to help me. That's what he says."

"And what about you? Do you want to be helped?"

"He's not as tough as he looks," Newt said. "Did you know that he meditates every day?"

Aidan nodded, noting that Newt hadn't answered his question. "I think Freddie has gone through a lot in his past," Aidan said. "Meditation can give you some quiet space while you figure that stuff out."

"I think he's sad," Newt said. "And so am I. I hope we can make each other happy."

"I hope so too, Newt."

The big man heaved himself up. "I'd better take a shower. Please take care of Freddie."

"We will," Aidan said. "That's what we do."

Newt nodded and walked toward the bedroom. Aidan looked down at the screen and saw that the article was in Spanish, but there was an option to translate to English. He clicked that button.

According to the article, Reinaldo Echeverria was a mid-level drug dealer in Ensenada, in the Baja California district of Mexico. Above the guy on the street but below the well-known leaders.

Aidan's heart rate accelerated as he read the translation, which was rough but understandable. Reinaldo Echeverria was noted as a dangerous man, called *el serpiente*, or the snake, and he had a reputation for delivering field justice. If someone dared disobey him, he took matters into his own hands rather than delegating them to an underling.

He was thought to be very wealthy and lived behind high walls in Ensenada. His wife, Silvia, was a virtual prisoner in the house, either because of her husband's personality or because of the dangers of being a drug dealer's wife. Reinaldo's only child was a son named Javier, who was believed to have escaped his father's iron hand for the United States, though the author had no proof.

Aidan stood up and took the laptop with him to the guest bedroom, where Liam had finished his shower. He sat on the side of the bed, wrapped in one of Freddie's big white towels, with his cell phone at his ear. He held up a hand to Aidan as he said, "Thanks. I'll see you then," into the phone.

Then he turned to Aidan. "That was Louis. He dug around for information about that warehouse fire in LA. The cops got a couple of partial prints from the bottle used to hold the Molotov cocktail, but they didn't match anyone in the system. It wasn't until about six months later that Carl Ousterhout got picked up for a drunk and disorderly and had his prints taken."

"The straight guy that Freddie said went apeshit during his shoot," Aidan said.

"Yup. Carl admitted that he was pissed off at everybody involved with that movie, and one night he got drunk and made himself a Molotov cocktail. He insisted that it was justifiable, because he was retaliating for what he called a sexual assault. The judge didn't see it that way and ordered him held for trial. He was waiting in jail when he pissed off the wrong guy and got shanked. Case closed and another lead down the toilet."

"Here's a new lead to replace that one," Aidan said. He turned the laptop toward Liam. "Take a look at this guy. I think he's Javier's father. And if he is, I can see that he'd have a motive to kill Freddie."

"How do you figure that?" Liam unwrapped the towel and used it to dry his hair. Aidan was momentarily distracted by his partner's awesome physique. Liam was so gorgeous, his body sculpted like Michelangelo's *David*, and Aidan sometimes had a hard time accepting that Liam was his.

"Earth to Aidan? Put your tongue back in your mouth and engage your brain." Liam tossed the towel into the bathroom and strode across the bedroom, his half-hard dick swinging.

Aidan swallowed. "According to Freddie, Javier Echeverria died a few months ago from AIDS. We know that Mexico is a very macho culture, right? Suppose Javier's father wants to kill whoever infected his son, and he's starting with people his son associated with in the porn business."

"Don't you think that's a stretch?" Liam asked as he stepped into a jockstrap and pulled it up to his hips.

"No more than one of Freddie's brothers trying to kill him to protect a political campaign. We're grasping at straws here, Liam. Don't you think this merits looking into?"

Liam pulled on a pair of khaki slacks. "Yes, I do. Louis wants to meet with me this morning about some information he found, and I'll ask him to look into this El Serpiente. If he's really a drug dealer, then some federal agency has got to have a dossier on him."

"What kind of information has Louis found?"

"Nothing related to this case, at least Louis doesn't think so. When Louis went looking into Freddie, his name popped up on the fringe of an active federal investigation into money laundering."

"Money laundering?"

"I don't understand the details yet, but I'm going to try to pry more information from Louis. I'll let you know what I find out. And I'll text Louis El Serpiente's name so maybe he can have something by the time we meet."

"That's good," Aidan said. "I have a feeling that whoever is after Freddie could mount his next attack any time."

28 – The Banana

Before he could leave the house to meet with Louis, Liam had one more thing to do. He walked down the hall and rapped on the door to Freddie's editing studio. "Come in!" Freddie called.

When Liam walked in, he was impressed by the array of equipment, from a high-end computer to the multiple screens and the expensive audio gear.

The view through the large windows was similar to the one from the living room, sloping down toward Nice and the Mediterranean. Bees buzzed and butterflies fluttered around the random collection of lavender and flowering plants Liam had noticed earlier.

Freddie pushed back from his computer. "I have to think about calling my brothers," he said, looking at Liam. "You can't push me."

"I didn't come in about that." Liam nodded toward a chair. "Can I sit?"

"Go ahead." Freddie crossed his arms over his chest in the classic defensive posture. This wasn't going to be easy, Liam thought.

"I have a friend who works for the US government," Liam said. "I asked him to do some investigating on your behalf. He was able to get hold of the police and fire department reports for that explosion at your warehouse."

"Wasn't my warehouse," Freddie said. "But go on."

Liam told him what Louis had discovered, about Carl Ousterhout, the Molotov cocktail, the deadly shiv in jail. "Fuck me,"

Freddie said. "It was that crazy bastard straight guy." He shook his head. "I knew that was a dumb idea from the start. It's one thing to get a cocksucker to play straight for the camera, but tricking a meth head? That's a recipe for disaster."

"I can see that." Liam leaned forward. "You've been around the block a few times, Freddie. You know how things work in the real world. You ask someone for a favor; then you owe him one in return."

"And?"

"My friend put out some feelers to find out about the warehouse fire, including your name. He paid his part of the favor by telling me what he found out. But some additional information showed up unrelated to the fire, and now he's asked me for a favor back, to learn more about that information."

"What do you mean?"

"Did you know that your name is connected to an ongoing federal investigation back in the States?"

Freddie shook his head. "Come on, dude. All I do is edit this shit these days. If there's somebody underage, it's not on me. And unless they've changed the Constitution since I left, there's still a right to distribute materials. The Supreme Court decided that back in 1973. It's called freedom of speech."

"As far as I can tell, this isn't about the nature of the work," Liam said. "It's about how you get paid for it."

"What does that mean? I report my income, and I file my taxes. Everything is legit."

"But not everybody in your industry is so clean," Liam said. "That friend of yours you mentioned. His name is Mario Dellarosa?"

"Yup. Mario's always taken care of me. I owe him a lot."

"Enough to launder money for him?" Liam asked.

Freddie frowned. "What the fuck?"

"He ever tell you where the money comes from to fund his operations?"

"I assumed it came from sales of previous movies and investors. There are always guys hanging around the edges of porn, guys with some spare cash who want to hobnob with the talent. You invest some cash in my operation, I invite you to parties, maybe hook you up with some cute young thing who needs a mentor. That kind of thing."

"The Feds think there's more to it than that," Liam said. "He's never asked you to launder money for him?"

Freddie shook his head. "I'm strictly a work-for-hire guy these days," he said. "I do my job, I get paid, and I move on. And I haven't been back in LA for five years, so I don't know what Mario might or might not be getting up to."

"I need something, Freddie. Maybe your friend Mario is a good guy. But my contact has put himself on the line for you, and he needs to be able to justify his nosing around by giving something back. You must know a scumbag or two you could throw under the bus. Give me a name for my friend, and I'll be even with him, and he won't get in trouble."

Freddie snarled. "You guys are all alike. You think because I make porn I'm slime under your shoe. But then you go into the back room of a bookstore and pull your dick out, and you're just like the rest of us."

Liam was tempted to retort that he'd never pulled his dick out in a bookstore, but then he remembered an incident that would make a liar out of him. And he did sympathize with Freddie. From everything he'd seen so far, the guy was a decent sort who happened to work in a business people disapproved of.

Hey, he'd been in the military, and there were still a lot of people in the world who'd call him a baby killer. He took a deep breath, let it out.

"I understand how you feel," Liam said. He stood up. "I'm going to meet with my contact now. To thank him for the information he provided about the warehouse bombing, and to ask him for even more help. I hope I can rely on my personal relationship with him to make that happen."

"Hold on," Freddie said. He let out a big breath. "There was this one guy."

Liam sat back down. "An investor? Or a producer?"

"An investor. Only in the straight shit, nothing gay. Big goombah from New Jersey, loaded down with gold rings, bracelet, watch. I met him once, through that chick Holly who worked on *Straight Suckers* with me. But he gave me a vibe, you know. Like if I was willing to make a straight movie, he could come up with the cash, as long as I didn't ask too many questions about where it came from."

"You have a name for this goombah?"

"They called him The Banana," Freddie said.

Liam was tempted to laugh. A guy named The Banana who was interested in porn? Come on. He usually had a pretty good bullshit meter, but it wasn't going off. Freddie was being honest about what he knew, even if it wasn't much.

"Holly might know more," Freddie said. "I think she was doing him."

Liam nodded. Had he already given Holly's name to Louis? He didn't think so. All he'd asked Louis to do was look up Freddie. But if Louis had come up with Freddie's friend Mario, could he already have found Holly too?

"Appreciate it," he said and stood up. "I'll let you get back to work."

He stopped back in the living room. "What was Holly's real name?" he asked Aidan.

"Elizabeth Angstrom. But I haven't been able to find anything recent on her."

"Maybe Louis can." He told Aidan what Freddie had said. "Do me a favor? Text both of those names to Louis."

Aidan agreed, and Liam moved on to the master bedroom, where Newt was at work on his computer. "Can I borrow your car for a run into Nice?" he asked. "I have to meet somebody near the Zone Piétonne, and parking the Jeep anywhere near there is a real pain. Your car can slip into a tiny spot."

"No problem," Newt said. "But are you sure you can fit?" His face reddened. "I mean, because you're so tall."

"I'll manage," Liam said. He took the keys from Newt and walked outside where the little red car was parked to the side of the driveway. He felt like he had to fold himself into a pretzel to get in, slumping a bit so his head didn't hit the ceiling. Yeah, Newt had called that one. But Liam would suffer the cramped space because of the convenience in parking.

As he navigated the curving roads down into Nice, he thought about what Freddie had said. He didn't look down on people who made or watched porn. But yeah, he did have an attitude that the business was corrupt and therefore the people involved in it were too.

Freddie was brusque and outspoken, but he seemed to have a good heart. Look at the way he'd taken in Newt, who wasn't most guys' wet dream of a boyfriend. And anybody who was generous to outcasts ranked high in his book.

One of the traits that had attracted him first to Aidan was his kindness. Sure, he was handsome and smart and could think on his feet. But his empathy, his ability to understand people in trouble and how they would react, was vital to their partnership. Liam had a tendency to bull his way forward in an operation, a trait drummed into him as a SEAL. It took Aidan to remind him periodically that their clients were human beings with hopes and fears.

He tried not to take his partner for granted. He still remembered the first time he had seen Aidan, in a bar on the Rue Mamounia in Tunis. He had mistaken Aidan for the client he was to meet there, and his heart had given a flip at Aidan's good looks.

He had to admit that had colored their first meetings. Then Aidan admitted that he had misunderstood Liam's motives, that he'd thought Liam was trying to pick him up in the bar. He still remembered Aidan saying something like *"you probably aren't even gay,"* and how he'd laughed, thinking that observation had come out of left field.

Then he'd seen the hurt look in Aidan's eyes and realized that the attraction between them was mutual. Though he'd been in the middle of a crisis, searching for a client he'd thought was lost, Liam had stopped for a moment to kiss Aidan, an impulsive gesture meant to say a whole raft of things Liam didn't have words for.

Fortunately, Aidan had understood.

Liam swerved around a slow-moving truck, leaning on the horn of the tiny car. He was embarrassed that he had to slide back behind the truck because he didn't have enough space or power to pass it.

That was the key, he thought, when his mind got back on track. Finding someone who understood you. Sex was just a physical act, and handsome faces or buff physiques only got you so far in a relationship. But if you could look at the person beside you and understand him, feel he really got you, that was gold.

It looked like Freddie and Newt had found that in each other too. Which made Liam that much more determined to protect them.

29 – Phone Home

Freddie didn't want to call either of his brothers. But if he had to call one of them, he picked Gerald. Gerald was the businessman, the most rational of the three of them. And if Earl had something going on, Gerald would know.

The other advantage was that if he called the office, he wouldn't have to worry about his number showing up on his brother's cell phone caller ID and Gerald letting the call go to voice mail. A glance at the clock, and some quick calculation, told him that if was four o'clock in the afternoon in Nice, it was eight in the morning back in Nebraska.

If there was one thing he knew about his brother Gerald, it was that he was a workaholic. Gerald was often the first one in the office in the morning and the last to leave. He was Mr. Inside to Earl's Mr. Outside, and it was rare for him to leave the office during the day unless Earl dragged him somewhere.

Freddie grabbed his phone and dialed before he could talk himself out of it. He stood by the window of the editing suite, looking out at the city below. Omaha was a long way from Nice, but in the end they were both cities, and business went on in much the same way in both.

"Thank you for calling Ventura Insurance. How may I direct your call?" The receptionist's vowels were as flat as the plains, and he channeled the accent of his boyhood.

"Gerald Ventura, please," Freddie said.

"Who may I say is calling?"

"His brother."

"Oh, sorry I didn't recognize your voice, Mr. Earl. I'll put you right through."

Freddie didn't bother to correct her. He tapped his fingers in time to the hold music as the bodyguards' little dog came into his studio, and he put his hand down so the dog could sniff it.

"What's up, Earl?"

Freddie turned his attention back to the phone. "It's not Earl. It's Freddie. And don't hang up, Gerald, please. I need to talk to you."

"Is it money? Because you get your deposits regularly."

Freddie could visualize his brother in his big office with a view of the Omaha skyline behind him, including the Woodmen Life tower. He snickered to think that he and Gerald would have very different definitions for wood.

The last time he'd been in that office, Gerald's large desk had been empty except for an in-box and an out-box, a telephone, and a computer. The walls were covered with framed photos of him and Earl with various local dignitaries, with the Little League team the agency sponsored, at the site of disasters, ready to provide an insurance check.

"No, the money is fine, and I'm healthy. But somebody's trying to kill me."

Gerald was silent for a moment. "We're not still holding your life insurance policy, are we?"

Freddie didn't know what to say to that. He stroked the little dog's head, and she rolled on her belly to have it scratched.

"A joke, Freddie. Come on, lost your sense of humor out there in La-La Land?"

Gerald wasn't a bad guy, Freddie thought. When they were little kids, before Earl arrived, Gerald had followed Freddie everywhere on his fat little legs. Freddie recognized now that it was love, but back then he'd just found his brother annoying.

"I left LA five years ago," Freddie said. "I live in France now. You didn't know?"

"Forgive me if I haven't kept up with your illustrious career."

The dog jumped up and scurried over to the French doors to the garden, then wagged her tail. Freddie stood up and opened the door for her, and she rushed outside. "Does Earl know where I am, what I've been doing?"

Funny, he thought, how he had always been Freddie, but his younger brother had never been Gerry. After Earl was born, Gerald had abandoned Freddie, always playing with the baby. That was fine with Freddie back then because he had so many secrets, and the last thing he wanted was a nosy little brother snooping around.

"Freddie. What do you want?"

"I want to know if one of you put out a hit on my life to protect Earl's Senate campaign."

It was Gerald's turn to be silent. Freddie waited. Gerald was a classic middle child, weighing his words, trying to keep peace in the family. That responsible attitude had served him well in business, and

Freddie was sure that the agency's success was due to the balance between Gerald and Earl, Mr. Inside and Mr. Outside.

Finally, Gerald said, "I can't say that either Earl or I approve of your lifestyle, Freddie. Not just the fact that you're gay. I know some very fine gay people here in town, including the young man who cuts my hair. But the way you make your living turns my stomach."

Gerald sighed. "From what I've seen, voters in Nebraska are smart enough to realize that every family has its black sheep. And even though you broke two of my ribs the last time I saw you, you're still my brother."

Freddie choked up for a moment, until Gerald said, "Of course, if I ever see you again, I owe you two broken ribs."

"They weren't broken, just fractured," Freddie said. "I'm the dramatic one, remember?"

"I remember a whole lot more about you than you think, big brother," Gerald said. "Whatever made you move to France? Did you have problems back in Los Angeles?"

"You could say that," Freddie said. "I needed a break. I stopped acting and directing. Now I just do contract work—video editing. I keep a low profile."

"Not so low, apparently, if someone's trying to kill you."

"I know." Freddie looked out at the empty sky, not a cloud in sight. He realized that it was good to talk to his brother, that he'd missed that connection to blood kin, even though he knew it was far too late to return to those days when the three of them were boys together.

"I don't know what to say, Freddie," Gerald said. "I can't offer you a place back here, because I can't take the risk that you'd put the rest of the family in danger. And I don't know anything about France or the police there. You say you have enough money?"

"Yeah, I make a good living, and I've been putting away the agency money. I have a pair of bodyguards to look after me for a while."

"That's good," Gerald said. "You take care of yourself, Freddie. I like the idea of having a big brother around, even if I don't ever see you."

"I'll do my best." Freddie hesitated, then plunged in. "Send my love to Earl and his family and to your wife and kids. And e-mail me some pictures of my nieces and nephews sometime."

"Will do. Gotta go, Freddie. I have another call."

Gerald hung up, and Freddie sat back. That call hadn't gone quite as he'd expected. But he trusted Gerald, and what his brother had said sounded pragmatic. Freddie believed that neither of his brothers was behind the attacks on him.

Who else could it be? The bodyguards had thought it was Newt at first. Then Gerald or Earl. Did they have a clue? He had to admit he hadn't given them much to work with. What demons from his past could still be hanging around, trying to destroy his future?

Mario had occasionally teased Freddie about his Midwestern values. *"You have a kind of corn-fed goodness to you, boy,"* Mario said once, before Freddie met Rodney and began his downward slide. *"You're a wild man, and I don't think there's a drug you haven't tested or a sexual position you haven't tried, but I've never seen you deliberately hurt someone."*

Freddie had seen too much of that kind of behavior. Even Mario, who was a good, loyal guy at heart, had an ambitious streak that caused him to use other people to get what he wanted, what he felt he deserved. Freddie, on the other hand, had always believed that others didn't have to fail for him to succeed.

He had tried to help other actors build their careers. He had been kind to even the creepiest fans, signing photographs and DVD cases and even the occasional piece of flesh. As a director, he'd tried to get the best performances from his actors, but never by harassing them or forcing them to do things they didn't want to do.

And look where it had gotten him. Mario had often said that good guys finished last. And here was Freddie, hiding out in France, afraid that some crazy stalker was trying to kill him.

Maybe he should take a trip. Get away from all this madness. He had the money. He still had work to do on this edit, but he could push it back a couple of weeks, lie low for a while. Leaving LA had kept him safe for five years. But how long could he run?

30 – Not by Inches

After Liam left for his meeting with Louis, Aidan e-mailed Richard for a report on Reinaldo Echeverria, El Serpiente. He made a note that the first thing he wanted was confirmation that Reinaldo's son, Javier, was the same age as the actor in Freddie's film and that he was dead.

Then he went back to research Echeverria Senior. Everything he found was in Spanish, and he had to rely on online translation, which lost the nuances of the reporting, but the point was clear. El Serpiente was a bad guy, and that made Aidan very worried. He hoped that Richard would find that the Javier they were investigating was no relation at all.

Eventually, his mind began to wander. He kept thinking back to that truck, the way he'd seen the danger to Liam and the client and been powerless to prevent it.

There was an element of luck in any operation, and Aidan worried each time things got scary that this might be the time their luck ran out. How long could he and Liam keep doing this bodyguard work? They were both in good shape and could manage the physical and mental challenges. But it would only take a minor miscalculation to ruin everything they had. Being in the wrong place at the wrong time. A bad guy with more resources than expected. A client who acted stupidly, putting them in danger.

There was a sudden emptiness at the bottom of his stomach, and he got up. The sun was a brilliant yellow, searing the dry landscape.

He opened the sliding door and walked outside.

The blue-green Mediterranean shimmered in the far distance, and the quiet was almost palpable. It was so different up here from the frenzied activity of Nice, where there were always car horns, keening police sirens, the ruckus of cell phone conversations.

A roar that grew in intensity with every second ripped the quiet open, and Aidan opened his eyes. A jetliner on its descent trajectory swooped past, and Aidan remembered that desperate flight he'd taken from Philadelphia to Tunis. The overwhelming sadness and fear he had faced after spending eleven years with Blake and then discovering how easily Blake could toss him aside.

He crossed his arms protectively over his chest and closed his eyes. He wasn't sure he could go on living without Liam. The breakup with Blake had been so sudden and so damaging that if he hadn't met Liam almost immediately, he thought he might have crashed and burned in Tunis.

He'd felt rudderless, unloved and unwanted, and that first time he'd made an overture to Liam, when Liam had unthinkingly rejected him, he'd felt so miserable. Only Liam's kiss had brought him back from the edge. Those first days he'd spent with Liam, chasing a Bedouin tribe through the desert, had made him feel more alive than ever before. The adventure, the adrenaline rush, the developing love between him and Liam. The sex, better than he'd ever had before.

Even though he and Liam didn't make love as often as they once had, the bond between them was strong. He knew that despite any small problems that cropped up, Liam would never leave him.

No, his relationship with Liam wouldn't end by inches, a gradual drifting apart. It would be sudden and catastrophic, the way things had ended with Blake. One day he'd be part of a couple, and the next he'd be alone. He had staked so much of his identity in this partnership, making himself into a bodyguard in order to be Liam's true partner.

Was it too much? Would he end up without any identity at all if things fell apart? Would he be a grieving widower adrift in a foreign country?

He wondered, not for the first time, what Blake was doing. It was hard to wipe out his memory completely; they had loved each other once, lived together for a big chunk of Aidan's life. So many of his attitudes had developed during those years. His need to please, for one thing. He had taken classes in cooking, flower arranging, foreign languages, and dozens of other topics so that he could make a beautiful life for himself and Blake.

He had learned to pack a suitcase quickly, to deal with Blake's moods, to keep the house to Blake's standards. He'd done it all because he thought that was the way to keep Blake's love, or at least affection, to maintain his place by Blake's side.

Had Blake found someone else? What did it matter to Aidan?

He remembered the Oscar Wilde quote: "I can resist anything except temptation." What would it hurt to do a quick search on Blake Chennault?

He looked around to make sure that Hayam hadn't snuck outside with him, and when he didn't see her anywhere, he went back inside and closed the door behind him. He hesitated for a moment, his fingers hovering over the keyboard; then he took the plunge.

Blake still worked for the same law firm in Philadelphia, he discovered. Still lived in the same apartment off Rittenhouse Square. He had won several patent and trademark infringement cases in the past five years and spoken at a number of professional conferences.

But was he dating anyone else? Why couldn't Aidan figure that out? He switched to an image search, looking for recent pictures of Blake at social events, hoping to see a boyfriend by his side. Or did he want to see that at all? Did he want Blake to have moved on with his life, or did he want Blake still pining after all he had lost when he'd kicked Aidan to the curb?

Aidan finally caught himself. This was ridiculous, he thought. He closed the browser displaying images of Blake in his neatly pressed suits. He looked at the clock. Would Richard have made any progress on El Serpiente? He picked up his cell phone and called.

"Oy, mate, I'm still working on the last three things you asked me for," Richard said.

"I know, Richard, and I hate to rush you. But I have to know if the Javier Echeverria who acted in porn is the son of El Serpiente."

"I haven't been able to nail it down yet," Richard said. "I found the kid's birth certificate and death certificate. The Javier Echeverria who was born in Mexico City to this gangster bloke and his wife is definitely the same one who died in LA. But the porn acting? That part doesn't click."

"What do you mean?"

"The dates are screwy. If he's the same bloke, then it means he started acting at fifteen. Was your client into kiddie porn back then?"

"I don't know, but I can ask," Aidan said. "Keep looking and let us know as soon as you have the evidence."

He ended the call and stood up. He didn't believe that Freddie had been into kiddie porn; all the movies he'd seen had featured Freddie with other guys who were clearly over twenty-one. But perhaps Freddie had a side business separate from his own acting.

He walked down the hallway to the editing studio and stood in the open doorway for a moment, watching the action on screen. Typical porn fare, the kind shown in back rooms of gay bars, X-rated bookstores, and online. Two naked guys, young and slim, sucked each other in a bedroom somewhere. Boring.

Freddie hit a couple of keys, and the screen shifted to one guy's index finger snaking into the other's ass as he sucked. Even though he'd seen similar stuff hundreds of times, Aidan couldn't help getting hard. He rapped on the door frame.

Freddie hit the pause button and turned around. "What?"

"Sorry to bother you, but I heard something very disturbing, and I wanted to check it with you."

"Disturbing how? You found out who's after me?"

Aidan shook his head. "No, but we're working on leads. One of them is that kid Javier from your last movie. What do you know about him?"

Freddie shrugged. "It was years ago, and I didn't really know him. I only worked with him on that one scene. I remember he was

Mexican and that he sucked like a pro."

"You remember how old he was?"

Freddie crossed his arms over his chest. "Everybody had to supply proof of age. Mario ran a quality operation." He sighed. "But I learned after the fact that the kid's ID was faked. He wasn't even eighteen."

"Try fourteen, going on fifteen," Aidan said.

"Yeah, that's what he told me. I got pissed off at him. Told him he could have gotten all of us arrested and that I was going to spread the word not to hire him until he could prove his age legitimately."

"Did you?"

Freddie shook his head. "Right after I found out, the warehouse blew up, and I was scared shitless that the authorities would get hold of him and I'd get blamed for hiring him. Tried to cut all my ties back there, and by the time I felt safe enough to get back in touch, he was the last thing on my mind."

"Well, it looks like his father is a drug dealer in Mexico," Aidan said. "And he has a reason to have a grudge against you if he knows you were involved with his son doing porn, and maybe even blames you, and everybody else Javier worked with, for his death."

"But that was five years ago," Freddie protested.

Aidan shook his head. "Javier only died a few months ago. His father could just be getting started on his revenge."

31 – Straight Guys

"I have something for you," Liam said as he slid into a chair across from Louis at the café a few blocks from the embassy.

The server appeared, and they both ordered. "You get the text from Aidan?" Liam asked.

"The Banana?" Louis said, and Liam could tell he was trying not to laugh. "You believe him?"

"I do. He said that woman whose name Aidan texted you could tell your agents more."

"Elizabeth Angstrom? Aka Elizabeth Angstrom Wilson?"

"Don't know about the Wilson part."

"She's the woman you're looking for. Her name has already come up in the money-laundering investigation."

"Good. They can ask her about The Banana."

"Not possible. She was a housewife in Thousand Oaks, married to a social worker, with a five-year-old son. She was walking out of her house one day about a month ago, and someone shot her with a sniper rifle."

Liam's heart skipped a beat. He'd seen so much death in his career, but anytime there was a kid involved made it so much worse. "Was she flipping on somebody?"

"Nobody wants to say, but it looks like a hit, so that's my guess." He shook his head. "Your client has a lot of dead colleagues popping up. What film did he work on with her?"

"*Straight Suckers.*"

"Oh, yeah," Louis said. "A classic of its genre."

"You haven't actually seen it, have you?" Liam asked as the server delivered their coffees.

"Hassan has a thing for straight guys," he said. "Or straight-appearing ones."

"Like you," Liam said. "I didn't even know you were gay until Aidan told me."

"That's more about you than me," Louis said. "But yeah. So let's say he and I have more than a passing acquaintance with that type of film." He picked up his cup and sipped. "What about you guys? What do you watch?"

"We don't. At least, I don't." Liam looked down and felt his face redden.

"Come on, we're just guys here," Louis said. "You can tell me."

"Aidan has a thing for military porn. Anything with a uniform involved. Cops, soldiers, sailors. I've come in on him watching stuff sometimes."

"Does he get you to dress up?"

"I'm not comfortable talking about this," Liam said. "Can we get back to business?"

"So the answer is yes," Louis said. "Oh, to be a fly on the wall in your bedroom."

"If you were a fly in my bedroom, I'd swat you. Did you come up with anything on El Serpiente?"

Louis laughed. "Not much makes you squirm, does it, McCullough? But sex does. Very interesting."

Liam sipped his coffee and waited. Waiting was something he'd learned in the SEALs, the ability to settle his mind and body for as long as he needed to before whatever he was waiting for happened.

"He's quite a colorful character, this serpent." Louis pushed a sheet of paper toward Liam. "And you know what's interesting?"

"What's that?"

"My sources think he might be in France. And he's in the market for a semiautomatic weapon."

"You're shitting me," Liam said.

Louis drained the last of his coffee. "Nope. I know this wasn't exactly the news you were hoping to get." He stood up and said, "Thanks for the coffee. I've got some more feelers out. I hope to have a line on where he is soon. In the meantime, you need to be very careful."

He walked out, and Liam let out a deep breath. Well, at least they had an idea of who they were up against. He reached for his cell phone to call and warn Aidan, but the battery was dead.

He nearly smacked the phone against the table, but tamed his temper. This was the second indication he'd gotten recently that he was going soft. First his need to have three square meals a day. Now letting his phone run out of charge. Would the next mistake be one that cost his client's life? Or worse, Aidan's?

He left some euros on the table and stood up. He could go after Louis, ask to use his phone to call Aidan. Or he could get his ass back up to Freddie's house, where he belonged.

He stepped out into the pedestrian zone. A skinny white guy

with blond dreads spilling out of a jumbo-sized ball cap was playing a flute on a blanket, a cup of change in front of him. Chic young mothers with infants in strollers, businessmen and women in dark suits, and the ubiquitous tourists streamed around him. He skirted them all and hurried to the garage nearby.

He had borrowed Newt's tiny car because he'd thought it would be easier to park, but the spot he'd found was big enough to handle the Jeep. And dumb ass that he was, he'd left the car charger for the phone plugged into the Jeep's dashboard.

Any one of his mistakes would have been enough to get his ass reamed by his SEAL commander. Maybe it was a good thing that Don't Ask, Don't Tell had pushed him out of the military when the act was still in effect. What kind of a SEAL would he make today?

He couldn't even blame Aidan. He had embraced the creature comforts Aidan had brought to his life, loved their physical intimacy and the deep sense of connection they had. But all that good living had gotten to him. Gone was the soldier who could walk for miles without food or water, whose every sense was attuned to danger.

Maybe he needed to get out of fieldwork. Talk to Jean-Luc, see if there were administrative jobs for him and Aidan. He'd hate it; nothing made him antsier than being stuck behind a desk. But he'd have to suck it up, for Aidan's sake if not for his own.

32 – Taking Control

After his shower Friday morning, Newt was about to reinsert the butt plug, but Freddie stopped him. "I'm changing things around," Freddie said. "I don't need to hurt you to be happy with you. I don't need to assert my dominance or any of that shit. I just want to be with you."

"I'm willing to do whatever you want," Newt said. "But that after that first time, the pain wasn't really turning me on."

His back and butt still tingled with the memory of the cat-o'-nine-tails and the flat of Freddie's hand. He couldn't look down and see his dick; the protruding shelf of his belly got in the way. But he could feel that he wasn't getting hard, even standing there naked with Freddie in the bathroom.

Then Freddie kissed him, one of those long, lingering kisses that Newt had imagined between Fledglis and Ulric. The feeling of Freddie's skin against his, the moist, probing tongue, Freddie's hands on his back. That made his dick jump, and Freddie pressed his thigh against it. "You are a horny bastard, aren't you?" Freddie said.

"As you keep reminding me, you're a porn star. Who wouldn't get turned on by a handsome, sexy guy like you?"

"Ex-porn star, as *you* keep reminding *me*," Freddie said. He backed away from Newt and flicked his finger at Newt's hard-on, which bounced back and forth. "Hold that thought. I have work to do."

Then he strutted out of the bathroom, his butt tight, those angel wings tattooed on his back flexing as he walked, and Newt had to resist the urge to jerk off right then.

Instead he turned to look at himself in the mirror. Was it his imagination, or had he lost a few more pounds? His man boobs looked tighter, didn't hang down as much. And when he turned sideways it looked like his belly was a bit flatter.

With trepidation, he stepped on the scale. Sure enough, he'd lost another five pounds. He was still as big as a hippo, and it would take a long time before he felt good about his body. But he was making progress.

He got down on the floor, resting his back on the hard marble, and stretched his legs out. Then he put his hands behind his head and tried to raise his upper body.

He was stunned that he could do five sit-ups before he crashed. He hadn't exercised like that since he was in his teens. He rested, caught his breath, then rolled over onto his belly. Could he do a push-up or two?

Yup. His upper arms, though fleshy, had always been strong, and he managed ten pushups—though he didn't get that far above the floor, just enough to raise his belly from the marble.

He was doing it, he thought with glee. He was taking control of his body, pushing it into something better. He had to grab the counter to pull himself up from the floor, though, which deflated his positive feelings a bit, but still he was pretty happy with himself when he got dressed and went into Freddie's bedroom to get back to work.

That good feeling hadn't translated into words on the page,

though. By early afternoon, Newt hadn't written a word. The master bedroom was at one side of the house and had side windows that looked down toward the neighbor's house. The window straight ahead of Newt faced the ocean, and though it was distant, only a scrap of water, it was almost mesmerizing.

He couldn't focus on Fledglis and Ulric; he was too caught up in his own fantasies of Freddie. It was hard to realize that he'd only met Freddie less than a week before. Since spotting Freddie at the hypermarché on Sunday, he'd been on a roller coaster of highs and lows—desperation at the way he'd been caught jerking off in Freddie's yard to the awesome sex between them. His writing had reflected the same pattern. Sometimes he was inspired and the words flowed; other times he felt almost constipated by his inability to get his feelings out on the page.

Something had changed between him and Freddie the night before. They had talked, really connected, and then Newt had been able to make Freddie come. No whips or ball-busting involved. Did that mean they were falling in love?

Newt had experienced crushes before, usually on very masculine straight guys or anonymous porn stars. He'd certainly crushed on Freddie Venus. Now he was getting to know the real man who hid behind those angel wings.

But every time he tried to imagine a future for the two of them, he remembered the threat hanging over their heads. Someone was out there who wanted to destroy any chance of happiness for them, and it pissed Newt off.

What would Fledglis do if Ulric was in danger? Newt knew his unicorn. Fledglis would come up with a plan and then carry it out, rescue his half-man, half-angel lover. It was up to Newt to do the same thing for Freddie, but he had to let Fledglis guide him.

He positioned his fingers over the laptop's keyboard, and suddenly the words began to flow.

33 – Strange & Wonderful

Freddie sat back in his editing chair as the rays of the setting sun began to infiltrate the editing room. He had tried to concentrate on work, but every half hour or so his thoughts strayed back to Newt.

How had he let that big guy get under his skin so quickly? Was he going to end up with his heart broken again, the way it had been when he discovered Rodney had been cheating on him?

Working in porn had taught him to remove emotion from the sexual act. It was just a physical thing, two or more bodies coming together. His dick had always been reliable, able to perform on command. He rarely even needed a fluffer between scenes. He was a horny bastard. Director after director had told him so.

Then it was over. Rodney was dead; Freddie let himself go, porking up, spending most of his time high on alcohol or drugs. His reliable dick disappointed him time after time. Sometimes he couldn't get hard. Sometimes he'd stiffen but couldn't come. And even when he did, the orgasm was such a localized experience that he hardly noticed.

He had accepted that that part of his life was over. He was happy there in his little house in the hills, doing editing work because it was something to keep his mind occupied. Now he realized that he'd been using the work to shield himself from having any emotional involvement.

He knew some people in Nice, but none he could call friends. He had joined a team that played *petanque*, the French version of bocce, but dropped out after a couple of weeks. When he went to the movies or ate out, he went by himself.

Then Newt Camilleri had come into his life, and everything got shaken up. On the surface, the guy was a hot mess. He was fat and sensitive and just this side of plain old weird. But he had rung Freddie's bell, and Freddie was back to square one, following his dick.

He remembered what it had felt like to fuck Newt, to be so determined to give pleasure to another human being, and he realized that he was hard. Watching Justin and Colt get it on did nothing for him, but thinking of the pitiful tub of lard gave him a stiffy that demanded attention.

What a strange and wonderful world it was.

He closed his eyes and pictured Newt. Not as the big guy saw himself, a whale unworthy of sexual interest. Not even as he was, a porker who could stand to lose about a hundred pounds. But as Freddie knew he could be.

He had already seen the transformation start. Newt's clothes were getting loose on him. His legs had to be strong, to support all that weight, and he was able to run a little farther each morning. The more muscle mass Newt built up, the more calories he could burn. With his diet controlled and a routine of regular exercise and sex, the pounds would be falling off him. But was it up to Freddie to change Newt? Did Newt want to become this guy that Freddie saw in him?

He recalled the pictures he'd seen of Newt back home. He had weighed much more then. And he knew that Newt had been walking every day since his arrival in France. It wasn't like Freddie was pushing him somewhere he didn't want to go, just helping him get there.

In his mind's eye, Freddie saw Newt naked on his king-size bed. Newt's balls were wrapped with the leather strap, and he had weighted tit clamps on his big, fleshy nipples. Another strap connected his tits to his balls. He was waiting for Freddie to do whatever he wanted.

But Freddie didn't want him that way. No leather strap, no tit clamps. Just Newt, who was strong and sweet and only needed someone to show him that true vision of himself.

Freddie realized that his big dick was stiff, leaking precome. In his imagination, he swaggered forward to Newt naked, his dick slapping against his belly. Newt's dick was standing up like a flagpole, and he was playing with his tits and looking at Freddie with eyes glazed in lust.

Freddie realized that he was breathing hard, that his dick was pulsing in his shorts. What the fuck was he doing by himself, imagining sex, when there was a guy in his bedroom waiting for him?

He jumped up so fast that he knocked over his editing chair, but he didn't care. He hurried out of the studio and down the hall, shedding clothes as he went.

By the time he pushed through the bedroom door, he was as naked as the day he was born, though significantly better endowed. "I need you," Freddie said. "I don't know why, but I do."

Newt pushed back his chair and stood up. His dick thrust

forward against his baggy shorts, and he pushed them down. "Come to Papa," he said as his dick sprang out.

Freddie crossed the room, pressed his belly against Newt's, and wrapped his arms around Newt's back. Freddie's dick was only half-hard, but it felt hot and strong against Newt's skin.

Freddie didn't lean in for a kiss, though. Instead he focused on Newt's eyes.

Newt's lashes were thin, and his eyebrows needed trimming. His eyes were a deep, dark brown. They kissed, and it was another of those earth-moving kisses, made that much more awesome because their bodies connected at so many points. Newt wrapped his hands around Freddie's back and cupped his butt, and Freddie squirmed in closer to him.

Freddie's dick stiffened against Newt's thigh. "I want you to fuck me," Newt said, when he broke the kiss.

"I can't," Freddie said. "That other time, that was a fluke."

"Sure you can. Pretend you're the little dick that could."

Freddie laughed and backed away a bit, palming his stiff dick. "Not exactly little."

"Then be the big dick that could," Newt said. "Stick it in me. Take possession of me completely. Please, Freddie?"

"I don't..." Freddie stopped. "What the fuck. We'll give it a try. Oh, but fuck me, I don't have any rubbers. Haven't needed them in years."

"In my bag," Newt said. "In the bathroom. Lube too, if you want."

"Good deal," Freddie said. When he returned from the bathroom with the bottle of lube and a condom, he said, "Lay down on your side. This is going to require some engineering."

Newt did as he was told. Freddie popped the top off the lube bottle and squirted som gel onto his index finger. He began tickling it around Newt's hole. "It's cold," Newt said.

"Don't worry, it'll warm up soon," Freddie said. It was a struggle to get Newt's cheeks open enough so that Freddie could slide in. Jesus, he hoped the guy trimmed down his ass. Maybe Liam could come up with exercises to firm Newt's glutes and slim him down back there.

"Freddie," Newt said in a pleading tone. "Come on."

"I'm working on it," Freddie said. "You don't exactly have easy access." He slapped Newt's butt. "But don't worry, I'm an expert. And the more you exercise and eat right, the easier this is going to be."

Finally, Freddie made contact. His dick head pushed up against Newt's hole, forced its way in. Newt grunted and wiggled and then Freddie was inside. Newt's chute was tight, and Freddie had to adjust. He couldn't slam in and out like he wanted to; instead he'd have to make sure his dick stayed inside, then thrust and shimmy.

Since he wasn't likely to get off, this was about giving Newt pleasure, letting him see what it was like to be on the receiving end of all the love and desire Freddie could push into him.

Freddie's body was right up against Newt's, and he reached one hand around to pinch one of Newt's nipples. The big guy wiggled and bucked, and Freddie gave up thinking and let his instincts take over.

He began to pant and moved faster and faster, slamming into Newt's ass. Newt's body shook, and Freddie knew he was hitting the big guy's prostate. "Oh, oh, Jesus," Freddie said, and his body exploded with a power he hadn't felt for years.

He pulled out of Newt and collapsed on his back, and Newt squirmed around, the bed shaking, so he could face Freddie. "Are you all right?" Newt asked.

"Fucked to death," Freddie said, smiling. "But oh, what a hell of a way to go."

34 – Lost Dog

Aidan was pacing nervously in the living room, worrying about Liam, when Freddie dashed past him on his way to the bedroom, shedding clothes as he ran. The bedroom door slammed shut, and within a few minutes, Aidan heard what sounded like Freddie's bed banging against the wall.

At least the client was busy, and presumably happy, he thought. But where was Liam? It had already been a couple of hours, plenty of time to drive into the city, have a quick meeting, then come back up to Freddie's house. Had he learned something from Louis that required immediate attention? Or had something happened to him on the way into or out of the city?

Whoever was after Freddie must have realized by now that he'd hired bodyguards. Suppose this stalker had decided to take out Liam? What could Aidan do? Call Jean-Luc? Call the police and see if an accident had been reported?

He closed his eyes. He needed to calm down. Liam could take care of himself. He had already called Liam's cell twice, and both times the call went straight to voice mail. He just had to wait.

He was relieved when he heard Newt's tiny putt-putt car come up the steep driveway. "Hayam! Daddy's home!" he called, and wondered why the little dog wasn't rushing out with him to greet Liam. He stepped outside and shielded his eyes from the bright late-afternoon sun.

"Sorry I didn't call," Liam said as he emerged from the smart car, unfurling himself like one of those clowns in the circus. "Phone died, and the charger was in the Jeep."

"That's okay. What did Louis have to say?"

"Looks like El Serpiente could be our guy. Louis has heard rumors that he's in France and in the market for semiautomatic weapons."

"That sucks," Aidan said. "But at least we have an idea who we're up against."

"We're going to need reinforcements," Liam said. "And we need to lock down the house. I'm going to call Jean-Luc and see who can we pull in. You make sure that all the doors are locked and all the windows shut, with curtains or blinds drawn. We're going to hunker down in here for the time being."

Aidan always had the urge to salute when Liam went into his operations mode, barking orders, but he knew the situation was too serious for snarkiness. He started in the guest room, then knocked on the door to Freddie's bedroom.

"Come in," Freddie called.

Aidan opened the door gingerly, afraid of what he might see, but both Freddie and Newt were sitting up in bed with the covers pulled over them. "Bad news," Aidan said.

He explained about Javier Echeverria's father, that he had been sighted in France looking for weapons.

"Who is Javier Echeverria?" Newt asked.

"I'll explain it later," Freddie said. He swung out of bed, naked, and looked around the room. "Where are my clothes?"

"There's a trail of them from the editing suite to here," Aidan said. "I need to get this room locked down and then continue through the house."

He started with the French doors as, behind him, Freddie walked out and Newt got dressed. Aidan realized that he still hadn't seen Hayam. "You haven't seen our dog, have you?" he asked Newt. "She usually comes whenever I call her."

"Sorry. I was writing, and I'm in another world then. But I can help you look for her."

"We'll look while we lock down the house," Aidan said. He went into Freddie's bathroom and made sure that the window was closed and locked, then lowered the blinds.

"It's like a bunker in here," Newt said when he came out. The master bedroom was dark with slivers of light coming in.

"Let's hope it's as safe as one," Aidan said.

He stopped at the guest bathroom and made sure it was secure, then continued into the living room. Liam had Aidan's cell tucked between his head and his shoulder, and he was talking to Jean-Luc as he closed and locked the big French doors.

"How many men can you get us, and how fast?" Liam asked.

Aidan didn't wait to hear Jean-Luc's response. He and Newt hurried down the hall to Freddie's editing room. Aidan kept calling for the dog, with no response.

"She was probably in with Freddie, and maybe he locked her in accidentally," Newt said. "I've seen the way she likes to cuddle up with him. He should probably get a dog of his own."

When they got to the studio, Freddie was standing by the open French doors, staring out into the backyard. He had picked up his clothes on the way there and was dressed in his shorts and T-shirt. "Come on, Freddie," Aidan said. "You've got to stay away from the windows." He tugged on Freddie's arm.

"Have you seen their dog, Freddie?" Newt asked as Aidan began pulling down a window shade.

"Yeah, she was here a while ago. She wanted to go out, and I let her. She must be out in the yard somewhere. I'm sorry. I wasn't thinking."

"She's a good dog," Aidan said. "She'll come back. I'll call her."

He stepped outside and called for the dog. He heard an answering yip from somewhere up the hill. "That's her," Aidan said.

"Who?" Liam asked as he came into the room.

"Hayam. I need to go find her. She might be in trouble."

"I'll go with you," Freddie said. "It's pretty wild back there, and there are hidden dips and humps."

"Freddie has to stay here," Liam said. "Inside. You two close these doors and don't open them again until we come back. We have some additional bodyguards coming, and once they get here, we'll come up with a game plan."

"I'll look after Freddie," Newt said. After Aidan and Liam stepped outside, he pushed the French doors shut, and Aidan heard the bolt slide.

Aidan and Liam hurried up the slope. "Where are you, girl?" Aidan called. "Hayam!"

She yipped eagerly but didn't seem to be moving. "Oh God, I hope she isn't hurt," Aidan said. He stumbled over a rock and lost his balance, but Liam grabbed him.

"Take it easy, Aidan. We'll find her."

At the sound of her daddies' voices so close, Hayam began yelping and barking. "She's right up there," Aidan said.

They found the little dog lying in a long depression in the ground, her foot tangled in a pile of rope. "Oh, sweetie," Aidan said. He leaned down to untie her. "What did you get into?"

Aidan was having trouble with the rope. "Could you help me out here?" he asked Liam crossly.

"You realize what this is, don't you?" Liam said as he squatted beside Aidan. "This is a sniper's nest." He nodded downhill. "And it has a perfect view of Freddie's editing room."

He quickly undid the knot around the little dog's foot; then Liam lifted her up and handed her to Aidan. "We'd better get back to the house. I want to sit down and brainstorm with you before the rest of the guys get here."

Aidan heard the sound of a car coming up Freddie's driveway and looked over there. "Whoever you called got here awful fast," he said, pointing downhill.

A single man stepped out of the nondescript sedan. It was too far to see clearly, but Aidan had a sinking sensation as he watched the man move.

"He's not reinforcements," he said. "That's El Serpiente."

35 – Don't Think, Act

Newt tugged on Freddie's arm. "Come on, Freddie. We need to get away from these windows. It's not safe even with the drapes closed because somebody could shoot right through."

"But we have to be here to open the doors for them."

"I'll stay here. You find a good place inside where you're out of trouble."

"I'm never out of trouble," Freddie said. "But my throat's as dry as the Sahara. I'm going to get a bottle of water, and I'll meet you in the living room after you let them back in."

Newt lifted the side of one of the curtains to look out. He saw the bodyguards climbing the hill, then squatting by the ground. "I hope the little dog is all right," he said to himself. Then he added silently, *And the rest of us too.*

He heard the sound of a car coming up the driveway. Good, he thought. The extra bodyguards are here already. He took a couple of deep breaths. It was going to be all right. Freddie would be okay. The bodyguards would protect him.

He looked back outside. Aidan and Liam had stood up, and Aidan had the little dog in his arms. He heard a rap on the front door and hurried out of the editing suite. He wanted to get to the door first, so that Freddie wouldn't have to open it himself.

He was too late, though. Freddie had already opened the door, and the middle-aged man facing him didn't look like a bodyguard at all. His face was scarred with a long slash from his right eye to his mouth, and he wore a military-style vest with multiple pockets. He had a heavy-duty handgun aimed at Freddie.

The gunman was speaking in rapid Spanish, too fast for Newt to understand even if he'd spoken more than a few words of the language. But his anger was clear.

Newt barreled down the hall like Fledglis charging bad guys in one of his stories. His footsteps were loud against the stone floor, and he pumped his arms to keep his momentum going. As he got close, he leaped at Freddie and pushed him out of the way as the man with the gun began to fire.

The sound reverberated in the narrow hallway. Freddie fell to the floor with Newt on top of him. Newt rolled his body toward the man with the gun. He barely registered the sound of the gun firing, the bullets ricocheting off the walls.

Newt lashed out with his right leg, connecting his foot with the man's groin. The man fell backward, out the front door and backwards onto the driveway. Newt rolled again. He slammed the door shut, then leaned his back against it.

The whole encounter had taken less than a minute, but it seemed to have gone on forever. Newt's heart was racing, and he was having trouble catching his breath. It didn't feel like he had broken anything, though. That was the benefit of a lot of padding.

He looked down and saw the pool of blood. Oh God, was Freddie hurt? He looked across from him where Freddie was sitting up. "What the fuck?" Freddie said.

"Did he shoot you?" Newt asked. It was hard to breathe, but he had to know that Freddie was all right.

"I'm fine, just had the wind knocked out of me. But where'd all that blood come from?"

Newt looked down at the stone floor. Then everything went black.

* * *

Liam galloped down the hillside and leaped over the low stone wall that divided Freddie's yard from his neighbor's. From around the corner of the house, he heard a man's voice speaking in Spanish and then a fusillade of gunfire.

Another mistake. They had waited too long and let this El Serpiente get the drop on them.

He pushed forward, ran around the corner and into the driveway. The Jeep was parked to the side, then Newt's little red car. An unfamiliar dark sedan sat behind Newt's.

Ahead of him Liam saw the man in the doorway firing into the house. Then suddenly someone inside the house kicked out at him, and the gunman fell backward, hitting his head on the driveway. The door to the house slammed shut.

The driveway's pebbles scattered under Liam's feet as he raced around the Jeep toward the man. The gun had fallen a few feet from him, and Liam was determined to grab it before the man came to his senses.

The man sat up, shook his head, then looked around. He saw the gun and reached toward it. Before he could get it, though, Liam leaped on top of him. The man went down again, and Liam used his weight to keep him pinned to the ground. But the man was wiry and strong and struggled to throw Liam off.

Liam leaned forward and tried to pin the man's arms to the driveway, but the stranger was fueled by a passion that glowed in his eyes. He brought his legs up behind Liam, struggling to kick out. Liam was determined not to make another mistake. He was going to subdue this man or die trying.

He reached back and grabbed the man's right leg. With a quick twist, he broke the fibula. The man howled in pain but kept on bucking Liam with his midsection, trying to throw him off balance. Liam leaned forward and placed his arm across the man's windpipe, but the man resisted, struggling to get enough purchase to twist or break it.

Aidan's voice rang out behind him, over the noise of the two of them scuffling on the ground. "*Levanten los manos o te pego un tiro!*"

Liam saw Aidan standing over them with both hands on the grip of the man's semiautomatic gun. He was aiming straight at the man's head, and at that close range, there was no way he could miss.

Liam looked up at Aidan. "Good job. I thought I was going to have to bang this guy's head into the pavement a couple of times."

"I wish you had," Aidan said.

The man began to spit out a stream of Spanish expletives but kept squirming and struggling. Clearly the threat of his own gun wasn't enough to stop him.

The front door swung open. "Help me!" Freddie cried. "Newt's been shot."

Aidan's aim never wavered, and Liam admired Aidan's cool, how far his partner had come in the years they had worked together. Without looking away from the man on the ground, Aidan called, "Freddie, I saw some rope under the sink in your kitchen. Can you bring it here? We need to get this man immobilized. Then I'll look after Newt." To the man he said, "*Dejar de luchar o te pego un tiro, pendejo!*"

El Serpiente wouldn't shut up. Since the man spoke Spanish, Liam began grilling him. His command of it was rough, but he'd interrogated men in that language before. "Are you alone?" he demanded. "Is there anyone watching us?"

The stranger cursed and spat.

"You are Reinaldo Echeverria," Liam said, and the man turned to face him, his eyes wild. "Father of Javier."

It seemed like something inside the man's brain had switched on. He began talking about his son, how the homosexuals in Los Angeles had killed him. Liam felt sorry for him, but he used that moment to flip El Serpiente onto his stomach.

Echeverria began shouting obscenities again as his broken leg hit the pavement. Liam sat on the man's back, immobilizing him. "*Cállate!*" Aidan said. "Nobody wants to hear anything more from you. Save it for the *policía*."

Freddie rushed out of the front door, holding a coil of rope and a cell phone. "I called an ambulance," he said. "And the cops. You've got to come look at Newt. He's bleeding."

"In a minute," Aidan said. While Liam kept the Mexican immobilized, Aidan took the rope from Freddie and tied El Serpiente's hands together.

"Come on," Freddie said impatiently. "What if he dies?"

"Give me the rope," Liam said. "I can finish up. Aidan, you go see what you can do for Newt before the ambulance gets here."

The Agence had required them to renew their CPR credentials as a condition of employment, so he knew that Aidan could do as good a job at saving Newt as he could. As long as Newt could still be saved.

* * *

Aidan handed the rope to Liam and hurried into the house, conscious of the blast of cool air. He realized that he was sweating profusely, and he wiped his hands on his shorts before he knelt to the stone floor. Newt was lying on his side, and a pool of ruby-red blood was gathering around his abdomen.

"Is Freddie all right?" Newt asked, his voice hoarse.

"He's fine," Aidan said. "We need to get you taken care of, though."

"It hurts," Newt said.

Freddie was on Aidan's heels. "Aidan's going to take care of you, baby," he said, kneeling down. He took Newt's hand. "You've got to hold on."

"I'll get the first-aid kit," Aidan said. "Don't let him move."

He ran down the hallway to the guest room. The first-aid kit was right where it belonged, and he grabbed it and raced back to the foyer.

Freddie sat by Newt's side, still holding his hand and repeating encouragements. Aidan sat on the floor cross-legged beside Newt's belly. He dug a pair of scissors from the kit. "Hope you didn't like T-this shirt too much," he said as he sliced the fabric from the neck down and pulled it aside to examine Newt's wounds.

There were three of them, though most of the blood seemed to be coming from one of them. "Lot of fat there," Newt mumbled.

"That's a good thing, baby," Freddie said. "Maybe it's just a flesh wound."

Despite all the flesh there, it appeared to Aidan that the bullets had penetrated more deeply. Aidan didn't attempt to remove the bullets; that would be up to a surgeon. He folded a piece of gauze from the first-aid kit and placed it over one wound, taping it down. Then he repeated the process twice more. His hands were covered with blood by the time heard the sirens approaching.

"It hurts," Newt moaned.

"Stay with us, big guy," Aidan said. "You've lost a lot of blood, but they can give you a transfusion at the hospital."

"He took those bullets for me," Freddie said. "Oh, Christ, Newt, you didn't have to do that."

"What…Fledglis…would…do," Newt said. Then he passed out.

* * *

Freddie wanted to go to the hospital with Newt, but the police wouldn't let him leave the house until they understood what had happened. The first cop to respond to the call immediately took the Mexican's gun from Liam and radioed for more help as the ambulance pulled up.

Liam had to help the two attendants lift Newt onto the stretcher. He was still breathing but falling in and out of consciousness, mumbling incoherent phrases about a castle and a farmhouse.

As the ambulance pulled away, four more cop cars had arrived, lights flashing and sirens whooping. A plainclothes detective directed the officers to preserve the area around the driveway, to put Freddie, Liam, and Aidan in separate rooms.

Freddie was sitting in the living room with a uniformed cop to guard him when the detective finally appeared, nearly an hour later. "I need to know what's happened with my friend," Freddie demanded in French. "Where are my bodyguards? Do I need an attorney?"

"All in time, monsieur," the detective said in English. "I have some questions for you."

Freddie answered as clearly as he could, reciting the events of the past week, from the stalking incidents to that day. He tried to keep Newt's situation out of the conversation, but it was too complicated, and eventually he admitted that Newt had only appeared at his door on Sunday. He left out the part about Newt spanking his monkey in the lavender patch, though.

The cop went over everything again and again. How did Freddie know that Newt was not connected to the Mexican with the broken leg? How did he know the man? His son? The man blamed Freddie for the death of his son. How did it happen? Why would the man blame Freddie?

The questions, his worry over Newt, and the stress of the day eventually wore him out. He kept yawning during the questioning, and he started getting confused. Eventually, he simply refused to keep speaking because he knew that it was more and more likely he'd say something that would hurt rather than help.

Through the front window, he saw a constant flow of men and women arriving and departing, collecting evidence. He did not see Liam or Aidan, though, until Liam stepped in the front door, accompanied by an official-looking Frenchman in a suit.

The suit spoke to the detective in rapid French. Freddie could only follow bits and pieces, but it sounded like the Mexican had been identified and his criminal record revealed, and that the bodyguards had been proved to be legitimate.

The detective said, "All right, we are finished here for now. But we will need to speak with you again." He walked out to the driveway, and Freddie turned to Liam.

"Have you heard anything about Newt?" he asked. "How is he? Nobody has been able to tell me anything."

"I spoke to a nurse at the hospital," Liam said. "He's in surgery to have those bullets removed. He's a strong guy. He'll make it."

"I want to see him. I want be there when he gets out of surgery."

"The police are almost finished. As soon as they let us leave, we'll drive you down to the hospital."

Freddie looked around. He could smell the tang of blood from the foyer. He didn't want Newt to have to return to the house and see his blood everywhere. "I better call my maid," he said. "She has a key to the house. I hope she can get over here and start cleaning this up."

The maid arrived as the last police were leaving. "*Mon dieu!*" she said when she stepped inside. She was a tough-looking woman in her sixties, and she'd worked for Freddie for years, keeping the house well. She shook her head and moved toward the kitchen to get her cleaning supplies.

"Let's roll," Liam said. "We'll take the Jeep."

Freddie held on to the door as Liam zoomed around the curves and down into the city to the massive stone Hôpital St. Roch. "You think he'll make it?" he asked Liam.

"He's a sturdy guy," Liam said. "I think it will take more than a couple of bullets to wipe out Newt."

"But what if they hit something important? Stopped his heart or something?"

"He was still breathing when they took him away," Liam said. "If the bullet had hit an artery or his heart, he'd have been dead before the ambulance got there. You just have faith, all right?"

"It's all my fault," Freddie said. "I never should have let Newt come stay with me once I knew there was someone after me."

"You couldn't have known what was going to happen," Aidan said from the backseat. "The best you can do now is stop blaming yourself and focus on being strong for Newt."

They parked near the entrance marked *Urgences* and hurried inside. It took some negotiating, but eventually they found a sympathetic male nurse, as queer as a three-dollar bill as Freddie's father would have said, who told them that Newt was already in recovery. "His wounds were not too serious," he said. "But he lost a great deal of blood and required a transfusion. He will go to a regular room as soon as he awakes."

Freddie felt his legs go weak, and he was glad he had Aidan and Liam on either side of him to hold him up.

36 – Take the Lead

Liam drove Aidan and Freddie back up into the hills to Freddie's house. "I want to go to sleep for about a day," Freddie said. "You think Newt will be okay until I wake up?"

"We'll keep tabs on him with the hospital," Aidan said.

"Good. I'm going to take a handful of pills and try to forget today ever happened."

Freddie gave them a two-fingered salute and disappeared into his bedroom. It was evening, and Liam thought a good night's sleep sounded like a great idea. Then his stomach grumbled.

Aidan laughed. "Your tummy wants to be fed. Let me see what we have in the kitchen." Liam followed him in, and Aidan assigned him to chop up some peppers, mushrooms, and zucchini for a quick stir-fry. They moved easily around the kitchen, and Liam thought that this was all he wanted—this man, this ease together.

His father wouldn't have been caught dead with a chopping knife; he thought all cooking was women's work. He wouldn't even have a grill in the backyard. But then, his parents' relationship was a lot different from his with Aidan. He wasn't sure that Doris and Big Bill had ever loved each other. Liam had been born only six months after his parents' marriage, and Big Bill had blamed Doris for trapping him. *"I'd be footloose and fancy-free if it wasn't for you,"* he often grumbled.

His parents never kissed or hugged each other, at least not in the presence of their kids. Liam still had a hard time being as affectionate as Aidan wanted. Sex was one thing; intimacy was another, and he was still learning that.

Aidan threw the vegetables into Freddie's wok, accompanied by strips of raw chicken, and the kitchen filled with the aroma of soy sauce and the sound of the sizzling food.

Aidan opened the blinds to the starlit night, and lit a fat candle on Freddie's kitchen windowsill. After he delivered two plates of stir-fry to the table, he dimmed the lights, and they ate in the flickering candlelight.

"This is good," Liam said after a couple of bites. "I didn't realize how hungry I was."

"Food always tastes better after drama," Aidan said. "When I saw you go galloping down the hill this afternoon, my heart nearly stopped beating. I was so scared for you. But I kept on going because I knew you'd manage."

"I'm not sure I can do this much longer," Liam said. He didn't know why he'd had that impulse, but once the floodgates had opened, there was no stopping what he had to say. He put down his silverware and looked at Aidan.

"I'm getting old and soft. My muscles ache. I need to eat three meals a day. Pretty soon my reflexes will be shot. I don't want to ever make a mistake big enough to hurt you. I've been thinking about asking Jean-Luc if he can find me an office job somewhere at the Agence. Then you can go back to teaching, and we'll both be out of danger."

Aidan put his hands out on the table, and Liam grasped them.

"I worry about you all the time," Aidan said. "I love you so much, and I'm scared of losing you. I know what you're saying, that every case that goes bad could be our last one. And that's an awful thing to consider."

"So you want to quit?" Liam asked.

Aidan shook his head. "I have never felt so alive since I've been with you," he said. "Yeah, I like teaching. And I might go back to it sometime. But right now, I only want to be with you."

"That sounds like the lyrics to a song," Liam said and then smiled.

"It is. Dusty Springfield. But I'm not going to let you derail me. I know you, Liam McCullough. You would hate having a desk job, meeting with clients, making assignments, doing paperwork. It would kill you almost as fast as some sniper's bullet or an out-of-control truck."

Liam's emotions were all over the place. "But what can we do?"

"We can take each day, and each job, as it comes," Aidan said. "As long as you're happy with me, and with what we have, I'll always be by your side."

"Oh, sweetheart," Liam said. "I'm more than happy with you. You're the best thing that ever happened to me."

"Then why don't you want to have sex with me?"

Liam felt blindsided. "Excuse me? Didn't we have sex twice in the last couple of days?"

"I know you think I'm oversexed, Liam," Aidan said.

Liam started to protest, but Aidan stopped him. "And I know

that that initial burst of sexual sizzle has to die out eventually. We've had a great run. I don't want us to end up as roommates, bickering like a pair of old queens and never touching each other."

"I sure as hell don't want that," Liam said. "What's your idea? More porn? More role-play? Whatever you need, I'm there."

"I don't want to be the one to call the shots all the time in the bedroom," Aidan said. "You know I like it when my big, strong, sexy lover takes over."

"And I haven't been doing that enough." Liam nodded. "Yeah, I get it." He felt his dick hardening in his slacks. "We both had that kind of upbringing, I guess. That the man is the one to take the lead when it comes to sex."

"Excuse me?" Aidan said. "In case you haven't looked lately, I'm as male as you are."

"You know what I mean. You want to have sex with a real man. One who takes charge." He smiled. "Though I know you like to be the pushy bottom sometimes."

Aidan faked a look of outrage, then laughed. "You must have been talking to Louis," he said. "To come up with a term like *pushy bottom*."

"I don't talk to Louis about sex," Liam protested. "Well, he tries to talk to me, but I clam up."

"Talking is good," Aidan said. "If we're going to be partners in life, and whatever else, we have to be able to communicate." He smiled. "What does Louis say when he talks about sex?"

"He says that Hassan is a size queen, and he gets his rocks off over masculine men."

"I knew that Hassan and I had a lot in common," Aidan said.

"And that Hassan has a crush on Freddie." Liam shook his head. "I don't see it. But maybe I need to become more familiar with his body of work."

He stood up, aware that his stiff dick was tenting his khakis. "What do you say we postpone cleanup for a while and get some porn on?"

Aidan was so eager he knocked over the kitchen chair when he stood up. "Last one naked is a rotten egg," he said and dashed for the guest room.

Liam let him run. There were few things he liked better than walking into a bedroom to find Aidan naked there, waiting for him. And after this week, there was no way that Aidan was going to accuse him again of shirking his duties.

He remembered the box of sex toys he and Aidan had discovered in Freddie's storage room, and instead of going directly to the guest room, he went to look for the box. He recognized Aidan's handwriting in magic marker, the word *Toys*. He pulled it down, then began digging through it, looking for inspiration.

A two-headed dildo rested on a coiled leather leash with a cock ring attached to it. Blindfolds and ball gags and anal beads and nipple clamps and items whose function he could only guess at. What the hell, he thought. He picked up the whole box and carried it to the guest room, his stiff dick leading the way.

Aidan was sitting up in bed naked when Liam walked in, just as

Liam had hoped. "I was afraid you'd changed your mind," Aidan said.

"I remembered this box of magic tricks and thought we might experiment." Liam put the box on the bed in front of Aidan. "You take a look while I get naked."

"Oh no," Aidan said, sitting back against the pillows, his legs stretched out and his dick waving in the air. "I want to watch the show first."

Even though he knew he had a great body and he loved being naked, Liam sometimes felt bashful about stripping in front of someone else. He figured it went back to those high school locker rooms, when he'd get a stiffy from seeing other guys naked and didn't want anyone else to know.

But Aidan already knew.

Liam found his cell phone on the dresser, opened the music player, and picked one of Aidan's favorite songs, Jane Birkin and Serge Gainsbourg singing "Je t'aime."

"I like this already," Aidan said.

"I can tell," Liam said, smiling. He began to sway his hips as he untucked his polo shirt from his slacks. He contracted his abs as he lifted the shirt up slowly, and he heard Aidan groan with pleasure.

"Don't get started without me," Liam said as he lifted the shirt over his head. He stretched his arms and swung the shirt around on one finger, then tossed it aside.

Birkin and Gainsbourg were coming with each other in breathy voices, and Aidan's mouth was open like a dog in heat.

"If you don't want to be a bodyguard anymore, you could always be a stripper," Aidan said. "Though I wouldn't want to share this view with anyone."

Liam looked at him and licked his lips. His dick was throbbing in his pants, and he unbuckled his belt. He pulled it out of its loops and twirled it for a moment. Then he moved up to Aidan. "Hands up, you varmint," he said.

Aidan lifted his hands over his head, and Liam wrapped his belt around his partner's wrists. Aidan was panting with desire, his chest rising and falling, his dick bouncing.

Liam undid his pants and let them hang open as he toed off his deck shoes. Without touching his slacks, he began to shimmy his hips until the pants were around his thighs, then dropped to the floor. The pouch of his jockstrap was already wet with precome.

He reached over to the box of sex toys and pulled out a pair of nipple clamps, each with a set of small weights attached. "Lean back," he said to Aidan.

He opened the package and gently clipped one clamp around Aidan's tit. Aidan moaned with pleasure. Then Liam attached the other.

"Feeling submissive yet?" Liam asked.

"I am all yours," Aidan said.

Liam saw that Aidan's cock was leaking fluid too. He went back to the box and retrieved the ball weights. "Lift up your legs," he said. Aidan did, and Liam wrapped a cock ring around the base of Aidan's dick, then attached the weights.

He stood back and surveyed his work. "Looks good for starters. Now stand up."

Aidan was having difficulty getting his balance because his hands were tied, so Liam leaned down and lifted him under the arms. Aidan put his cuffed hands around Liam's neck, and they pressed their bodies closer, dicks against skin. Liam put his arms around Aidan's back and cupped his partner's butt with both hands. Aidan groaned again.

"How's that weight?" Liam asked.

"Nothing I can't handle," Aidan said. "Bring it on, big boy."

"You haven't seen big yet," Liam said. "Turn around and assume the position."

Aidan lifted his cuffed hands over Liam's head and did as he was told, leaning against the wall with his bound hands flat, his legs spread. Liam pulled out a round rubber doohickey with tiny bumps around the edges and read the package description. "Good. This is what I thought it was."

"What's that?" Aidan said.

"You'll feel it," Liam said. He dropped his jock and his dick sprang out. It took some maneuvering, but eventually he slipped the rubber cock ring around the tip of his dick, just below the head. Then he squirted some lube in his hand and began massaging Aidan's hole.

"Oh God," Aidan said. "Oh, Liam. That feels so good."

Liam coated the head of his dick and the rubber ring and then positioned himself behind Aidan. "Take a deep breath, baby."

He could feel Aidan relaxing before him, and he slipped the

head of his dick into Aidan's ass. "Holy shit," Aidan said as Liam's dick popped back out. "What the hell? Did your dick grow or something?"

"Or something," Liam said. "Come on. You know you can take it." He pushed back in, and this time he made it past Aidan's anal ring.

Aidan grunted and moaned.

"I'm not hurting you, am I?"

"Only in a good way," Aidan said. "Jesus, that thing is big, whatever it is." He tried to twist around. "Are you using a dildo on me?"

"Nope. That's all me. With a little help."

He leaned forward and nipped Aidan's shoulder, then reached around to tug on the nipple clamps. Aidan writhed and squirmed, and Liam felt his control slipping. He pushed forward as deep as he could, and Aidan pushed back. They didn't speak anymore, just moaned and grunted as Liam increased his pace and felt the weights on Aidan's balls swing back and forth.

Aidan was so clearly enjoying himself that Liam redoubled his efforts. The cock ring felt strange around his dick, but every time the head of it nosed against Aidan's prostate and Aidan jumped, Liam felt his own endorphins rising. He pushed and pulled, his sweaty hands gripping Aidan's waist, and Aidan began to whimper and cry. "So close," he said. "Fuck me, baby. Push me over the edge."

Liam was very willing to oblige. His guts began to churn, and he was desperate to come, but he wanted Aidan to come first. He reached around and grabbed Aidan's dick, and almost immediately his partner spurted. Liam closed his eyes and saw stars as his orgasm surged.

His body sagged against Aidan's, and for a moment he felt his partner take his weight. Then Liam stepped back, and his dick pulled out of Aidan's ass with a squishy sound.

Aidan let go of the wall and half-turned, and then his legs must have given out because he was falling into Liam's arms. Liam slung one arm under Aidan's ass, the other around his shoulders, and lifted him onto the bed.

Though he felt himself staggering, Liam reached up and undid the belt, then the nipple clamps, then the ball weights. Aidan had sprayed Freddie's guest-room wall with his come, so Liam grabbed one of those cloths that Aidan had called trick towels and used it to wipe the wall.

Only then did he collapse in bed next to Aidan. Aidan snuggled into him, resting his head on Liam's chest, and Liam wrapped one arm around his partner's shoulders.

* * * *

Liam woke first. He and Aidan were a sticky mess, and he could see that he'd only smeared his partner's come in a big circle on the wall. He got up and padded silently to the bathroom, returning with a couple of warm, wet towels.

He used the first to gently wipe Aidan's dick and belly. Aidan opened his eyes and looked up at him. "Mmm," he said. "I could get used to waking up this way."

Liam turned to the wall.

"And the view from this angle is pretty impressive," Aidan said. "Even after all these years, I bet I could still bounce a quarter off that ass."

"I'd rather have you fuck it," Liam said, still cleaning. "You seemed to enjoy that cock ring I used last night. Made me want to see what it feels like to be on the other end."

Aidan picked it up from the bedside table. "This is what you had in me? Very kinky." Liam turned around, and Aidan smiled. "Awesome too. I'll be happy to oblige you. But we'll both need to recharge our batteries first."

"Agreed," Liam said. "You want to take a shower first or you want me to?"

"How about together?" Aidan swung his legs out of bed. "After I empty my bladder." He looked at Liam. "Unless you've been thinking about trying some water sports too."

"I'll pass on that," Liam said.

Aidan walked into the bathroom and stood before the toilet. Liam came into the bathroom, turned the shower on, and then stepped in. Aidan joined him a moment later, and they took turns soaping and rinsing each other.

Liam couldn't imagine feeling better. A positive resolution to the case, awesome sex, and a good night's sleep. And of course, having Aidan there with him.

They dressed and walked out to the kitchen. Freddie appeared to still be asleep. "Think we should check on him?" Aidan asked. "He said he was going to take a bunch of pills last night."

Liam sat at the kitchen table as Aidan began assembling ingredients for breakfast. "Freddie strikes me as a guy well acquainted with pharmaceuticals," Liam said.

Aidan prepared omelets and bacon while Liam called down to the hospital to check on Newt. He was put through to the man himself. "How are you doing, big guy?" he asked.

"I feel like somebody shot me," Newt grumbled.

"What time are they letting you go?"

"The doctor wants to keep me here through the weekend," Newt said. "My blood pressure is up, and he wants to monitor it."

"Freddie won't like that," Liam said.

"What won't I like?"

Liam turned to see Freddie in the doorway of the kitchen. His eyes were clear, and he was freshly showered himself, wearing a spaghetti-string T-shirt that showed off his muscles and a variety of tattoos.

"Here's Newt," Liam said, and handed Freddie the phone. Freddie took it and walked back to the living room, and Liam sat down to eat breakfast with Aidan.

It was nearly a half hour before Freddie returned to the kitchen. "I'm going down to the hospital to look after Newt," he said. "Your company's going to send me a bill, right?"

Liam nodded and stood to take the phone back from Freddie. "We don't get too involved in that. If you have any questions, you can call the office."

"I won't argue, whatever it is," Freddie said. "You saved my fucking life, and Newt's too."

"It's what we do," Liam said.

"A handshake doesn't seem enough," Freddie said. "Either of you get jealous if I give you both a hug?"

"Aidan's been hoping for one since we got here," Liam said.

Freddie started with Liam, wrapping his arms around him. Freddie was almost Aidan's height, and he fit into Liam's body almost as easily as Aidan did. Liam put his arms awkwardly around Freddie's back as Freddie hugged him. Yeah, he was a pretty fit guy, Liam thought. But Freddie could keep his ropy muscles and his rock-solid abs; Liam preferred his partner's embrace to anyone else's.

He backed away, and Aidan stood up. Liam watched Freddie hug him, and over Freddie's shoulder Aidan pretended to swoon, and Liam laughed.

"You should be all right on your own from now on," Liam said. "We'll pack up our gear and head back home."

Freddie looked emotional. "You guys have to keep in touch. Once Newt gets better, we'll have you up here."

"Will do," Liam said.

He and Aidan went into the guest room, and they were packed and ready to go when Freddie was ready to drive himself down to the hospital. He had changed out of his revealing T-shirt and shorts to a conservative pair of slacks, button-down shirt, and sports jacket.

"Very snazzy," Aidan said.

"You know the way it is," Freddie said. "You get more respect from people when you look like you deserve it. I want to get the best care for Newt."

Driving down to the city in the Jeep, Liam remembered they were supposed to have dinner with Hassan and Louis that night. "They're going to be disappointed that Freddie won't be with us," he said to Aidan.

"They'll get over it. And Freddie said he wants to keep in touch. They'll all meet up eventually."

"Nice really has become our home," Liam said. "I think you're right; it's time to buy a house and settle down."

"You're sure?" Aidan said. "You're not just doing this because I want to?"

"I've been thinking about it," Liam said. "I've been stuck not wanting to have the kind of life my parents had. Both of them felt trapped—Big Bill hated all the restrictions, and he took his anger out on my mom and us kids. And Doris wanted to get out, but she had no skills and no place to go."

He turned to look at Aidan. "But we're not Big Bill and Doris. Neither of us is trapped here, and buying a house together isn't going to change that. At dinner tonight, we'll ask Hassan to keep an eye out for someplace for us."

Aidan reached out to take his hand. "Just like on Freddie's tattoo," he said. "I have come home at last! This is my real country. Further up and further in!"

Thanks for reading! I'd love to stay in touch with you. Subscribe to one or more of my newsletters at my website, www.mahubooks.com, and I promise I won't spam you!

Follow me at Goodreads to see what I'm reading, and my author page at Facebook where I post news and giveaways.

If you liked this book, please consider posting a brief review at your vendor, at Goodreads and in reader groups. Even a short review help other readers discover books they might like. Thanks!

Dedication

To Marc. Sail away with me, to another world.

Acknowledgments

Thank you so much to all the readers who have enjoyed following Aidan's and Liam's adventures, and for giving me the opportunity to keep writing about them. Special thanks to my editor, Maryam Salim, who made these books so much better, and all the staff at Loose Id who line edited, proofread, designed terrific covers, and got the books out into the world. Kelly Nichols created the new cover.

About the Author

Neil lives in South Florida with his husband and two rambunctious golden retrievers. He is a four-time finalist for the Lambda Literary Award in Best Gay Mystery and Best Gay Romance.

A professor of English at Broward College's South Campus, he has written and edited many other books; details can be found at his website, **http://www.mahubooks.com.** He is also past president of the Florida chapter of Mystery Writers of America.

www.ingramcontent.com/pod-product-compliance
Lightning Source LLC
LaVergne TN
LVHW011946060526
838201LV00061B/4232